Fire Line Aleaqida العقيدة of the Golden Dragon Vol. 1

Marques Bowden

Edited by
Sabina Cooper
Linda W

Dedication to My (Late) Father

Dear Dad,

I was halfway through writing this book when I got the call that you were being admitted to the hospital for heart surgery. I remember calling the hospital looking for you, and when I finally did, you felt that you would not make it. I told you not to worry about it and let the doctors do their thing. You see, a year prior to that, we spoke, against conventional wisdom, for four hours. It was no secret that I grew up not knowing who you were and what you were doing, so much so that I resented you. However, I told you never to push me away again at the pinnacle of that deep conversation; I told you that you are my dad, and as a new father, I understood that in order to be what I missed in my life to my son, I had to come to terms and accept you for who you are. Fast forward to our last coherent conversation, we had. You made it through the procedure on December 20th, 2022, and I called you. The First words I said to you when you picked up the phone were Happy Birthday Pop. I heard the smile in your voice when you responded thank you. You then asked me how I was doing, and I said, "Well, considering that it's negative 24° outside in Montana, I'm good." He laughed and said, "Yeah, I don't miss those MP days being stationed in Ellsworth AFB." After that, you said we'll talk again soon.

Unfortunately, 2 days later, you suffered another heart attack and had to get a call from your favorite niece. It took me 3 days to drive from Montana to Philadelphia to see you in a comatose state, and one of the hardest things to do was slowly watching you die without us talking like before. I grew up hearing so much of your failures, faults, and that (even after your passing) I was a liar like you were. It hurt me deeply the resentment you had. As I saw you take your last breath, I found it somewhat poetic that on the day I was born in the same place 4 and 5 (respectfully) generations of your family lived, I would be there with you when you went on to glory. As for those who deemed us as flawed, liars, etc, I wanted to take the time to oblige those who felt this way while sending you off to glory with the truth in this dedication.

The truth is, at that moment, I realized that you were a flawed individual with dreams and aspirations but didn't have the support or extra (umph) to see things through to the end. At those moments with just the two of us, I completely understood the toll and heartbreak of not being able to break certain generational curses and circumstances that led us apart for many years. Instead of leading back at those who said those things about us (because to keep unfiltered, raw, and unapologetic, I felt that our character was under attack with little or no empathy), I remembered the principles of the Buddha while researching for this novel. The first chapter is fitting because it deals with the source of suffering so that it can be investigated, overcome, and leading to the path of nirvana. Few people can rise above circumstances when those who criticize live in glass houses themselves. No one in this world is perfect; therefore, we should take the time to expound on the good (if not the great things you contributed). You touched so many hearts and minds around you. Little did I realize the irony of being told that I had the (worst) qualities from you, that I inherited your best qualities. I learned that you loved writing and would write articles in The Philadelphia Inquirer. You were also a student of history and wanted to write a memoir; I also realized that even though we went 23 years without seeing each other, we went through similar paths of life. So, to end this letter, not only do I dedicate this book to you, I'm going to remind people that your legacy lives on through me and through Dreadon. That failure isn't an option; it's opposition; operate in this world like a target; learn to take a punch so you can get back up; and, most importantly, finish what you start. I love you, and regardless of how people perceive you and I, what you gave me will one day infect this world with our presence, insight, competence, and empowerment. Now rest knowing that your son got this from here on out! Until we meet again,

Sincerely yours,

Chapter 1

Samudaya

The symphony of crickets and other insects infects the misty air. Birds flutter their feathers as they prepare for the greeting of a new day. As the sun begins to rise, several monks stand outside of a huge Temple painted with fire-yellow rooftops and blood-colored walls, standing by a giant gong to show the appropriate respect for their gift of life.

Slowly the night gives way today. The light of a new time exposes the lush green Bamboo and Deciduous Forests. The twinkle in the minute drops of water gives the leaves the illusion of sparkling diamonds, refracting the same life-sustaining light upon which all living creatures rely on.

As the sun fully erects, one of the monks gets out of his stance as the line of others remain in their postures. Each holding their left hand in a prayer position while keeping their balled fist behind their backs. The lowly monk grabs a big stick and braces himself. After a short moment of peace and harmony, the monk hits the gong three short and steady times. GONG…GONG…GONG… After the last echoes of the gong migrate into the wind, each monk bows in reference without making a gesture or a sound.

The monks walk inside the Temple in an orderly and unified fashion. The main monk, who hit the gong, continues to face outward while his companions enter the structure. As the last monk makes his way inside, the main monk closes his eyes and bows his head.

Suddenly, the sound of footsteps fills the air. The main monk notices the subtle disturbance to nature yet remains unphased by the commotion. Closer and closer the source of the steps comes. The feet of the stranger get louder and louder as he makes his way toward the top of the stairway. As he reaches the top, he stands in front of the monk.

With the power of the Dracocernentia, Malik is able to associate the bio-electrical pulses surging in the body along with the sounds associated with behaviors and thoughts. This allows Malik to quickly deduce and pick up every language of the world, after hearing a few words. He learned this ability in his travels to Africa and Spain, which allows him to communicate with the locals.

"*Speaking in Chinese* (***Good Morning. Is this the Temple of the Golden Dragon***)?"

The monk says nothing. He stands before the stranger as if he didn't hear, see, or acknowledge his presence. The stranger speaks again, this time with a more direct tone.

"*Speaking in Chinese* (***I have searched for many weeks to seek the Temple. The world is at stake as well as my people***)", he exclaims, "*Responding in Chinese* (***I don't have time for this; is this or is this not the Temple of the Golden Dragon***)?"

Again, the monk says and does nothing, standing still with his hand in a prayer position. Finally, imprudence gets the best of the stranger. He removes his hood, opens his eyes, and activates the Dracocernentia.

The stranger is Malik. Weary of his weeks of travel and unsettling in his appearance. His face is covered with a short, thick, and entangled beard, hair partially locked into small dreads, and his fade all but gone. Despite his access to resources, Malik sent most of his possessions back to his family in Jacksonville to better conceal himself from the ever-so-lurking eyes of the new Elite 8.

The monks look at the eyes of Malik, and then closes his eyes, bows, and turns to the direction of Temple. With his soft spoken voice, he instructs Malik to follow.

" *Responding in Chinese* (***Follow me…Dragon Moor***)".

Having understood the small opening, Malik slowly follows the monk through the giant doors of the Temple.

The monk walks towards the structure in the back of the Temple courtyard. The building is equally as impressive, with symbols and calligraphy masking the borders of the door. Malik becomes anxious about the possibilities that may be inside. His breath is nonexistent, the sweat carries grind and grit down his face, and his lips scrape against each other for relief. The monk faces Malik, bows, and moves his head towards the building without uttering a single word.

"Xièxiè (***Thank you***)," Malik responds as he bows his head.

The monk remains stoic and walks away. Malik stands facing the door. He hesitates for a moment, hoping to compartmentalize past, present, and future events.

"*I know it's been about 8 weeks, but it feels like 8 years*," Malik reflects, "*I can't shake this feeling of defeat, nor those last chilling words of Audrey...*"

Malik can still see the sword, once held by his ancestors, plunge through the back of the unfortunate woman. The sight and smell of blood is as fresh to Malik as the slight mist covering the air. Then, Malik takes a deep breath, closes his eyes, and calms himself down.

"*Somehow, I have to get past that and see this journey through. So here goes*". Malik opens his eyes, regains his resolve, and walks towards the building.

Malik reaches the building and slowly enters inside. The room is lit with several candles, each shining a small light inside the vast void. In the middle of the room is an old man sitting down underneath a huge structure of a Golden Dragon. The statue beast has a furry nose, with two protruding whiskers, sharp claws, big teeth, and eyes as red as blood.

When Malik gazes upon it, his eyes begin to not only illuminate but cause the eyes of dragon to activate as well. Strange series of lights penetrated the room, as Malik is once again flooded with images of his past, the past of his ancestors, and the potential futures. The old man continues to sit as he remains calm and unaffected. Malik holds his head in pain while forcefully bending the knee down to the ground.

"AGH..." he complained, "The pain...the suffering..."

After a few gruesome moments, the lights disappear. The statue is again non engaging, and Malik catches his breath. Again, the old monk says and does nothing. Feeling out of place, yet emboldened by his quest, Malik slowly walks towards the man before sitting down. He clears his throat, reactivates his Dracocernentia, then begins to speak.

"*In Chinese* (***Excuse me, Master. I have traveled far and have been flooded with images***)," Malik pleads, " (***I seek the source of these images in hopes of better understanding them. Can you help me***)?

The man curves a micro-edge of his right lip upward. His demeanor personifies acumen; never rushes to speak nor to judgement. He looks ahead as if staring at the future while Malik awaits his response. After about 10 seconds of silence, wise words begin to enter Malik's plane of consciousness.

"*Responding in Chinese* (***So quick to find the answer, instead of understanding the question***)," the master elaborates, " (***The Buddha teaches us that we can be filled with suffering, but we can also be filled with joy and happiness. What you seek, Dragon Moor isn't something out in the world, but the very place that you always had access to***)".

"*Responding in Chinese* (***Access to what? I know what I need to do. I know that I needed to overcome my pain and the pain of my people***)", Malik answers. "(***But do you truly know the source of your suffering? Why do your enemies make you suffer, and why cause them to suffer***)"?

Before Malik could retort, he hesitates and thinks to himself, "*What do you mean the source of my suffering? And why my enemies suffer? What does it matter?*"

The old man sits quietly as he takes a deep breath. He continues his explanation without any prompting from Malik.

"*Speaking in Chinese* (***I sense that you are confused with not my words, but the meaning of them***)," the man further explains, " (***A tiger can suffer when it is hungry. The deer suffers when the tiger catches, kills, and eats it. Yet the tiger does not hate the deer any more than the deer hates the tiger. Like the stripes on a tiger, hatred can be visible, or like the shadows of the night, hatred can be hidden, but so can the source that determines whether that feeling goes on the path of happiness and joy or suffering and hatred***)."

Malik takes his time to comprehend the messaging. The old man's words give him a sense of ease and calm, despite not fully understanding the angle he is taking. Again the old man senses this and speaks again.

"Explaining in Chinese (***You are a dragon. Your instincts are to show your power. The fire within you burns for justice. However, in order to find what you seek, you must tap within the realm that came naturally to your ancestors. You must understand the suffering***)."

" Wǒzěnmezuò (How do I do that)?" Malik asks.

" *Thinking, then responding in Chinese*…(***You must do what you've mastered long ago. Seek the guidance of those before you. Allow yourself to embrace the suffering as well as joy. In time***…)," the monk then gets up, bows his head, and finishes, " (***May Buddha grant you the peace at the end of your journey***)."

Afterwards, the old man leaves Malik and out of the room. Malik sits down for a while, pondering the words of an old man who has seen several lifetimes to gain the perspective of a prudent being. His lack of comprehension partially paralyzes Malik in place, as if he were stuck in between two buildings of time while trying to squeeze out. Then, Malik begins to reflect.

"*So I need to see the source of my suffering. I can make a case it's White Supremacy, but is it that simple? To understand my enemies and their source of suffering?*" Malik sighs, " *Maybe I do need to take my time to meditate on these things.* Well, I'm alone in front of a dragon statue, surrounded by candles. Might as well make the best of it."

Malik looks directly at the dragon. The room stands still. The fire from the candles begin to flicker, and then a gust of wind flows inside the room. Malik's golden hue eyes begin to light up, matching the intensity of the dragon statue.

After a brief time, Malik's eyes fully illuminate and fill the room. A roaring sound can be heard from the statue, yet nothing moves. A vortex of light and energy swirl around as Malik remains spiritually connected to the transfer from one plane to another.

Once the lights subside, Malik finds himself in another plane. Filled with light red and pink colored clouds, lightly tinted blue skies, and air as thick as mud, Malik swirls his head around to see if anyone is sharing this plane.

"Hello?! Hello?!" Malik yells, "Is anybody here?!"

As Malik continues to look around, a mysterious figure reveals himself from the pink shadows. He is an imposing man: heavily melanated with a bald head and full beard. He lacks a top to cover his big, ripped chest but makes up for it with his iron wrist braces, red and yellow colored pants and no shoes.

Feeling something off in the air, Malik swirls his body around until he sees the shadowy figure. Slightly alarmed and not recognizing the figure, Malik slowly speaks to the stranger.

"Who… Who are you?"

The man laughs and smiles, " So THIS is the one destined to be the Golden Dragon Moor…HA HAHA!"

"Golden Dragon Moor?" Malik asks, "Why me?"

"You are here to find out," the stranger responds, " Who knows but you, whether you last…or not…"

The man takes his heavily built right arm, lowers it towards the void, and responds.

"So…Shall we?"

Malik, determined to see this through, nods his head a little as he approaches the man. The man chuckles again then smiles, "Excellent."

Chapter 2
The Power of Awarelessness

The void is vast and calming. The atmosphere is a conglomerate of soothing colors: light pinks, orange, and blues. A thick, milky, cloudy mist surrounds Malik and this muscled but humble man. He smiles again. He is wearing a yellow sash that covers half of his torso while exposing his right arm. His head shines like a gem with no hair confined to the lower half of his face. His course beard is black with some streaks of gray that seemingly swim down the trails of kinks. Finally, his eyes are golden beige: filled with purity, certainty, and detachment.

"Welcome," he says. Stunned at the figure, Malik musters up the nerve to inquire about his guest. "I've never met someone like you before," Malik continues, "Who are you?" "Heh heh heh…" the man continues, "I am no one. I do not perceive myself to the illusion of perception. However, in the realm that we live in, something doesn't exist until we put a name to it. So, to comfort your soul, I will reveal the name I was given to me by my father. Bodhidharma." "Bodhidharma," Malik responds, "I've… read some text about you. You were also known as Daruma, who created the Zen and credited with the foundation of Shaolin Martial Arts."

Bodhidharma chuckles as he briefly closes his eyes. Then he states his views while ascertaining the concerns that brough Malik to the Temple.

"Men want to be remembered or acknowledged in some way. Often times, we can waste our lives trying to obtain something that can be touched, yet hold no value," he continues, "However, in you, I sense a disturbance in your ying and yang. You have discovered your past yet fail to understand how your suffering completes the circle." "(Sigh) I am troubled," Malik answers, "I lost the Harq Alqadr, and soon, the world will soon begin it's genocide of my people." "I see…but is that the source of your suffering?" "Suffering?" Malik retorts, "What does that have to do with…"

Bodhidharma interrupts by generating smoke by moving his arms. His stances mirror that of the Grand Masters; despite not moving his legs, his arms control the mist and smoke until the veil creates a world which Malik looks on in amazement. He is surrounded by a miniature version of the Earth: in his view is a desert, followed by lush rain forests, and then a mountain range. Afterwards, Bodhidharma ends his pose with his right hand in a prayer position.

"What you seek Moor cannot be obtained unless you understand the source of your suffering," Bodhidharma says, " In order to do that, you must know without knowing, ask the right questions, then forget it all at the same time." "Know without knowing? Asking the right questions? I don't understand?" Malik responds while scratching his head. "I want to tell you a story about my life in the living realm Moor. Direct your attention below as the images convey my words."

Bodhidharma's eyes begin to glow like flashlights. Then his words begin to manifest images and characters in the mini world below.

"When I was about your age, I was given a vision. I did not understand the meaning of the vision, nor could I tell you the message. However, I knew that it was meant for me to seek something beyond what's understood," Bodhidharma continues as his mini representative travels through the desert and forests, "For many years, I traveled through many lands, meditated for hours, and I observed nature at it's purest. From the smallest insects to the fleetest of antelopes, to the birds in the skies and to the snakes crawling below. Then, I began to meditate a different way."

The mini character would face miniature versions of different animals and mimic their movements.

Malik watches with interest and intrigue as Bodhidharma continues his story.

"In time, I was able to derive and mirror the movements of everything I saw in nature. But then, something happened," Bodhidharma changes his stance. He bends his right knee down while pointing his left toe downward. His right arm curves at the elbow, allowing his right hand to point straight underneath his face while his left arm points towards the mountains. Malik is confused, yet remains silent as Bodhidharma continues his story.

"One day, I decided to climb the highest mountain. It was bitterly cold, it was snowy, and most of all, it was steep. It took nearly every ounce of strength to climb the cliffside of the mountain. At one point, I believed I was going to die."

Afterwards, Bodhidharma changes his stance again. This time he extends both arms and legs out while curving his middle fingers in both hands.

"When I reached the mountain top, I was confronted with a magnificent beast. A Golden Dragon with immense strength, size, and power. It's snake-like body curled in the wind while it's wings kept it afloat in the thin air. His teeth were perfectly ivory while it's whiskers swim in the air. But what kept me mesmerized was it's red eyes." he continues, "As it began to roar, I slowly crouched in submission, not knowing if the beast saw me as a meal or a threat."

Miraculously, Malik develops the prudence to ask a question. "What did the dragon do next?" "Well, heh hehheh, it's eyes illuminated mine." Bodhidharma answered, "When I begin to see like the dragon, I begin to move like the dragon. I began to move the same, like, like a mirror image. I was no longer in control of my mind nor body. For a week, I continued to do this until the storms stop. Afterwards, my eyes, head, and heart were purged with anything that led to the attachment. Then the Golden Dragon flew off."

Bodhidharma moved his arms again, manipulating the mist in the void to bring it back to it's original color. Then he relaxes his arms, then approaches Malik.

"After that moment, I soon realized that the power we possess isn't meant to quell our petty desires. You see this…Elite 8, as you call it… as a component of current Power when in actuality, it is a sign of their weakness. Their inability to confront the truth about themselves, thus using this illusionary system to distort their own reality about themselves."

"Well illusion or not, the suffering caused by their system has devastated this world and my people," Malik responds, "How do you combat that?"

Again, Bodhidharma chuckles with patience and understanding, sensing that Malik is missing the point. "So, you have seen these…visions correct? Of a Golden Dragon?"

"Yes, I don't know what they mean?"

"Because again," Bodhidharma reiterates, "You don't know the right questions, nor the source of your suffering. You must learn how to achieve the power of knowing without knowing. Just like I didn't know that the Golden Dragon was not going to eat me. How I dance with the Golden Dragon, thus meditating for a week without any conscious thought or sense of identity, only then was I able to gain the insight…"

"Insight?" Malik asked.

"Yes…that to know everything means to know nothing," Bodhidharma continues, "I will teach you how to move, how to seek within, and how to probe for the right questions to set you on the right path. Then, you will obtain the power of Awarelessness."

"The power of Awarelessness?"

"When you achieve this, your fears, your desires, and your goals will not be attached to the point you block your full potential. Then you will be able to be a beacon, a shining light, a sun to those who choose to follow you."

Malik ponders on the words of Bodhidharma. His eyes drop as easily as his head. So much to take in that the very weight of information allows Malik to slightly comprehend the words of the would be master.

"He's right," Malik realizes, "I have so much on my mind, body, and heart that I can feel the weight crushing me. I'm going to need to learn how to compartmentalize…but perhaps…" Malik looks up at Bodhidharma. He begins to smile and lighten his face. Bodhidharma returns the gesture, acknowledging the conclusion Malik has reached.

"I understand now," Malik says, "and…instead of saying I'm ready, I'm going to do exactly what you did with the Dragon, allow myself to fully immerse myself without attachment." Bodhidharma nods, then places his right arm on Malik's shoulder and commands him.

"Let us begin…and…allow yourself to fully engage to the possibilities."

While Malik is in deep meditation, his body is still in a seated position in front of the Dragon structure. The old monk walks back in and notices the candles not lit. Despite this, he smiles, as he sees Malik's body sitting in front of the structure. Another monk, much younger and more inquisitive, begins to question the old master.

"Shīfu, Conversing in Chinese (***Master, why is he meditating without the light? Won't he get lost?***)"

"Responding in Chinese, (***Darkness is not just an enemy to the light, it is also an ally to find the light***)," he continues, " (***When we are lost, most people will confine themselves to a corner because to find their true selves shows them the darkness they try to hide. However, when we have to courage to face ourselves, including the darkness, we begin to realize the truth.***)"

"Shīfu, *asking in Chinese*? (***What is the truth, Master***?)" The old man smiles as he concludes his message.

"*Replying in Chinese* (***The truth is we each are attached to our suffering. We are molded by the pain we experience but do not understand. Everybody on Earth feels the pain and remembers how that pain. It can prevent them from seeking to the true meaning behind it. It weakens us and makes us vulnerable because we will refuse to take power from it. What this stranger is attempting to do, is to confront the source of his suffering and find a way to redirect the energy to save himself and his people. As students of the Buddhah, we must provide a place of meditation so that he can achieve his 4 Noble Truths; then he can continue on his journey to finally seek peace in his existence.***)"

Moved by the words of wisdom, the young monk bows in acknowledgement and walks away. The old monk continues to look on as Malik continues his meditation. Then he whispers to himself.

" (***The source of your pain will make you stronger if you learn to know it and forget it. Only then will you achieve the Chi necessary to achieve a level beyond comprehension.***)" Afterwards, the old monk bows, then walks away, leaving Malik to confront the source of his struggles.

Chapter 3
Flowing with the Universal Self

Malik sits down on the non-existent floor. His attention is fixated on Bodhidharma as he begins to explain the purpose of the teaching. He takes a deep breath and closes his eyes. A few moments seem like days. The atmosphere is still. The waiting tests Malik's patience.

Then, Bodhidharma opens his eyes, changes stances, then moves from pose to pose. "What you call Martial Arts isn't about mastering a kick or learning how to defeat your opponent", he continues, "It's about mastering all of you, the good and especially the bad. In order to achieve Awarelessness, you must learn how to accept all aspects of yourself, including what you think you perceive as failure."

"Perceive as failure?" Malik tries to grasp as he continues to listen with intensity. Bodhidharma's perception is keen to the micro expressions Malik exhibits but continues to lecture as he moves.

"I sense in you a level of peace in who you are. I suspect that you had to endure training in order to understand yourself," Bodhidharma continues, "However, your source of suffering isn't as easy as just who disrespected you, hurt you, or tried to kill you. What you must understand Malik is that who you are is but a single grain of sand in the beach of what you truly are." Bodhidharma stops his movements by standing in his prayer stance. Then he prompts Malik to get up from his seated position.

"What I want you to do is to close your eyes and allow the Fire Line from within to guide your movements," he instructs, "but be warned, what you see will not be ideal nor pleasant. This is necessary in order to progress to the next step." Bodhidharma then takes that hand that was in prayer position, then extents it to the void. "Go now, and see what your Fire Line takes you."

Reluctantly, Malik walks a few paces towards the space where Bodhidharma demonstrate his movements. He begins to breathe shakenly. His body begins to quiver with nervousness. After a few tense moments, Malik closes his eyes and takes a deep breath. He stands motionless until he is able to get his body under control. His heart beats in a constant rhythm, the breath becomes consistently slow, and Malik is at peace. "Alright…here goes."

Malik closes his eyes and begins to move. His body reacts by directing Malik into several stances and poses. As he becomes immerse in his movements, voices begin to enter the Moor's head.

"You were too predictable…I can't believe you actually thought you were my hero…" the feminine voices continue.

"Au…Audrey?" Malik continues as his body begins to produce balls of sweat.

"Why fight for people who don't give a damn about you? They are destined to remain subservient and incompetent."

"NNN…NO! That's not true…" Malik retorts as his skin becomes tight and his movements more erratic.

Then suddenly, the voices begin to change. Each representing a different person or character in his past.

"I love you not as Marshall Benson, but as what God intended you to be…Malik Rasheed Wilson…"

"Mom?"

"Your whore of a mother cast you out…"

"No…NO!" Malik struggles, until finally a voice appears, louder and more profound than the last.

"You want me? Heh hehheh? Come on…and meet the same fate as my Caramel Candy. No matter what you do, you can't defeat me. For I…control the destiny of men…for I…am Elite!"

In a fit of rage, Malik's eyes turn red, he lets out a fire blast from his mouth and roars.

"GGGGGGOOOOOOOTTTTTTHHHHH!"

Meanwhile, his physical body emits a fire blast that lights all of the candles in the chamber. The old monk notices a sudden wave of heat outside of the building, then proceed to walk towards the entrance of the Temple. He stands there quietly. Holding his beads in one hand while keeping his other in a prayer position.

Suddenly, a younger fellow monk runs behind to investigate the burst of energy. Despite the hectic amount of energy, Malik's body remains in place in front of the Dragon statue while the old monk continues to watch. The younger monk questions the elder in Chinese.

" (***Master, what is going on***)?" he asks, " (***Where did this energy come from***)?"

With his stoic demeanour, the old monk answers the young monk while fixing his eyes on both Malik and the Dragon statue.

" (***When we are confronted with regret, it comes with suffering. However, what follows is anger. We direct our anger towards the one who caused the suffering, but fail to understand***…)"

“ (***Understand what, Master***)?” the young monk asks.

“ (***All suffering has a source. Even an enemy with evil intent is suffering because something triggers with it to cause suffering. Suffering is like energy. One cannot destroy energy; only direct and guide it. Our young Moor must understand this if he is to unlock his full potential***.)”

“Wǒdǒngshīfu (I understand Master),” the young monk answers, “ (***can he do it***)?”

The old monk smirks alittle while maintaining his posture and composure. Despite his seemingly apathetic stance, his confidence could not be hidden. Still, he concludes his thoughts by answering the young monk in Chinese.

“ (***We are taught not to run away from what causes pain, only to seek out its source and understand it. I can sense his chi, and I know that he is strong. He has endured pain and suffering and still chooses to fight for his people. He must now learn how to confront it without resorting to anger. By achieving this, he will gain the power of knowing without knowing***).”

Moved by the clarity of this instruction, the young monk bows in reverence then leaves the old monk.

Meanwhile, in the veil, Malik begins to sweat profusely and breathe hard. His eyes are stained with the overflow of blood vessels to his reddish-brown eyes. Then tears begin to trinkle down his face as he crashes down to his hands and knees. Bodhidharma looks on with some level of concern but remains objective as well as optimistic.

“I…could feel…nothing…but rage,” Malik explains while catching himself.

"This is what I believe your Fire Line is trying to show you," Bodhidharma continues, "What you heard is what you think is the source of your suffering."

"But he killed Audrey! And he's going to…"

"That's just the result," Bodhidharma interrupts, "But did you even think about why this person did what he did?"

"What does that have to do with what they hear and now?" Malik asks.

"Because to understand your enemy, you must understand what motivates him. What caused him to suffer, and what lead him to generate suffering to others? If you face him right now, your anger will blind you, and he will take advantage of that."

"Just like he did before…" Malik remembers.
"I suggest we stop for today. Go and seek solitude. Then, when you are ready, we will resume."

Malik gets up and nods to Bodhidharma. Afterwards, Bodhidharma smiles, performs 3 rhythmic stances, then generates flashing lights that send Malik back to the present.

When Malik opens his eyes, he sees that nearly all of the candles are out of wax. He slowly looks around and begins to catch his breath. Standing in the doorway is the old monk. He continues to remain in his prayer pose as Malik gets up and greets him.

Malik bows and speaks in Chinese, to the resourceful master. " (***I…was confronted by my recent source of suffering***)," Malik says, " (***and I respond in anger and rage***)."

The old monk remains silent for about 5 seconds, then he smiles before responding.

" (***It is natural to meet an adversary with rage. When armies fight against each other, we only think of the battle itself. However, you are not simply fighting an enemy, you are fighting yourself***)."

" (***I've fought that battle before, master***)," Malik answers, "(***and I was able to conquer that side of me***)."

" (***I can sense that in you. What you must fight now is the source of suffering for your ancestors…and your people. All suffering comes from a single time, a single moment, or sometimes a series of events that could not be controlled. We cannot control the heavens when it decides to rain or when the sun melts all of the snow. All we can do is allow our energies to flow with the stream of change***)."

"Wǒdǒngshīfu (I…understand, master)."

The old monk then moves out of the way of the doorway and escorts Malik out. As the two walk together, the old sage gives Malik one last piece of advice.

" (***Focus not so much on your mission***) Dragon Moor," he states, " (***Learn from the ordinary. How do the trees remain alive after years of hardship? How do the birds continue to fly despite the weather? How the life we cling to continues to endure. Then you may realize that suffering can be diverted with the right thinking and right action***)."

Malik bows with appreciation and responds with saying Shifu. Then the old monk treks away to walk around the monastery.

Malik looks at the dimming light transitioning to night. The stars give him a sense of calm and quiet that allows him to recenter his frame of mind.

"I think I understand…" Malik reflects, "Maybe I am going about this all wrong…"

Suddenly, something beeps in his pocket. Malik looks down, inserts his left hand in his left pocket and grabs a flip phone. When he opens the phone, he sees a message from an anonymous person.

"**How is the journey going**?" Malik uses both hands to text back.

"**I can't believe people use to text like this. Ok, let me respond. The training is alot harder than I expected**."

"**Hard how**?" the person responds.

"**Instead of teaching me how to fight, they're teaching me how to find the source of suffering. It doesn't make any sense to me so far**."

After a few moments, a text responds to Malik's message.

"**I think they're teaching you how to conquer your enemy by conquering yourself. There's only so much I can say. Just keep at it and let me know when you're ready to come home.**"

"**Understood**," Malik responds, "**We'll talk again soon**."

Malik then puts the phone back in his pocket and stares at the sky. He allows the wind to blow and the rustling of the trees to play through his ears. Malik begins to close his eyes and purge his mind of all thoughts. As the night fully transforms the sky, Malik then begins to spread his arms like an eagle, ready to take fight towards the path of his current journey.

Chapter 4
Inner Nature

The night has reached it's epicenter of darkness. Before the sun can rise, Malik is sweating profusely as he tosses and turns on his humble bedding. The images of Audrey continue to fulfill it's quest to purge any optimism out while defiling the logical incentive to keep fighting. He continues to moan unconsciously, meanwhile continuing to rock back and forth in a futile attempt to go back to sleep.

"No…No…" he groans.

"You…stupid…naive little man…" the voice inside his head whispers, "Why did you think someone like me would ever think you can be any more than that?" Over and over again, the subtle but vile words continue to ring in Malik's head like a migraine.

"No…no…NNNNNOOOO!" he yells.

After a few minutes of rustling, Malik violently raises up, with eyes bulging, mouth wide open, and heavily breathing. Still in the discontent with the inner turmoil, Malik shakes his head. With small tears in his eyes and wet skin, Malik wipes his eyes, gets out of bed, and stares at the walls.

"I can't shake these feelings of guilt," he continues, "The whispers…the anger…the pain…the suf…"

Suddenly, a flash of white light blinds Malik. He hears a lowly screech that brings him into an alternative reality. Afterwards, a calming voice enters the plane like wind and eases his pain.

“Step aside, my heir…and breathe.” the feminine voice commands.

“Who..who are you?” Malik asks.

The voice again commands, this time faiding as it concludes into the wind.

“Step outside…and breathe.”

Afterwards, an orange phoenix with fiery white feathers appears, flapping it’s wings and screeching before disappearing from Malik’s sight.

After the slight episode, Malik again wipes his face off with the last remaining remnants of sweat. He takes a deep breath while closing his eyes. He stands up, silently, allowing the few breezes of air flow through to calm him down. Without any thought nor sense of assurance, Malik grabs his shoes, puts on a sleeveless shirt, and walks out of his room.

The crickets continue their orchestra of songs as the full moon begins to migrate. Malik uses the cover of night to walk towards the front of the gates. As he continues treking towards the entrance, the old monk is strangely strolling by awaiting the morning sun. As he witnesses Malik climbing the walls out of the monastery, he looks on with confident, pure eyes, smiles, and bows in his normal prayer stance.

“Xiànzàishìshíhòule (Now is the time),” he whispers in Chinese, “ (***To understand the guilt and the suffering, to purify your heart and mind, and seek one with your nature***).”

Afterwards, stands and waits unit the rays of the sun overcome the night.

Malik scales over the walls and begins to climb up the nearby ginkgo and conifer trees. Gracefully, Malik maneuvers through the forest as he finds a place to quell his mind of the inner demons he has yet to overcome. The pain that is hidden until his most vulnerable moments has Malik in a state of idleness.

“The same voices continue to haunt me,” Malik ponders, “I don’t know how to let go of this feeling. I…don’t know if it’s anger…or if it’s hate that I feel.” Malik continues to skim through the trees like a gibbon as he continues to think to himself. “I know that this feeling is what’s stopping me. I need to figure this out.”

Malik approaches a bamboo forest. Suddenly, he hears a sound coming towards his left side. His senses heighten up, he calms his breathing, then activates his Dracocernentia. The vibrant colors of receptors show an unusual but rare sight. Intrigued by the sight, Malik decides to stand in a tree about 150 yards away from the source of his attention. Rustling in the Bamboo forest, a peaceful creature is sitting down, eating the stalks like spaghetti while watching a cub a few feet away. The black and white coating makes no mistake of the identity of this humbling creature.

“Wow…a Giant Panda.” Malik whispers as he continues to observe.

The receptors of the bears show only colors of green, matching the food they are eating as well as the temperment. Seeing the animals gives Malik a small level of calm and peace as he continues to observe the animals minding their business.

Then, another receptor shows up in Malik’s plain of view. This receptor has the colors of orange, but the body is more streamlined, with a dirty grayish and white coat with dark spots. The graceful predator is slowly moving in on the unsuspecting pair. Malik’s eyes scrunch down as the predator draws near it’s intended victim.

“Oh no…” Malik whispers, “that leopard is probably aiming for the little one. I don’t think I can watch this.”

Suddenly, a gust of wind blows towards Malik. A voice in the air whispers as the breeze gets closer to Malik.

"Wait..." it whispers, as Malik looks around to try to find the source of the voice.

Not feeling overly surprised, Malik again thinks to himself.

"I should've known. Alright, let's see how this plays out."

The breeze blows past the bears. The keen nose of the mother picks up the scent of trouble and immediately rushes towards her cub. Seeing that it's opportunity slipping, the erratic leopard pounces in a feeble attempt to outpace the mother. Malik witnesses this moment like a movie, noticing every frame of action.

"This is incredible," he whispers.

As the leopard gets closer, the mother catches up to her cub, puts it in between her legs, and turns around to her attacker. The mighty panda stands her ground, growls at the leopard, and shows her canines. The leopard tuffs it's ears backwards and returns the gesture with teeth and fangs. Both animals show their formidable poses as predator and prey.

However, after a few seconds of show, the mother's resolve to protect her own create anxiety in the leopard. With a swipe of her mighty paw, she dissuades the leopard and it retreats back up into the nearby cliffsides. Once the threat is gone, she and her cub resemble eating the bamboo. Malik takes a moment to reflect upon this.

"It's strange," he continues, "despite the fight, neither animal showed receptors of hate nor disgust for one another. Normally I'd see different receptors in humans but these only showed the desire to eat and the desire to live. It was as black and white as the fur on the panda and yet, neither creature hated or disregarded each other's life, to the capacity that the mother didn't bother to chase the Snow Leopard away." After making the association, Malik heads towards a nearby lake.

The glimmer of sunrise is beginning to creep behind Malik. After an hour of trekking through the forest, Malik reaches a lake at the edge. Malik sits on the banks and stays silent. He listens to the soothing flow of the water, the rustling of the trees, and the wind in the air. Malik then closes his eyes one last time.

After a few moments, something prompts Malik into action. The cool mountain breeze blows in his face. The smell of the water marks it's purity and freshness. Malik then takes off his shoes and socks. Still with his eyes closed, he grips the loafy clays and sands with his toes. He stands up as he raises his arms to embrace the air blowing against his body. Then he slowly makes his way into the cold, calming waters of the lake. He then turns around to face the east. With his eyes still closed, he begins to take short deep breaths. With each breath, his body lightens up. The outer layer of his skin is coated with a small heatwave. With each breath, the heatwave becomes brighter and brighter. After the tenth time in deep breath, Malik's eyes explode into a white light, changing his plain of view and perception into a clear, white veil.

The sight of the veil is unlike anything Malik has experienced at this moment. The walls are pure white and the ground nearly nonexistent. He looks around and feels a level of comfort he hasn't experienced in a long time. Then a voice echoes, grabbing his attention.

"Welcome, my heir." the feminine voice greets.

"Who's there? Where are you?" Malik asks.

All of a sudden, a great white phoenix appears in front of Malik and screeches at him. The magnificent bird fixes it's blue eyes at Malik, syncing their connection like magnets. After a few flaps of it's wings, a fiery flare transforms the phoenix into a beautiful, tall, dark-skinned woman wearing no shoes, covered in white robes and a hijib. Malik squints at her as she gives a subtle smile and a nod. Then, something that Malik remembered long ago prompts him to engage the woman.

"Are…you…Muqadas?" Malik asks.

The woman walks up to Malik and hugs him. Then, with her soft hands, she caresses Malik's cheeks, moves his head closes to her, and kisses him on his forehead. Malik briefly closes his eyes and smiles as she takes a step back.

"Very perceptive my heir," she responds, "Seems you are in an impasse in your journey."

"Yes, honorable…"

"Please child," Muqadas interrupts while giggling, "I am your many times great grandmother, not a queen or some empress. I don't need a title."

"Right…I feel guilty…and angry…"

"And sad that you couldn't save someone, especially of our own kind."

Muqadas, again, interrupts.

"Yes…" Malik says, still drowned in the seep of sorrow or remorse. Muqadas recognizes his distraught attitude but continues to instruct with positivity.

"Come…I want to show you something." she commands. Malik nods as Muqadas extends her hand.

After a few seconds, a small, blue phoenix emerges and hovers over Muqadas' hand. Malik raises one eyebrow while making a distinction.

"Wait a minute, that's the same phoenix that exited her mouth!" Malik exclaimed, "How did it.."

"You thought that her essence was gone forever no?" Muqadas continues, " As you may know, the phoenix and dragon are interlocked like, what you may say, DNA. Our ancestors understood the value of each other in order to ensure the longevity of our legacies. As I explained to your sister some time ago, one cannot function effectively without the other. Observe."

Muqadas prompts the small phoenix to spit fire at the abyss, projecting images that timeline Audrey's life.

"As you can see, the one you call Audrey grew up not understanding the events that surround her. She only knew half of the truth about the man you call Hauss. Do you remember why he went into exile?"

"Yes, he said it was because he tried to prove that dragons existed, and they called him crazy." Malik answered.

"It was more than that, my heir," Muqadas prompted the phoenix to spit more flames, creating a new series of images, "When the professor did collective research with other researchers around the world, he not only discovered our legacies but discovered remains of a strange painting."

"What painting?" Malik asked.

“This one…” Muqadas points to the image.

The painting has a red backdrop with a black man in a golden cloak standing, an army of black hands holding golden swords, and a large golden dragon behind him.

“WAIT A MINUTE,” Malik yells, “That dragon…it’s the same dragon that has been haunting my visions. But how?”

“Because your mentor Hauss did not know that not only was his ancestor Riaahn, the original Golden Dragon Moor; his ancestors also led to his decisions to pursue the depths of this heritage, even though he didn’t know it at the time. Such as your father wanting to fly, as you say, jets and you, my heir, wanting to know where you came from.”

Malik ponders while absorbing the vast amount of information. He is slowly putting the pieces together in his mind while making the connections that draw him closer to the source of part of his suffering.

“So…because he had access to this information, he knew that there were others that would silence him and his family…”

“Precisely,” Muqadas adds, as she shows new images, “ Getting a tip from his colleague in England…”

“(*Adebayo*)” Malik connects.

“Hauss left his family with no word or contact, fearing for their lives and safety. In order not to leave any trails, Hauss dilebrately hid away anything that can link him to his wife and daughter.”

“So that’s why he never mentioned family to me,” Malik realizes, “It was to protect them and his granddaughter.”

Then the phoenix flies towards Malik and lands on his left shoulder. Afterwards, Muqadas walks towards Malik.

"The essence of the phoenix still remains because memories of not only Audrey but Hauss still remains inside you," Muqadas continues, "As long as you keep these memories alive, you will have access to their Fire Line. Such access can be dangerous but useful in your journey to the power of Awarelessness."

"Awarelessness, you are aware…"

"I am my amir," Muqadas continues, "Malik…understanding the pain of others is what makes us not only human but intune with the world around us. We did not isolate ourselves or confine ourselves to a corner of the world. We spread our wisdom, knowledge, and legacies. You must understand that not every burden can be taken or held. Sometimes, you have to understand and learn to let go."

"Let go, but are you saying…"

"No, letting go is not the same as forgetting," Muqadas concludes, "It is releasing the source of your pain and allowing the light to shine upon it. When we learn how to deal with our pain and put it in it's proper context, we learn one crucial thing, especially as Moors…"

"What is that, many times great grandmother?" Malik asks.

"(Giggles) As our old saying goes, the dragon is the muscle for our people, strong, solid, and durable. It also needs blood, which is pumped from the heart, which is the phoenix. Learn this well, Malik. Then your journey will flow like a river to your destination."

Suddenly, Muqadas begins to disappear. Malik doesn't overreact but simply heeds the words from his ancestor. Muqadas then grabs Malik's chin once more, kisses him on the forehead, then Malik wakes up in the present plane.

The sun is starting the rise, and the birds begin their morning ritual. The slightly orange seam begins to color the surface of the lake with the reflection of the sky. With a new sense of understanding and pride, Malik now looks at the rising sun as what it is, the beginning of a new day. "I get it now," Malik says, "When I go back to that chamber, I need to approach my lesson from a different perspective. This time, I will explore this new power, and then I'll be one step closer to achieving what Bodhidharma was trying to teach me."

Malik then walks out of the lake, takes off his top to wipe his shins and feet, puts his socks, shoes, and top on, and then returns to the sanctuary.

Chapter 5
The Mark of Bodhidharma

Malik enters the sanctuary. The room is completely dark with a new set of candles. The Dragon continues to remain motionless as Malik takes another deep breath.

"I think I'm ready to follow through with this," he assures himself, "Alright, let's do this."

Malik slowly paces himself towards the same spot in front of the dragon. He sits down and closes his eyes. The room remains still, and the air is nonexistent. The perpetual cycle of silence allows Malik to concentrate his Fire Line: his chest rises and falls with each slow breath, his skin is dry, and his ears become awakened to the sounds not present in the living realm.

Suddenly, darkness is invaded by a slimmer of light. The heat from Malik coats his body into a small wave. The glowing layer continues to illuminate the room as Malik remains motionless. As his consciousness gets ready for deep meditation, his Dracocernentia activates and blows a heat wave, lighting all of the candles while giving the room a red glow. Then, the eyes on the statue of the dragon begin to sync with Malik as he is once again transported deep within the confines of his own mind. A cylinder road of flashing colors leads Malik as his mind flows through like a leaf in a stream. The vibrant colors of blue, yellow, green, and orange don't surprise the warrior as he embraces the transition.

After a few moments, Malik is once again sent to the completely white veil. The representation of his body lands in a space that neither has corners, walls, or boundaries. He doesn't look around or swing his head from side to side. Instead, he remains stoic, motionless, and calm. Seconds later, a familiar voice echoes behind Malik.

"Ah…so you have returned. Have you found your conviction, Young Moor?"

Malik smirks for a bit and shakes his head. Then his attitude turns serious: his eyebrows move downward, his mouth clinches, and his eyes focus as he turns around.

"Bodhidharma, I'm ready to try again."

Bodhidharma notices the face of determination painted on Malik. He straightens his lip and rubs his beard with intrigue.

"And what if you fail?" he asks.

"Failure isn't an option. It's a part of suffering, and in order to achieve the Power of Awarelessness, I need to understand not only my pain but the pain of others."

Bodhidharma nods and smirks. Then he gets into a fighting stance by keeping his left hand behind his back, spreading his legs slightly less than shoulder length apart, and keeping his right hand in prayer postition.

"Very well," Bodhidharma responds, "Follow my movements and allow yourself to let go."

Malik gets into the same stance and focuses his attention on Bodhidharma. Then Bodhidharma begins to move into a series of fighting stances.

As Malik continues to follow Bodhidharma, Bodhidharma instructs Malik through the movement while preparing Malik for the inevitable.

“The root of Martial Arts is to conquer yourself,” he continues, “As you move, think not of what troubles you, but what your mind and heart allow you to flow. They will guide you towards the sources of suffering that, in turn, will lead you into a way of confronting them.”

Malik begins to slowly close his eyes. Despite them being shut after 3 moves, he is still able to follow Bodhidharma as he continues to move and instruct.

“Good Malik…good,” he continues, “You are now about to enter into a new set of memories, and with it, you will find the source that plagues your consciousness with the poison of doubt and unworthiness. Soon, you will be forced to confront it without the power to change the outcome, only to embrace what has happened.”

After 5 moves, Bodhidharma stops moving and gets into a rest position. Despite this, Malik continues to move on his own. The sweat from his body pierces through his skin. His muscles bulk up, but his eyes remain closed. Bodhidharma waits with anticipation as Malik dwells deeper and deeper into meditation. Bodhidharma smirks as he knows what is about to happen next.

“Malik, whatever you do, allow the vision to playthrough without judgement or doubt. What you see is what you were meant to see.”

Suddenly, a blue flame begins to emulate from Malik's body. As the flames converge towards his chest, they form a shape of a small phoenix. The silhouette then screeches like an eagle, allowing Malik's eyes to open. However, the eyes are different from his usual Dracocernentia. The entire eye is covered in a cloudy blue hue with a darker indigo round pupil. This is a different Avemcernentia; Malik is able to dive into the memories of the source of his recent suffering.

"I…I… don't believe…No. I must see this through."

The eyes flash back into the mind of Audrey. Malik is able to hear, see, feel, and smell the memory as vividly as if he was living through it. The time represents a moment in Audrey's past.

The year is 2016. Audrey is driving feverously home from college towards the hospital. She is weaving through traffic as she continues to wipe the excess leakage from her eyes. The cell phone continues to ring and ring. She glances at it, but ignores it as she continues to drive.

After reaching the hospital, Audrey looks for a parking spot in the area near the emergency room. After driving around for a minute, she finds a parking spot about 40 yards away from the front entrance. She gets out of the car, slams the door, and runs towards the building.

When Audrey gets inside, she looks at the wall of directions to the rooms. A nurse receptionist recognizes the young adult and offers her services.

"Miss, can I help you?" she asked.

The nurse is a pleasant-looking white woman with yellow highlights in her brown hair, blue eyes, and rosy cheeks. She is also wearing green scrubs and black croc slides.

"Yes, um… my grandmother was admitted about 3 hours ago. I need to find her."

"Oh I think I know who," the woman responds, "Once I press the button, It'll be down the hall, to your first right, and should be within the first 3 rooms or so."

"Thank you, " Audrey responds.

The woman presses the button, and the doors automatically open. Afterwards, Audrey speeds walks through the doors and down the hall. Her breath is heavy and rushed. Her pace is unorthrodox and out of rhythm. As she turns the corner, she sees a woman sitting face down by the 3rd room. Audrey hesitates for a moment until the middle-aged woman glances up. As she rushes up, her face is harden, her eyes widen, and her mouth drops.

"Audrey!" the woman yells, "I have been calling…"

Audrey blocks out all of the sounds and rushes towards the back of the room. The woman tries to stop Audrey by holding her, but Audrey continues to fight through.

"Audrey. Audrey!"

"MOM LET ME GO NOW!" Audrey yells with tears flowing through her eyes.

The pieces of saliva and snot from her nose could not hide the pain burning through her chest. Finally, her mother hugs her and softly whispers in her ear.

"She's gone sweetie," she says, "She's gone…"

"No… NO!!!"Audrey yells, then pushes her mom out of the way.

Audrey storms into the room as the Dr., a tall black man with a small bald spot in the back of his head, grey streaks in his hair and beard, and thick plastic glasses, begins the process of taking the i.v. out of her grandmother. Audrey then crashes her knees to the floor as she sees an elderly woman lie in peace.

"I'm sorry young lady," the Dr. says.

Ignoring his words, Audrey taps her grandmother on the shoulder while pleading with her.

"Grammy wake up. Wake up." she says delusionally, "You're alright. You just taking a little nap that's all."

"Ma'am," the Dr. says, "she left us about 10 minutes ago. I'm sorry."

"YEAH YOU ARE!" Audrey retaliates, "WHAT GOOD ARE YOU!"

"Audrey, that's enough!" her mom says as she once again tries to restrain her.

"Grammy…Grammy…GRAMMY!"

Audrey yells as she bursts into tears. Her head lowers as her mom gets her up. Then they both walk outside the room as the Dr. wipes his eyes and glasses over the lost patient. As soon as they leave the room, Audrey wails in pain like a battle cry, loosing every sense of herself in tears. Her mom closes her eyes and sheds a tear as she desperately tries to calm her daughter down. The women then walk away from the room towards the long hallway.

30 minutes later, the women are standing outside of the hospital as the cool air tries to calm them down. Audrey has her arms folded, still with wet eyes, as she shakes her head angrily at the world. Her mom can do nothing else but watch her daughter mourn in the type of madness concealed only by the love of a departed old woman.

"Why…why did she have to go…" Audrey says softly.

Her mom hesitates for a while, taking a deep breath before responding with an answer.

"You know, your grandmother was sick for a long time Audrey."

"So…why didn't you tell me?" Audrey asks with an attitude.

"Audrey…you didn't need to worry when you are at college. I thought it was best not to get you riled up." her mom answers, "She wanted you to have this."

Her mom takes a small booklet with some photos out of her purse. She attempts to give them to Audrey. Audrey, with her arms still folded, slowly looks in the direction of her mother and the booklet. Her mother tries to give it to Audrey. Then, in a fit of rage, Audrey snatches the book and throws it in the ground.

"REALLY MOM! DO YOU THINK I GIVE A DAMN ABOUT SOME STUPID BOOK?!" Audrey yells.

Her mom desperately grabs the book and the pictures. Then she reengages with Audrey.

"I swear, Audrey Hauss, that temper of yours…" she says, "look, your grandmother wanted you to have this so that you can always remember her."

"But…what if I don't want to?"

Again, her mom tries to hand her the booklet.

"You and I both know you don't mean that, young lady. Please take it."

Audrey's downward-looking eyes transition upwards. Her lips begin to whimper, and her eyes begin to flow with tears. She avoids eye contact with her mom while grabbing the booklet.

"Mom…I want to be alone." Audrey says softly.

Her mom nods while wiping her eyes, then begins to walk away.

"Baby I love you. Please call me when you decide if you need to stay or go back to your dorm."

Audrey again avoids eye contact and stands alone, facing the full moon for several minutes.

Hours pass and Audrey finds herself alone at a local coffee shop. She sits down and sips on her coffee as she slowly looks at the contents of the little booklet. After shifting through some loose photos, one in particular catches her eye. It is a picture of a golden sword with a curved blade and a red jewel at the center of the hilt. Then suddenly, a voice interrupts her concentration.

"That's a beautiful-looking sword." the young man says. Audrey turns around and breathes as she see a white man, wearing a fitted collared shirt, and blue jeans with brown hair smiling at her.

"Yeah well, It was given to me by someone special." "By who, if I may ask?"

"Listen…"

"Victor's my name," the man interrupts.

"Right…Victor," Audrey responds, "I had a very long day and right now, I just need…"

"Another coffee. A woman as pretty as you shouldn't be alone, at least without another cup of coffee."

"(Sigh)...That's sweet of you but…"

"Say no more. I take it you're a Frappuccino type of girl, with whip cream with a drizzle of caramel?" Victor says confidently.

Audrey tries to hide her blushing by putting on a hard exterior. However, her loneliness gets the better of her and she succumbs to his subtle charms.

"Sure…" she says.

"I'll be right back." Victor says as he precedes to grab another coffee.

Five minutes later, Victor returns with a grande-size Frappuccino with whipped cream with caramel. Audrey takes a sip, closes her eyes, then smiles.

"Mmm, that's good. Thank you." she says.

"No worries, my dear," Victor says.

"So, what's with the accent? You sound like you're from Europe somewhere." Audrey asks.

"Indeed. I live in London, but I'm here in a special exchange program at the University of Georgia."

"Really? I go there as well." Audrey responds, "I don't see you around, but then again, it is a big campus."

"Truly," Victor responds, "I'll be here for one more semester, then I have to head back home."

"I see." "Anywho, I noticed that picture. Are you into swords?"

"OH me? No, it was something passed down by my grandmother. She just died." Audrey responds.

"Oh dear, terribly sorry 'bout that love." Victor empathizes, "My parents died recently too."

"Oh no," Audrey says. "Yeah, but they left me with an inheritance to pass down their legacies. So I'm here to finish my education so that I can go back and keep what they built alive."

"I see," Audrey says, "So what is it about this sword?"

"Well, my dear. THAT sword is said to be held by those who conquered much of Europe during the dark ages."

"Dark ages? You mean Medieval times?" Audrey asks.

"Well yes, one in the same," Victor continues, "You see, during the end of the Roman Empire, Islam became a growing religion. With that, combined several tribes and nations into one purpose, the expansion of their beliefs. The leader of this army were known as Moors."

"Moors?" Audrey asks, "Never heard of them."

"Quite fascinating blokes, the Moors. Some legends say that they even rode dragons."

"Dragons? Really?" Audrey scoffs, "Victor are you high, sir?"

"I assure you I'm not daft," Victor responds, "You see here (Victor points at the picture), the handles resemble dragon scales, and that ruby is actually the eye of the dragon."

"Really. Victor, how do you know about all of this?"

"Well my dear, that's going to cost you another cup of coffee."

"Listen Victor, I appreciate it, and it's getting late."

"No worries, I just don't want this to be the last time I see such a beautiful woman." Victor says. "Well listen, since we go to the same school, maybe we can link up again. Here's my number."

Audrey gets up, takes out her cell phone, and exchanges numbers with Victor. Afterwards, Audrey addresses Victor one last time.

"It was good talking to you," she says, "and the name is Audrey."

"Such a lovely name," Victor responds, "Now, don't let this be our last meeting."

"I'm sure we'll see each other again," Audrey says.

"I'm counting on it." Victor responds as he winks at her. Then a fury of smoke clouds the memory as the phoenix screeches again.

Malik is panting hard: dripping with sweat, as the small phoenix moves from his chest and looks him in the eyes. As Malik regains himself, the phoenix screeches one last time before disappearing into nothingness. Bodhidharma then smiles as Malik relaxes himself.

"I…I…get it now," Malik reflects, "The first time I met her, she mentioned that her grandmother died. Then she mentioned that her grandfather abandoned her. But…"

"But?" Bodhidharma interrupts briefly.

"But she never knew the truth. The whole truth. She was lonely and Victor…"

"You see Moor, you have now tapped into more depths of your power that you have yet to fully understand. The power of Awarenlessness is about knowing all to forget all. In battle, you must remember the reason to fight without it drowning your senses and dulling your ability to respond. When driven by rage, you don't see the dangers that surround you until you are ensnared in the trap."

"Much like King Roderick in the battle with my ancestors. He overestimated his strength with his allies and was outflanked." Malik reflects.

"Truly. Now that you have found the source of your suffering, it is up to you to understand that suffering and how to stop it from infecting the world."

"Will you teach me, Bodhidharma?"

Bodhidharma smiles as he walks closer to Malik. He takes his right hand and places it on Malik's chest. His hand then leaves a golden mark, which illumates into a bright color.

"Your training here is complete," Bodhidharma says, "This is a path you must take. The mark will help you on your quest and expose itself to those who seek the same as you. Look for the answers within yourself."

Malik looks at Bodhidharma but doesn't respond. After grasping the essence of his words, he nods at Bodhidharma, balls his left fist and, covers it with the palm of his right hand, then bows. Bodhidharma returns the jester.

A split second later, Malik wakes up in front of the stone dragon. The candles are nearly completely melted to the floor; Malik sits for a while as a familiar figure stands at the doorway. The old monk stands in his normal stance as he continues to watch Malik, Malik uses this opportunity to reflect in Chinese, on what he's learned.

"Shīfu, (***I now understand that to find the solution is to understand the journey. That of myself, and my enemy's***.)"

" (***Understanding the pain of others is crucial, even amongst enemies***)," the monk continues in Chinese, " (***One cannot wage war on both fronts and expect to win. You must learn how to conquer yourself before the enemy can exploit it. Suffering does not have to be forever, but it can be a tool for enlightenment***)."

Malik gets up and faces the old monk. Then he finishes the conversation to gain further understanding.

" (***Does empathizing with my enemy make me stronger because he can't hurt me? Or does knowing that I too am capable of such depths of evil if I neglect the needs of my inner Fire Line***)?"

The old monk smiles as he can see the mark glow. Despite not shining to normal eyes, the monk can see it through a scope of consciousness that can't be view unless tapped within a deep level of spirituality. He then concludes his message.

" (***You are asking the right questions. Take heed, and do not confuse yourself about the true enemy and who isn't. You will learn someday that the one that confines themselves to defeat are those who refuse to acknowledge their true self***)."

Malik takes heed of the message, closes his eyes, and bows. The old monk returns the favor by bowing back.

Afterwards, he leaves the door and walks away. In front view of Malik, he sees a setting sun. Flashes of visions flood his eyesight of a land of the rising sun, images of melanated people lurking in the shadows, and a clue to his next destination.

"I can sense it now," Malik thinks, "And I know where I need to go next…"

Chapter 6
Kindred Moors

The sky is blue and clear. It covers the vast and calming seas that stretch throughout eternity. The smooth songs of the waves caress the air like a comb through hair.

At a lone island, with a peak stretching high while covered by a forest and a river valley, a lone deity enjoys a picnic with his wife. The godly figure stood 4 stories tall, wearing a brown conical sedge hat, with a turquoise sash with brown shoulder pads, and leg pads, armed with a katana sharp enough to cut through air while wearing socks and sandals. The deity also had silky black hair that flowed down his back, a goatee to match, and the eyes of a warrior. He takes his hat off, smiles, sits next to his wife and in Japanese, offers her a drink.

"(***I appreciate this substance, my love***)" she compliments, " (***Your presence warms me like the eternal fires from the sun***)."

" (***Nothing burns hotter in this existence than my heart…as it longs for you, Kushinada***)".

Kushinada blushes at his advances while stroking her long, jet-back, silky hair. She also adjusts her sandy orange kimono while both enjoy their lunches.

As they both continue to giggle and smirk at one another, the winds of change quickly blow past their comfort. The once clear skies give way to clouds shrouded with darkness and cloaked with despair. The shimmer of light gives an orchestra of clacking as a brewing storm quickly advances towards the island.

Kushinada sighs with concern as the deity stands up with the sword with the ready. She slowly gets up and curesses her husband's arms as she tries to ascertain the coming storm.

"(***This is unusual***)," she ponders, " (***We must go inside and wait out the storm***)."

The deity grunts angrily with distrust and curiousity. His daring personality senses something that has brought the storm.

"Kushinada, (***my love. You must wait here while I deal with this intrusion***)"

" Shikashi, watashi no ai (But my love…)"

"(***This is no ordinary storm***)," he interrupts as he partially unsheathes his sword, "(***I will return once this problem is dealt with…*** (he faces her with a smile) ***Go now***.)"

Kushinada releases her grip as the deity makes his way towards the shore.

Suddenly, Kushinada yells out one last thing to her husband. "Susanno!" she yells.

He turns his head slightly, glancing at her with his left eye.

" (***Fight well, and with honor. Come back to me with your sword or on it***.)"

Susanno nods, then faces forward to the direction of the incoming storm.

Susanno reaches the edge of the beach of his island. He unsheathes his sword and raises it towards the sky. The ring from his blade commands the waves to crash towards him as he steps on it to allow him to transport towards the epicenter of the storm. Quickly, the waves carry him. He boldly stares at the storm, never taking his eyes off of it. The crashing of the waves becomes a mosh pit of calamity and ruggedness. The storms alter the equilibrium into a chaotic series of events as the storms get worse and worse.

Then, Susanno begins to anticipate the encounter; the inner workings of his mind flood it with thoughts and outcomes that plague the warrior. "(*This is unusual indeed*)," he ponders in Japanese, "(*I sense a presence, yet familiar but also different in it's motive*)."

Despite his reservations, Susanno perceeds on as fast as the waves carry him.

When Susanno reaches deep within the eye of the storm, something catches his eyes. A golden flash appears and flies towards Susanno. It flies faster and faster as Susanno crunches his eyebrows downward, still with his sword on the ready.

The flash comes within a few feet from Susanno until it's true form reveals itself. Susanno is startled by the reveal. His eyes widen, he lifts his conical hat, and relaxes his right arm while still holding his sword. A large, golden dragon has flown towards the great deity. The eyes glow beige with a red outline, two large pretruding horns, and a wingspan that seems to cover half of the ocean. The majestic beast lets of a roar, as a series of thunder serenate it's voice.

Unperturbed and not intimidated, Susanno stares down the beast and begins to find his nerve.

“(***A great dragon dares to show itself on my domain***),” he declares in Japanese, “(***Very well beast, I will show you the might of Susanno, god of the seas and the storms. Prepare to meet Kusanagi.)***”

The ring of the sword as it’s name was called, signals the dragon of an impending doom. The great dragon does little to nothing, continuing to fly in place.

Susanno gets into position as he prepares to attack. The series of thunder continue to clash around like a crowd while the series of lightning provide the little light in the midst of the storm. Then, the dragon lunges forward towards Susanno, roaring and showing it’s glowing white teeth. The collaboration of thunder and lightning add the dragon's confidence as Susanno gets ready to engage.

Susanno raises his sword in the air. He looks at the charging dragon and grits his teeth. Then with a battle cry that rivals the storm itself, he makes a large, clean, and decisive swing of his sword and cuts the dragon in half.

However, when Susanno looks up, he is startled and amazed of the outcome. The magical beast not only splits into, but each section manifests into silhouettes of two black men: one dressed in traditional samurai armor, two swords, and dreadlocks protruding from the back of his helmet, while the other cloaked in a black suit that covers everything but it’s grayish blue eyes.

The storms settle into a stable flow of wind. The seas calm down, and the clouds turn from dark to light gray. Susanno, with the sword still at the ready, keeps his guard as the two figures stand by motionless for a few seconds.

Afterwards, the black samurai unsheathes his swords, places them on the water, steps back, and kneels in reverence. The other black man does the same.

Intrigued by this behavior, Susanno carefully sheaths his sword and glances towards the odd entities. As he walks closer, both of the men look up at Susanno and ignite their eyes. The samurai's golden eyes matches the light by the eyes of the other to shine in front of Susanno.

In this brief exchange, Susanno is given many visions of indescribable events. The images and foreshadowing overwhelm even the mightiest of gods as Susanno stumbles in an attempt to maintain his focus and footing.

After several minutes of processing, Susanno closes his eyes, lowers his head, then looks at the men.

"Rikaishimasu (I understand)" the deity whispers in Japanese, " (***I will teach you the art of the sword so that you can pass it down to your descendants to quell the ultimate evil***.)"

Afterwards, the samurai gets up and bows again at Susanno. The other gets up, takes his right hand, places it on his chest, and extents his first two fingers while balling the remaining three fingers towards the middle of the palm. He then bows his head and disappears into a mysterious cloud of black mist and smoke.

RING…RING…RING…Malik is startled and gets up from his sleep. The vision he'd experienced from sleeping once again causes him to sweat perfusely. The alarm on his phone continues to ring as he tries to gather himself.

"You know, you never get used to those kinds of visions," Malik reflects as he grabs the phone.

He turns off the alarm, maneuvers his legs towards the edge of the bed, then looks at the flip phone. His mind is once again cluttered with questions, concerns, and motives as he scans around his small Chinese hotel.

Malik had traveled on foot through the day and night in an attempt to avoid detection from possible eyes of the new Elitetion regime. Despite feeling the presence, Malik does what he can to suppress his abilities until he can fully understand the motive of the Golden Dragon. Malik then reopens the flip phone to scroll through the contents for a number.

"(Sigh) Let's see here…" Malik ponders, "I hope he's progressing better than I am."

Malik pushes a button, dials the number, and places it on his right ear.

RING…RING…RING…RIN (Click)

"How goes the journey?" the man answers.

Malik takes a deep breath before responding.

"Well, after I left the Temple, I continued to keep a low profile as I get ready to leave the country. What about things on your end?"

"So, Esmeralda and I are getting ready to fly to England. Even though it's settled, the presence of the Elitetion has already spread it's disease." the man says. "You mean the Elitetion already…"

"It's under the guise of a pandemic. Many people are getting sick, some are dying, but there's also some after effects."

"After effects?" Malik asks, "How?"

"It's too much to explain right now," the man says, "Here's what I want you to do, Malik. I suspect that you are going on your next flight?"

"Yes, I got another vision. The short version is that it dealt with someone by the name of Susanno."

"Susanno, the Japanese god of Storms, masters of the seas, and arguably the greatest swordsman in exsistance," he continues, "Alright, I will make another call. Once this conversation is over, I want you to destroy this phone completely. I don't care how. Afterwards you will meet a man once you reach Tokyo. Don't worry about seeking him out, he'll find you. Your powers will enable you to feel him out. He will give you another phone with only one number. Call it when you are ready."

"Understood," Malik responds, "As soon as I'm done there, I will dial the number. I sense that whatever is in Japan is meant to help me defeat these bastards once and for all."

"I believe it will," he says, "Malik…be careful."

"You too…Mason."

Malik hangs up the phone, clenches it with his hand, and methodically heats it up through his hands to completely burn the phone. Afterwards, he packs up his meager belongings, makes sure his backpack contains a laptop and makes his way out of the room.

In the otherside of the world, Mason hangs up the phone and stares at the window. He remains silent as the night sky completely takes over, showing the lights of the city. Slowly, footsteps creep closer and closer until soft words exit out of rosy lips.

"Buenas noches (Good evening) Mason, was that who I thought it was?"

"Indeed it was Esmeralda." Mason responds.

"How is he holding up?" she asks, "I hope that he is…"

"Seems you've grown fond of the idiota, more than you want to admit," Mason responds, "I think Malik has a long way to go. However, he'll be fine as long as he doesn't give up on himself. In the mean time, it's time for us to go to the airport."

"Already?" Esmeralda asks, "But I didn't think that…"

"The time has come to coordinate our efforts. I received an anonymous tip to meet a potential ally in London."

"How do you know if this isn't a trap Mason?" Esmeralda asks, "You know that there can be many of them out there."

"I do indeed, Esmeralda," Mason answers confidently, "But with the pandemic underway, we must move quickly if we are going to stop the operations at it's source. Besides, I have a Sombre de fenix to protect me, yes?"

Esmeralda nods in compliance and Mason gives her the phone.

"You know what to do," Mason instructs, "After that, we need to catch the next flight out of here."

"Comprendida (Understood)."

Esmeralda then looks at the phone, closes her eyes, activates the Avemcernentia and burns the phone in the palm of her hand. The intense flames and heat destroy the phone completely, leaving nothing but smoke as evidence of it's existence. Afterwards, Esmeralda and Mason gather their things together. Mason escorts Esmeralda out as he does a last-second look of the room before he turns off the lights and closes the doors.

Several minutes later, Mason checks out of the hotel and grabs a cab. Esmeralda follows and enters the back seat first. Mason then enters the car and shuts the door.

"Al aeropuertopor favor señor (To the airport please sir)" Mason requests.

The cab driver nods, then drives towards the airport.

During the drive, Esmeralda looks through the streets as Mason patiently looks ahead. Her eyes become moist, her face becomes tense and disturbed, and her attitude shifts of that of concern. Then she faces Mason.

"Mason," Esmeralda asks, "How did you know about us? I mean…you know (She nods towards the driver while trying to remain vague)."

Understanding the cues, Mason speaks in cryptic but concise language that he hopes Esmeralda can understand.

"When I worked for the agency, a mutual friend and I was working to fix a problem. We went to certain neighborhoods and found out that certain tools were missing."

"So, these tools were special?" Esmeralda inquires.

"Indeed they were. So much so that the friend was able to identify why they were special. So one day, this mutual friend showed me a secret to the tools that no one ever knew."

"Did this secret involve, you know (Esmeralda carefully points to her eye)..."

Mason nods as he continues his story.

"When we finished figuring out what happened to the tools, I knew that there were more out there. However, the friend knew that there would be people willing to do whatever to get the tools."

"*So, he knew about Eulalia's powers, and this is why he's helping us, because she trusted him*," Esmeralda connects, "Well I'm looking forward to this vacation."

"So am I," Mason responds as he winks at Esmeralda, "I hear that the castles are wonderful, and the people…are welcoming."

The cab reaches the terminal at the airport. The driver addresses passengers. "Serán 40 euros (That will be 40 Euros)" he says.

Mason gives him the Euros, nods and addresses the driver.

"Quédese con elcambio (Keep the change)."

"Gracias Señor." Mason and Esmeralda get out of the car with their small belongings and luggages. The cab then drives away as Mason and Esmeralda prepare to enter the terminal.

"Who are you expecting to meet in London, Mason?" Esmeralda asks. Mason smiles, hands Esmeralda her ticket and passport, then responds.

"Let's just say, they're kindred spirits. Alright now, let's get through baggage claim and security."

Esmeralda nods as the two get in line to fly out.

Chapter 7
Common Convergence

Several hours later, an announcement interrupts Esmeralda's napping. Mason is patiently looking through his several leads, documents, and messages on his laptop.

"(DING) Ladies and Gentlemen, we will be landing in London in about 20 minutes. We now instruct you to take your seats and fasten your seatbelts. Do not get up until the plane is at a complete stop and instructed to get up. We will do a final run through if you have any trash or empty plates. Thank you once again for flying with us."

"(YAWN) I'm starting to get a little tired," Esmeralda says, "How will we know who to meet or where to go?"

"I have a lead that will escort us to a secret place in the eastern part of the city," Mason explains, "You'll be able to know. The 'other' sense will kick in when the time is right."

"Yes, but these 'senses' are unpredictable," Esmeralda explains.

"Oh, trust me," Mason ensures, "You'll know it when you know it."

Esmeralda nods as the plane begins to descend from the clouds.

As the plane reaches the airport, Esmeralda looks at the window to see the spectacle of the city: with its rustic, old buildings, the lights that meander through the city streets, and the mighty Thames carving a path through it all.

"*Increíble. Hay una cierta belleza cuando observas desde los cielos (Incredible. There's a certain beauty when you observe from the skies*)," Esmeralda ponders, "Me pregunto si nuestros ancestros tenían la misma perspectiva al montar en las grandes aves *(I wonder if our ancestors had the same perspective when riding on the great birds)*?"

Mason glances at Esmeralda as she continues to witness the descend. He smirks as he too thinks about the eventual reunion.

"*I can feel it*," he continues, "*I know that the beginning of the end is coming. I know that if we pull this out, this will be the start of a long reckoning that is way overdue.*"

Time passes by as the plane lands on an airstrip. When the plane reaches the ground, the loud crash of air catches up as the plane decelerates to a normal speed. The passengers all wait patiently as the pilot maneuvers the huge 757 to a docking station. Esmeralda and Mason look ahead as they maintain their poise before reaching their destination.

Finally, the plane finds a loading dock to secure itself. With precision and skill, the pilot masterfully parks the huge plane by the docking station. Then another announcement comes through the intercom.

"(DING) Ladies and Gentlemen, the plane is now at a complete stop. Make sure you gather all of your things and personal items. Thank you again for flying with us, and welcome to London.

"Finalmente (Finally), my back is starting to ache," Esmeralda states.

"Yes, I agree," Mason responds, "I'm starting to get too old for all of this traveling. Come on, let's get our things and go." Mason and Esmeralda grab their backpacks, get up from their seats and escort themselves out of the plane.

The duo makes their way towards baggage claim. As they walk down the corridor, Esmeralda suddenly feels a sharp pain on the right side of her head.

"UGH…" Esmeralda complains, as Mason takes notice.

"Are you alright?" Mason asks.

Esmeralda's eyes quickly transform partially to the Avemcernentia before she closes her eyes. However, Mason doesn't miss the subtle gesture and quickly deduces the cause.

"*That's right, there's a correlation between Moors. But I need to keep her calm until the time is right.*"

Meanwhile, Esmeralda sees visions of a Moor with dreadlocks, with a silhouette of a woman behind him with blue eyes. She continues to rub her head to relieve the pain.

"UGH…¿Quién es este chico... y la mujer detrás de él? (*Who is this guy...and the woman behind him*)?" she wonders, "Sean quienes sean, siento una conexión cercana... especialmente con… (*Whoever they are, I sense a close connection…especially with...*)"

Mason taps Esmeralda.

"Esmeralda, are you alright?"

"Si, I just…"

"I know," Mason interrupts, "Do you think you can control it until we leave the airport?"

Esmeralda looks at Mason with a half-hearted face of confidence with trying to deal with the slight pain. Mason returns the gesture as they continue to go down the baggage claim.

Ten minutes later, Mason and Esmeralda reach the baggage claim. As Esmeralda waits for their luggage, Mason pulls out a flip phone from his pocket. He quickly opens the phone, texts a random number, sends it, then puts it back in his pocket. Afterwards, Mason's brown suitcase and Esmeralda's blue bag show up. Mason walks forward to grab the bags and hands Esmeralda her blue bag.

"Here you go, dear," Mason says, "Now, are you ready?"

"Si," she responds, "I think I can make it out of here without another episode."

"Or just until we get in the car. One of my contacts will be waiting for us."

Mason explains as they both make their way out of the area. Esmeralda is anxious about the lack of information Mason is letting on. Her face is tense, her hair ruffled, but she does her best to maintain her composure. Mason remains relaxed and confident. His demeanor balances Esmeralda, keeping her at ease as much as the situation dictates.

Moments later, Mason and Esmeralda make it outside the Terminal. Despite being after midnight, the night is still filled with lights, noise and vehicles. Esmeralda rubs her left arm while Mason remains composed. He doesn't move his head or show any sign of concern. Again, the pains begin to manifest in Esmeralda's head, but she does what she can by not drawing attention to herself. Instead, she smiles to hide her discomfort while Mason returns the smile.

Then, a black 2022 Jaguar F-PACE drives up next to Mason and Esmeralda. She notices the expensive SUV and begins to transform her eyes. Before the Avemcernentia is activated, Mason taps her on her shoulder and nods, prompting her to deactivate her eyes.

"This is it," he assures, "Let's get in."

The drive unlocks the trunk and allows the duo to put their bags in. Then, Mason opens the door for Esmeralda before entering the back seat. Mason closes the door, then the driver addresses them.

"We fight for the future of Black People, Mentor," he says.

"And our resolve is uncompromising," Mason responds.

Then the driver switches gears and drives away from the airport.

During the short drive, Mason eases the tension by introducing Esmeralda to his operation.

"So, now that we are away from potential prying eyes and ears, let me introduce you to our escort," Mason explains, "This is Lionel, code name Barbary Lion. Lion, this is Esmeralda, the one I told you about."

"Hola. Encantado de conocer finalmente a un miembro de la legendaria Sombra del Fénix. (Hello. Nice to finally meet a member of the legendary Shadow of the Phoenix," Lionel responds.

"Oh…Es un placer conocerte también (It's nice to meet you too)," Esmeralda responds, "Mason, how does he…"

"You see, Esmeralda, back in the states, we are OBR, a militia group dedicated to ending the Systematic White Supremacist machine that has oppressed black people. As you know, you're not the only one with powers. As a matter of fact, we have some within our ranks as we speak."

"So, you mean to tell me that Malik wasn't part of this group?" Esmeralda asks.

"Well, there are some variables that need to be wrung out about that," Mason responds.

"You see, Esmeralda," Lionel adds on while continuing to drive, " When Victor Goth captured the sword, we found out that he was able to cause the pandemic that is spreading all over the world."

"Yeah, I heard many of the residence in Madrid talking about it," Esmeralda says.

"The world calls it the Pustula Flu, but we call it…the Shroud," Lionel concludes.

Esmeralda intensifies her mannerisms by scrunching her eyebrows down and tightening her lip. Her anxiety has now turned to deep intrigue.

"What you need to understand, Esmeralda, is that this Shroud is having an alter effect on not only Black people, but everyone on Earth with a certain level of Melanin. We also notice that the white people not only seem to fare better, but acts of racism have expanded exponentially," Mason explains.

"So, you think that the sword is magnifying its power by linking everyone who shares the common lineage and bio-makeup of the Moor, thus using the same instrument meant to unite us against us?" Esmeralda asks.

"That's what some of our scientists and allies believe," Lionel answers, "We believe that one of the Elitetion facilities is harboring the chemicals to help spread the Shroud. That's where you and the others come in."

"Others?" Esmeralda asks.

"You'll see soon enough, Esmeralda," Mason concludes, "Paciencia Fénix (Patience Phoenix)."

Lionel continues to drive as the travelers remain silent throughout the remainder of the trip.

Five minutes later, the SUV makes it to a facility on the eastern bank of the Thames River. They are meant by two guards dressed in all black armor, combat boots, beanie hats and machine guns. Lionel rolls down the window to let one of the guards examine the passengers. He takes a good look at Mason and Esmeralda, nods, then gives a hand signal to open the gate. The compound is an old military facility. It houses 10 medium-sized buildings that surround a large building about the size of a football stadium. Lionel parks the Jaguar in front of the building before he turns off the SUV. Suddenly, Esmeralda feels sharp pains again.

"UGH!" Esmeralda complains, "It's happening again."

"I know, we're close," Mason says, "Soon, the feelings will go away. I promise."

"Well, ladies and gents, it's time we met our welcome," Lionel says.

The passengers agree, calm down, and exit the Jaguar.

Despite the short length to the doors, the walk seems like walking through a vast desert for Esmeralda. Each step is amplified in her mind, her breath is heavy and thick, and her nerves become shaken. Despite the feeling of anxiousness, she moves on as she awaits finding the source of her feelings. Meanwhile, Lionel continues to chat with Mason.

"Our base leader has been expecting you for some time, Mentor," Lionel says, "he wants to go over the plans for Operation Liberation with you."

"We have time, Lion," Mason responds, "but right now, this meeting is essential to that plan, hence why this is of more importance."

"Understood," Lionel says before opening the door for his guests.

Esmeralda and Mason enter the building with Lionel following behind. They walk towards several members of OBR, armed with bulletproof vests and guns, as they look on with a subtle awe of their guests. After a few moments and extra steps, they come across a large conference room with a tall, black man with a short haircut, a full goatee, and a stature that commands respect. Lionel opens the door, allowing Mason and Esmeralda to go in.

After Lionel closes the door, the majestic, 6'3'' man slowly raises his head. He stares down Mason and Esmeralda. He crosses his hands behind his back, takes a slow, deep breath, and then he walks towards Esmeralda. He stands in front of her and gets a good look at her. Esmeralda matches his intensity by looking him in the eye. She shows no notion of emotion; instead slightly changes her eyes from brown to blue to brown again.

"Hmph…" the man nods.

Then he walks towards Mason. Mason looks at the man and stares back at him.

After 10 seconds of intense silence, Mason breaks the ice with his charismatic charm. “We both know you still suck at keeping a straight face.”
The man nods, then does nothing for about 2 seconds, then bursts out in laughter before giving Mason a big hug.

“HA HAHAHAHAHAHAHA…Mentor Mason Richardson, here in the flesh, mate,” he joyfully says as the men continue to embrace each other like long lost brothers.

“Indeed, I am,” Mason responds, “Good to see you again, Terrance.”

After a few seconds of pleasantries, both men disengage and engage in catching up.

“Very good to see you again, mate. Still have that spark, I see,” Terrance says.

“I still have time in me to make things right,” Mason says, “Here’s the one I told you about.”

Terrance looks at Esmeralda as she relaxes her body. Then she allows herself to open up as Mason introduces her.

“Esmeralda, this is Terrance Ongolo, code name Black Tiger,” Mason continues, “We once worked together with a joint terrorist task force between the English Secret Service and the FBI.”

“And now we are back together to fight the biggest terrorist this world has ever seen,” Terrance adds, “Es muy agradable conocerte (It is very nice to meet you) Esmeralda.”

“El placer es todo mío (Pleasure is all mine) Terrance.” Terrance shakes Esmeralda’s hand before continuing his explanation.

“You must be wondering why Mason here brought you here, lass,” Terrance inquires.

"Well, I'm somewhat informed, but I don't know how this deals with me specifically." Esmeralda responds.

"Quite understandable," Terrance continues, "As you know, the man you know as Victor Goth created his biomedical company here in London. However, our intel has informed us that he left the country to go to America, leaving the facility vulnerable and open to attack."

"Why did he go to America?" Esmeralda asks, "And what will destroying the facility do?"

"Excellent questions, my dear," Terrance answers, "America is the premier influence of the world. If Goth can control the power structure in the states, he can usher in a worldwide genocide, then give the antidote at a price to give to the surviving population."

"Sound like the same sadistic bastard that..." Esmeralda stutters before remembering the traumatic events of that night.

Terrence closes his eyes for a moment, then follows up by expressing his plans.

"However, with the manpower we have, we are not strong enough to endure the effects of the Shroud without succumbing to some sort of sickness. We have certain herbal remedies, but..."

"But the ingredients are fastly becoming harder and harder to gather...And we're running out of time," a voice interrupts.

Esmeralda and Mason quickly move their heads towards the left to locate the source of the interruption. Terrance smiles as he begins with the introductions.

"Ah...I almost forgot you were there, mate," he says.

“You know I have a flair for the dramatic,” the voice echoes as the man with light brown skin, dreadlocks down his back, and the Dracocernentia reveals himself. Esmeralda’s eyes immediately activate as he comes into view.

“YOU! You are the one who’s in my visions!” Esmeralda reveals.

“Well, seems I have another fan,” he states, “Names Bakala love, and you must be Señorita Esmeralda.”

“Ok, saber quién soy mientras te acabo de conocer me hace sentir muy incómodo. (Ok, you knowing who I am while I just meet you makes me really uncomfortable).” Esmeralda scolds.

Then, another voice interrupts the tension that takes Esmeralda by surprise.

“Todavía tan temperamental y rápido para juzgar a mi pajarito (Still so quick tempered and quick to judge my little bird),” she continues, “¿No te he enseñado nada? (Have I taught you nothing)?”

Esmeralda recognizes the voice. Her heart sinks, her voice begins to crack, and tears begin to flow down her face. She becomes speechless as the rest of the room witnesses a woman coming out of the shadows. She has pale, tan skin with a few wrinkles. Her hair is cut short with finger length, some grey streaks with black, about 5’8’’ tall and with her Avemcernentia fully activated. Esmeralda begins to crack her voice with the reveal.

“Eu…Eulalia?” Esmeralda tearfully whispers.

Eulalia smiles, shedding one tear, then nodding yes. Esmeralda rushes towards Eulalia and gives her an emotional hug. She cries uncontrollably as Eulalia embraces her.

“estoy aquí mi niña (I’m here my girl)” she whispers, “Estoy aquí (I’m here)”

Esmeralda continues to cry as the room gives them room to catch up. Bakala steps towards Terrance and Mason as the women exchange a few words.

Esmeralda lets go of Eulalia and begins to question her.

"Eulalia…How…WHY?!"

"I couldn't reveal to you what I discovered that time to you," Eulalia explains. At the same time, she deactivates her eyes, "You see, I became a target of the United States because I discovered my powers only recently. The only person who knew was Mason."

"You see, Esmeralda," Mason adds, "Right before I met Malik…"

"Malik?" Bakala interrupts, "The Yank?!"

"One in the same Bakala," Mason answers, "Eulalia and I were tasked with a special assignment to find people who had the potential powers of the Fire Line. As we kept tracking, Eulalia discovered that she was descended from two different lines: One Moorish Line that became indoctrinated into a Spanish aristocratic family and another that led an expedition to build a mission around the 17th century in America. Then Eulalia began suspecting something that turned out to be correct."

"What was it?" Esmeralda asks.

"That the United States Government is not only in league with the Elite 8, but they were secretly funding them by overlooking the kidnapping of the girls to extract the genes necessary to replicate our powers."

"So that's why you faked your death!" Esmeralda pieces together.

"Si," Eulalia confirms, "Mason here needed to have a sacrifice as proof of my demise, so that he could retire and dedicate his full time to this…OBR…and us."

Terrance then shifts the conversation after the group has leveled their emotions and introductions. He then directs the attention back to the table.

"I know this is very emotional for everybody, but we need to solidify our plans for Operation Liberation if we are to stop the spread of this pandemic."

"I agree," Mason concurs, "We'll need the might of the Dragon and Phoenix Moors to use their powers to purify the air while we attack the compound."

"But with all due respect," Esmeralda interjects, "It took Malik all the rage he had to create a fire blast so massive, it counteracts the effects of the chemicals. I'm not sure if we can sustain a siege that long."

"There is a way Pequeña ave (Little Bird)," Eulalia says.

"We have to fight as one and match our heart signatures to maintain our control as well as support," Bakala adds, "In the meantime, I will have to show some of the ways our power can help in other areas."

"Understood," Esmeralda complies.

"Then, we will come back to our plans tomorrow midday," Terrance says, "In the meantime, Bakala and Eulalia will escort Esmeralda to where she will be sleeping."

"Come on, Pequeña ave (Little Bird)," Eulalia prompts.

Esmeralda looks back at Mason. Mason gives her the nod to go, then Esmeralda and Bakala leave the room.

Terrance looks on as the Moor leaves his view of sight. Mason stands next to him as they both contemplate the ramifications of the mission.

"You know, mate," Terrance ponders, "20 years ago, I would've thought these young'ns knew nothing about due process, or doing things the right way."

"Yes," Mason responds, "but because of the failures of our past generation, we were force to acknowledge the truth too late. I can still remember the seeds of change back in the 80s and 90s when the effects of drugs devastated our communities."

"Same here, mate," Terrance agrees, "Yet, it's good to know this generation isn't afraid to fight back. You should get some sleep as well."

"Hmph…a luxury we no longer have…or at least comfortably," Mason says, "Until tomorrow, Black Tiger."

Mason also leaves the room, leaving Terrance to look beyond the doors. After standing for a while, he turns around, sits down on his chair, and rubs his head. Then he continues to stare profusely at the plans on top of the table for the rest of the night.

Chapter 8
Brewing Stew of Change

The deeming yellow lights slowly rise from the east. As the weaning hours of the night transform into the morning, the blazing orange begins to overtake the purplish sky to signal a new day. Terrance stares at the river to witness yet another sunrise. His eyes are still sharp and alert, despite not indulging in the luxury of rest. Slowly, steps signal the arrival of another person as Terrance continues to maintain his posture.

"So, Black Tiger, another day in the war for freedom, hey?" Mason asks.

Terrance chuckles underneath his deep breath. Then he smirks before addressing his friend.

"You know, mate," Terrance responds, "About 5 months ago, the chap Bakala came to us wanting to ally with us. As you know, we were somewhat aware of him and those who possess those powers…(sigh) still boggles my mind how much of our history is like Science Fiction. Seems it's hard to know what the truth is anymore."

"Yes," Mason says, "When I was tasked to find and locate those who had the right lineage, I too began to question what was real and what wasn't."

Terrance then shifts his body towards Mason. He wipes his glossy eyes, then clears his throat. Mason squints his eyes in anticipation of the shift in demeanour as Terrance begins to lay out his concerns.

"Bakala briefed me on his adventure with the one known as Shadowmoor from America."

"Yes, Terrance, I know of Shadowmoor," Mason confirms, "He was 'ONE' of those that I was ordered to investigate back in the states."

"(Chuckling) I figured he had some association with you, which is one of the reasons why Bakala didn't detain him while he was trying to thwart a kidnapping attempt."

"The moment I met HIM," Mason emphasizes, "I knew he was a hero and the one who could change the course of this Race War."

Then Terrance crosses his arms and circles around. He looks up at the ceiling, then at the window. After collecting his thoughts, he looks back at Mason.

"When he informed me of the enemy's plans to use biochemical warfare to implement racial genocide, I immediately probed to see what could be done to counteract this."

"OBR has created organic substances that help keep the body's pH levels Alkaline so that we don't succumb to whatever it is that is killing us."

"You see, mate," Terrance responds, "the Pustula Flu doesn't have a single strain. It's as if it's being amplified somehow, like it's evolving faster than we can control it."

Mason rubs his beard and nods his head. "The Harq Alqadr!"

"The what?" Terrance asks.

"Terrance, do you remember stories of the Moors that reached England?"

"Yeah, but I thought that was just a legend."

"Well, the legend was rooted in fact, and the fact is that there was indeed a sword that had mysterious power. Some believe because half of the sword was forged by some long forgotten Gold Alloy…"

"That could be a conductor to absorb energy just like…"

"Melanin," Mason interrupts as Terrance walks towards the table to rest his hands.

Terrance leans on the table as he compartmentalizes the flow of information. His mouth twitches closed with each new thought that is moving faster than he can process in his mind. Mason then walks towards Terrance and addresses him.

"We need to contact OBR in the states through a secure line, Terrance."

"Agreed, Mate," Terrance agrees, "I'll get a Zoom screen set up in the conference room. We need to give this intel to Snake Sight so that he can prepare a counterattack that will protect his men."

"After you, my friend," Mason states as he pats Terrance on his shoulder.

Terrance smirks, stands up straight, and, with Mason, walks out of the office towards the conference room.

Meanwhile, in a secret compound, a group of militia men are in a secured building training. Armed with paint rifles, infrared goggles, and body armor. Inside the compound is completely devoid of light, as the men silently maneuverer through the maze. As the men reach the center, a lone soldier, armed with a black tomahawk, gives a raised fist. The other men stop and patiently await further instructions.

The compound is quiet, the air is still, and the nerves remain steady as the silence does little to distract the men.

Suddenly, a fire blast comes towards the militia. The lone soldier intercepts the blast by absorbing the flames. Afterwards, a tall woman appears from the shadows to attack the lone soldier. Her Avemcernentia glows in the dark, revealing her position as she attempts to land a flaming kick towards the soldier.

Not phased by the sudden attack, the soldier returns the gesture by activating his Dracocernentia and blocking the kick with a flame punch. As the combatants smile at each other, they both engage in a friendly sparring match.

During the fight, another shadowy figure sprints through to outflank the militia. One of the head militia members balls his fists, then flattens his palm to get the team ready. The eerie sound of silence is disturbed by slight sounds of movement. Then, one of the militia at the rear gets punched by a limited fire fist. The commotion causes two of the militia to fire their paint guns. The series of shots fired misses their mark, as the cunning assailant eludes the pursuers.

As the militia is trying to track the secret individual, the two combatants continue to spar. One has mastered new levels of Engolo by performing a series of back flips and kicks. The soldier dodges it with limited difficulty as he whispers through the fight.

"You know, I kinda missed the you that wasn't as agile," he says.

"Well, too bad, because your slow ass will be mine," the cocky woman responds.

As the two continue to spar, the militia his now down to two active members. The remaining militia members stand back-to-back in hopes of catching the crafty individual. Both remain quiet as they wait for an opportunity. The militia men get nervous, as the individual activates the Dracocernentia at a distance where the light won't give up the position.

"I can see the yellow receptors in one of them," the individual plots, "I'm going to take that one out, then go after my dad."

Like a panther, the boy sneaks his way towards the uncertain militia members. The militia members continue to stay back-to-back with each other. They take a single step at a time and stay still for 5 seconds. Then they continue to rotate around.

Two minutes later, the boy gets within 2 yards of the military men. They position themselves so that they don't see the boy. As soon as they stop moving, the boy uses his speed and silence to fire a punch at the weaker militia man to the ground. Then he slaps the back of the head of the remaining militia man as he rushes towards the other soldier. Slightly disoriented, the militia man yells out to warn the other soldier.

"SNAKE SIGHT!"

The soldier hears the yell, then takes his tomahawk from his holster. The woman hears it as well and tries to attack again by throwing a kick. The soldier anticipates the move, grabs her leg and subdues her to the ground. After the swift move, the boy jumps in the air to attack the soldier.

With only microseconds to react, he takes his right arm to swing his tomahawk at the assailant. Then, with the boy's left hand, he generates flames that form a fire version of a tomahawk to block the attack. Once the weapons clashed, a buzzer sounded off and the lights turned on. The soldier smiles at the boy, then chuckles with pride.

"You're getting better, son," he says, "You've come a long way, Asir."

"Thanks, Dad," he responds with a smile.

"AND YOU…are still overconfident, Emma. I would hate to see how you are when you're at your full strength."

"Ugh, you know I was going easy on you on purpose, D'Shawn," Emma responds as they all get up and patch themselves.

For the past 5 months, Emma and Asir have been training with OBR during the pandemic. The chaos that has ensued has force OBR into hiding, as the heightened tension forces them to strengthen their ranks. As the militia men get up from the floor, the remaining militia man takes his googles off and walks towards Asir.

"I agree. You're getting better, lil bro," King Cobra congratulates, "but did you have to slap me THAT hard in the back of the head? You know I just got this fade cut!"

Asir laughs it off as he and King Cobra perform a double tap, wave high handshake. Asir feels more at home, and his social skills have dramatically increased. Then he responds to King Cobra.

"You gotta be faster, KC," Asir jokes.

"Right on, lil man," Cobra responds.

Emma and D'Shawn see the interaction, then smile.

"I'm so glad that he's growing up," D'Shawn states, "he's getting more comfortable around people and is learning to adapt to situations he used to think of as uncomfortable."

"Well, he has a great father to show and guide him now," Emma responds with a smile.

D'Shawn nods as he puts his tomahawk back in his holster.

Then, a member of OBR walks in with news for the trio.

"Snake Sight, we received a Zoom from our allies in London. You're needed in the conference room."

"Understood," D'Shawn says, "I'll be there presently."

"Well, well, I was wondering if we were going to get in some good trouble," Emma says.

"Now, Emma, you know that we need to mobilize with strategic proficiency in order to combat this pandemic."

"Dad, is this something you have to do alone?" Asir asks.

D'Shawn turns his body to Asir. He pats and caresses Asir's left shoulder, then responds. "Son, you're coming too. I think it's time you begin to understand your role in this fight."

"But D'Shawn, don't you think that…"

"Asir is 13 years old now. His days of being a boy are fast becoming a memory, and he knows through his meditation that our ancestors were already in Maroon squadrons at his age."

Emma stutters, then nods in reverence at D'Shawn's words. Then she looks at Asir and notices a shift in his mannerisms. He looks at his father with focus eyes, slightly tense arms, and nods in agreement.

"I'm going to do my best, Dad," Asir says.

"That's all I expect from you, son," D'Shawn responds, "Ok, let's go."

D'Shawn takes the lead, as Emma and Asir follow behind as they walk out of the training room. They walk down the hallways past many members of OBR. Some of the members relinquish their previous concerns and show adoration for Emma and Asir. Emma not only notices the accepting behaviour of the fellow militia, but some even stop to salute them. Then she looks at Asir. No longer the shy, self-conscious boy she met months earlier, Asir walks with his head high, his eyes focused, forward-looking, and with a strut that too commands respect.

"Asir has changed so much in just the few months that he's been with his dad," Emma reflects, "Clearly, he needed a male role model in his life. I just wonder how his mother will take it when he finally sees her. More importantly, will he be ready for the events that will forever change our perspectives…will I, for that matter?"

As the trio continues to walk down the hall, D'Shawn keeps his cool while trying to anticipate the upcoming conference. His eyes remain alert and sharp. Meanwhile, he briefly converses with himself before reaching the room.

"I can sense Asir's power," D'Shawn continues, "but like me, he has untapped power that can be trigger by extreme situations. With his Autism, I just hope I can teach him to moderate his emotions. This isn't a war; even so-called Neurotypical children could function without some repercussion. Only time will tell if I am able to help him with that."

About 5 minutes later, D'Shawn, Emma, and Asir make it into the conference room. A large screen visually shows Mason with Terrance, along with 4 of the militia men standing guard. Emma and Asir look at each other for a while as D'Shawn unmutes the speakers.

"Who is that man with the mentor, Ms Emma?" Asir whispers.

"We'll just have to wait and see," Emma responds, "but let's not use our eyes just yet. Sometimes, we have to learn how to be patient, even with our powers."

Asir nods before looking at the screen.

"Mentor…Black Tiger…" D'Shawn says.

"You appear to be in good health, Snake Sight," Terrance responds, "Looks like I can say the same with the Las and Chap behind you, yeah?"

D'Shawn smiles with pride before responding, "I couldn't be prouder. What is the situation?"

"We have reason to believe that the secret facility here in London is amplifying the effects of the Pustula Flu. My men are doing what they can to arm themselves with herbs, alkaline-rich vegetables, and Vitamin C, but…"

"But what Black Tiger?" D'Shawn asks, "Something is making this strain harder to combat." Terrance responds.

"Mason," Emma asks, "I remember you saying something a while back about finding Malik. You also told us about the Harq Alqadr. So, you think that the hidden powers of the sword could cause this anomaly?"

"As astute as ever, Emma," Mason answers, "There's no doubt that the sword's components are somehow amplifying the effects and specifically targeting highly melanated people across the globe."

Then, an erroneous figure walks through the guards and enters the conversation to aid in Mason's explanation.

"Well, love, that's not all that's happening."

"Wait a minute," Emma asks, "Who are…"

Shaking his dreads and smiling, Bakala activates his Dracocernentia and stands between Mason and Terrance.

"Sorry for interrupting your touch-up, but I wanted to meet the other yanks with our glorious eyes."

The Dracocernentia, despite being shown through a Zoom video, triggers the responses from D'Shawn, Emma, and Asir to activate their eyes. The convergence of energies allows the Moor to understand better the levels that Bakala continues to explain.

"In the atmosphere, there's another substance in the air that has bonded with the Pustula Flu. This compound has the ability to heighten the primal impulses of those not as melanated."

"Maniacine!" D'Shawn acknowledges, "It makes sense why the level of anti black racism has increased. This is a…"

"Racial Genocide. Those decrepit bastards are trying to wipe us out once and for all."

Emma realizes. Asir is shaken up for a bit by the reveal of this information. Despite shivering with fear, he wipes his forehead from sweat, keeps his eyes open, and tries to retain as much information as possible.

"So, what you're saying is that what's killing us is making White supremacists stronger?" Terrance asks.

"The problem with Maniacine is, with enough dosage, it can kill by poisoning the blood and rupturing vital organs," D'Shawn explains.

"However, based on the intel received from Malik and his other comrade," Mason intervenes, "Victor Goth strikes as a guy who will purposely go to the end to secure total dominion over us and the world. To them, if they can dominate without resistance, even if it meant that the human race would be extinguished within a few months, if not weeks, then he would take that."

"So how do we stop this from happening?" Emma asks.

"I'm here to come up with a non-artificial herb-based vaccine to counteract the effects of the virus and Maniacine," Bakala answers. " However, time is short, and we don't have enough resources to grow enough of the essential herbs to counteract the pandemic."

Meanwhile, Asir is seeing the field down to the molecular level. Though he does not understand the complexity, he sees how different molecules have different color receptors. The receptors bond together in color patterns: light yellow to dark red, green to blue, orange to gray. Finally, he sees the bonds trek around a flaming circle. As the circle gets brighter, the stronger the bonds become. Suddenly, he develops the nerve to join in the conversation.

"Eh, eh, eh, excuse me…" Asir stutters as he gains the attention of the people in the conference.

"What is it, son?" D'Shawn asks.

"Um…Bakala?"

"Go ahead, moppet." Bakala responds.

"Our…Fire Line is like a ball of energy, right?"

"Indeed, it is," Bakala answers.

"Like…the sun…" Asir continues.

"What are you getting at, Asir?" Emma asks.

"If the Maniacine, or whatever, can make the virus worse…couldn't our own Fire Line make our medicine stronger, just like the sun makes plants stronger? I can see, but I don't really understand, how these things that make up everything bond. I can see the colors and what they are supposed to match with. Then I can see this ball of energy make them stronger."

Everyone in the conference room is stunned by Asir's revelation. Terrance rubs his beard; Mason slowly smiles and nods as the others soon follow suit. Bakala then enacts an idea based on Asir's observations.

"I think you are on to som'n there," Bakala responds, "Indeed, we do have the Fire Line, and perhaps our power can magnify and amplify the growing process of the herbs we need."

"So, it seems like with your powers, you can imitate the sun," Mason adds, " If you make it a point to meditate for some time each day in manmade greenhouses…"

"Then we may be able to help speed the growing process and biochemical enhancements to combat this threat," Terrance finishes, "that's a stroke of brilliance, lad."

"You have a bright young man there," Bakala compliments.

"Indeed, I do," D'Shawn smiles as he briefly looks at Asir before continuing, "We'll get started on building an indoor greenhouse. We will contact you with a list of fruits, vegetables, herbs, and spices needed to grow so that we can begin to supply the people with the means to fight back."

"Understood," Terrance responds.

"Let's keep in contact, but strategically so that we don't draw too much suspicion," Mason instructs, "We don't know the depths to which the enemy can access this information. In the meantime, Emma, know that Malik is ok and will contact you as soon as his own training is done. I can't say much, but I know that he is destined to obtain a power that can't be fully understood. Trust in him."

"I will," Emma says.

"Then it is agreed," Terrance concludes, "For we fight for the future of Black People…"

"AND OUR RESOLVE IS UNCOMPROMISING!" everybody responds.

The video shuts off, and the meeting is concluded. D'Shawn, Emma, and Asir deactivate their eyes, then debrief from the meeting.

"You did awesome just now, Asir," D'Shawn praises.

"Thanks," Asir responds, "Did you not see the same vision, Dad?"

"Well, Asir…" D'Shawn responds before Emma steps in, "Sometimes each of us has a unique power that separates us from other people with the Fire Line. Yours may be to see how the patterns of receptors affect the body's ability to heal. In time, you'll learn to control better and understand this power."

"Yeah, it seems hard to explain, but simple to see. So, are we going to build a greenhouse?"

"We have something similar in the compound already," D'Shawn says, "We'll just have to expand it and add special mirrors to the ceiling to allow continuous sunlight. We will also have to rearrange the plumbing so that we can make the greenhouse more conducive to faster growth."

"Ok, let's get on it," Asir says, "C'mon, Ms. Emma, I can better show you what I saw just now."

"Well, I guess I don't have a choice," Emma says as they perform their own signature handshake, "Let's go. Are you coming?"

"I'll join up later," D'Shawn says.

Emma nods as she and Asir walk towards the western part of the compound. D'Shawn folds his arms and looks on as King Cobra slowly walks next to him. D'Shawn senses trouble and asks his officer about the situation.

"Any news?"

"There have been uprisings of racial warfare brewing in Atlanta. The police are actually turning a blind eye, as White Supremacist groups continue to harass the black people there," King Cobra reports, "Are we going to deploy a squadron there until Shadowmoor comes back?"

Faced with a difficult situation and an even more difficult decision, D'Shawn wastes no time to respond back to King Cobra.

"We cannot mobilize without a full force. Shadowmoor is the key to ending this. As powerful as I am, I don't have the insight or power he has. (Sigh) Unfortunately, we are not in a position to help them yet."

"Understood. In the meantime, I will continue to train the recruits and volunteers that pass through the vetting screening."

D'Shawn nods as King Cobra returns to his station. D'Shawn shakes his head, closes his eyes and whispers to himself.

"I hate not being strong enough to help," D'Shawn sulks, "Shadowmoor…Malik…Wherever you are, I hope this training is worth it. The people, your sister, me…we need your help."

D'Shawn then stands in the middle of the hall, as he decompresses the amount of burden of making such a difficult decision.

Chapter 9
The Kuroikage

The plane is flying at over 20,000 ft in the air. The soothing sounds of jet engines propelling the 757 through the skies keep Malik asleep. For the first time in months, he is getting adequate rest. There are no visions, no dreams, no attachments, just the calming noise of nothing as he and the passengers enjoy an uneventful flight.

Suddenly, a monitor goes off with announcements. One speaker is speaking in Japanese, while screens give options to translate into a language that is understood by the passenger. Malik is awakened by the sound of the intercom as it is about to speak. Cunningly, Malik activates the Dracocernentia slightly while keeping his eyes 90 percent closed so that he can understand the instructions.

" (***Ladies and Gentlemen, we are fast approaching Tokyo and will be landing in approximately 20 minutes. At this time, we ask that you have a seat and buckle your seatbelts. Please do not get up as the plane is descending. If you have any trash or leftover cups, please assist the stewardess as they makes their way to the aisle. Once again, we thank you for flying with us***."

Malik closes his eyes, deactivates his eyes, and eternalizes the patterns indicative of the language.

Soon he opens his eyes, yawns, and stretches to unkink his muscles.

"*Boy, this flight seemed like an eternity,*" Malik reflects, "*Kinda miss sitting in first class, but keeping a low profile is key until this journey is over.*"

As Malik prepares for the landing, one of the stewardess walk next to his seat. She is a pleasant-looking woman: about 5'4'' tall with brownish, black hair, rosy cheeks, and deep brown eyes. She smiles at Malik before speaking.

"Trash…sir?" she says. Malik looks down his seat, picks up a napkin, a soda can, and an empty bag of chips. Then he responds in Japanese to her as he dumps the trash. " (***I'm sorry for the mess***)," Malik says, " (***Thank you for your help***)." The stewardess smiles, then responds in Japanese, " (***Your Japanese is impressive. Enjoy the rest of the flight***)." Malik nods his head and smiles back.

As the woman continues down the aisle, Malik ponders what awaits him when he lands. The nerves of the journey continue to plague his mind like mold in a wet corner. The expectations and the ramifications cause Malik to dwell on his mind.

"*I can sense the effects of the pandemic,*" Malik contemplates, "*Despite my body's effectiveness, I think there is something else. Something that I'm not able to sense just yet. (Sigh) I just need to see this all the way through.*"

The plane continues to decelerate downwards as Malik looks out the window. As the plane flies through the thin clouds, the visuals of skyscrapers appear in view. The assortment of buildings, lighted calligraphy ads, and the millions of people signal the arrival of Malik's destination. The sun is still en route towards the top of the sky. The time in which the plane reaches the runway seems inconsequential to the amount of time Malik feels he has.

As the plane gets lower and lower, a sudden crash of air feels his eardrums as the roar of the jet engines combines with the rush of air finally catching up to the plane. As is routine with flying, the plane slows down and circles around to find the assign terminal. Many of the passengers wait patiently as the pilots maneuver the plane towards an empty slot. Slowly and carefully, the plane inches closer towards the space. The plane's wings are only meters apart from the other planes, but the pilots masterfully move it until it anchors itself towards the walkway.

After 2 minutes of parking the plane, it comes to a complete stop. Afterwards, a ding signals one last announcement in Japanese. " (***It is now safe to gather your belongings and exit the plane. Please make sure you take everything with you. Thank you for flying with us. Welcome to Tokyo***.)" As many of the passengers scramble to get their things, Malik patiently waits in his seat. He wakes himself up and looks on as passengers make their way out of the plane.

After waiting for about 10 minutes, Malik gets up from his seat and makes it down the aisle. With only his backpack, Malik calmly walks towards the front of the Cockpit. The Pilots and stewardesses smile and bow as Malik walks towards them. He smiles back and nods in response to their generosity. Malik makes his way down the terminal and into the airport.

Despite it only being 10:00 am, the airport is consumed with travelers from all shades, ethnicities, and cultures. Most of the passengers pay each other no mind as Malik attempts to meander through the tough crowds. Using his 6'2'' frame, Malik slithers his way through to get to a moving floor that bypasses most of the walkway.

"You know, this traveling should come easier," Malik complains under his breath, "*I just want to get my bag from baggage claim and get the hell up out of here.*"

So, Malik keeps his ground as the floor moves him towards the section of baggage claim.

Twenty minutes later, Malik finally makes it to baggage claim. Because he waited, most of the fellow passengers had gotten their luggage and walked away. The machine continues to spin around and around. Malik patiently looks for his bag while looking through his cell phone for any messages. Not seeing any messages, he then uses an app that creates a secret inscription to secure his usage of the internet. After the program loads, he then uses an alias given to him by OBR to book a ride with a local taxi service. With a few quick swipes, Malik finishes his business and puts his phone away.

Two minutes go by, and Malik puts his phone away. Suddenly, his medium-sized blue bag comes up the incline and descends towards the turnaround. Malik patiently waits until the bag gets within his range. Malik grabs his bag, puts the strap on his shoulder and walks towards the exits.

The walk is steady and consistent. As many travelers make their way, Malik once again gets drawn into himself with thought. The eerie peace around him alerts him to the unexpected as he ventures into another world.

"*This feeling of calm is somewhat unusual…and disturbing,*" Malik senses, "*I think I'm going to go visit some landmarks first before going downtown. Whatever awaits me, I have to be ready.*"

Malik steps outside the airport. He looks around as many vehicles come and go with several passengers. Despite the urge to dwell in insecurity, Malik keeps his composure intact and his head up. He slowly swivels his head from side to side, looking for the car that matches in his app.

After a few brief minutes of looking, a white Mitsubishi Lancer with a Taxi sign pulls up. Malik pulls out his phone and looks to see if this is the same car shown on the app. After a nod of affirmation, Malik makes his way towards the car. The driver glances at Malik as he opens the back seat of the car.

"Kon'nichiwa (Hello)," the driver welcomes. He is an unassuming man with black hair, glasses, and slightly yellow teeth. He then addresses Malik in broken English.

"Where…to…go?" Noticing the slow English, Malik uses the powers he'd mastered through the Dracocernentia to engage the driver in Japanese as he sits in the back seat and shuts the door.

" (***If I may, I would like to practice my Japanese with you, if you would honor me***)," Malik continues as the driver gives a brief nod, " (***I would like to go to the Sensō-ji Temple, please***)?" The driver smiles, then starts to drive out of the terminal.

As the taxi cruises through the streets, Malik takes the time to see the wonders of Japan, the people, and the culture. Suddenly, Malik begins to speak to himself.

"This is a beautiful country," Malik says lowly. The driver hears him and responds.

"Do you…need something…sir?" he asks.

"(***Oh, don't mind me. I was complementing how beautiful your country is***)."

" (***I see. Thank you***)," the driver responds, " (***Where are you from***?)"

“ (***I’m from America***),” Malik answers while giving cryptic responses, “ (***I wanted to visit this country and enjoy the sights. I heard that a temple is a special place***).”

“Tashika ni sōdesu (Indeed it is),” the driver explains, “ (***Built to honor Kannon by Buddhist monks nearly 1500 years ago. Very old***)”

“(***I see. Do the Buddhist monks still worship there?)***”

“ (***Most people go there for spiritual healing and insight. If you drop a coin by the entrance, you can receive a fortune***.)”

“Ryōkai shita (Understood),” Malik says.

Halfway towards the destination, the driver again engages in conversation.

“Your Japanese…is very…good…sir,” the driver compliments.

“Oh, thank you,” Malik responds, “I wanted to make it a point to give the proper respect before coming here.”

“Very…honorable,” the driver responds, “Very wise indeed. Somehow, I sense the spirit of Buddha in you.”

Malik briefly looks down and holds his chest for a moment. Then he smiles and responds to the driver.

“A wise man once said that we should not judge the flower of what we see, but the things that make up and allow that flower to thrive: the air, the water, the ground, and the minerals.”

Once again, the driver smiles as he continues to drive.

Five minutes later, the driver begins to slow down. Malik anticipates that he’s near his destination. He pulls out the phone, encrypts the signal, then on the app, finalizes the payment to the taxi. Moments later, the driver stops right in front of the walkway towards the temple.

"We are…here," he says, "Are you sure you don't want to go to a hotel?"

"Watashi wa genki (I'm fine)," Malik says as he gathers his things before exiting the car, " (***I enjoyed the drive and the conversation. The payment should go to your account***)."

Malik steps out of the car as the driver confirms the payment, then bids farewell to Malik.

" (***Thank you for your business. Enjoy your stay here in Japan***)," he says.

Malik bows as the driver returns the nod before driving off.

A few yards away, 2 men and a woman look at Malik. Sensing something unusual, one of the men whispers in Japanese to the young woman.

" ***(Is he the one? The one destined to be sent by the Daruma***?)"

"Tabun (Perhaps)," she whispers, "(***We won't risk using it until we get a closer look***)."

" (***Then we will proceed with caution***)," the other man says.

Then, like smoke, they vanish seemingly in midair as Malik makes his way towards the temple.

Malik walks up towards the Sensō-ji Temple. The structure is immaculate: fire blood color tiles matched with yellow edges that illuminate with the lights in the dimming day. Malik feels a sense of ease and peace as he closes his eyes.

"*There's…something about this place,*" Malik reflects, "*It's as if…I was meant to be here. But why?*"

The mysterious trio carefully watches from a distance as Malik goes through a mini meditation. As they move closer, something strange begins to manifest in Malik.

The white mark that Bodhidharma placed on his chest begins to irradiate in a different plane. Unbeknown to others around Malik, the burst of energy begins to light up the area. When the lights reach the trio, the woman's eyes begin to transform into a distinct blue hue.

"(***I see. It is him***)," she whispers.

She looks at her other companions. They notice her eyes as she gives them the nod to proceed. Then, they all vanish in midair to get closer.

After Malik takes a deep breath, he opens his eyes and looks up at the temple. He remains silent and allows himself to immerse himself in the majesty of the temple. Then, a black, cloudy smoke surrounds Malik.

"*That's strange. I don't see a fire anywhere.*"

Before he has time to react, one of the mysterious men jumps out of the air and tries to attack Malik. Malik, despite his attempts up to this point to be discreet, quickly transforms his eyes into the Dracocernentia and counters the jump kick with a block. Afterwards, another man comes in to try to punch Malik. Malik pushes the first man back and parries the other attack, then pushes him away. Both men maintain their distance as Malik drops his back and gets into a defensive position.

Malik carefully keeps his eyes on his supposed attackers as they continue to circle him. Malik continues to remain calm and focus, trying not to draw too much attention to himself.

" (***Who are you and what do you want from me***?)" Malik asks.

The men continue to circle, not answering. As the men continue to circle Malik, a rush of air alerts him of another potential threat. The speed of the 3rd assailant is so fast that Malik is barely able to pick it up with his eyes.

"*Who is this I sense*?" he wonders.

Incredible, she has the Avemcernentia? Here...in Japan?
He truly has the mark of Daruma, and he's powerful! Maybe he is...

Before Malik can fully grasp what's happening, the woman appears directly in front of Malik with her fist cocked backward. With one smooth, powerful stroke, she and Malik punch each other's fists with engulfed flames. As their fists meet with a force strong enough to clear the surrounding smoke, their eyes sync with each other. Malik is amazed that the woman processes the Avemcernentia, while the woman is amazed at the white light that surrounds Malik from his mark. Both stand in complete silence as the other men lower their guard and watch.

"*Incredible, she has the Avemcernentia...here...In Japan*," Malik ponders while keeping his gaze at her.

"*He truly has the mark of Daruma, and he's powerful. Maybe he is...*" she responds as she does the same.

Both Malik and the woman ease off of each other. Both continue to look at each other, inspecting every strand of hair, every vein visible to the body, and even the sweat from their skin. Malik notices something unusual about the woman. Her skin is burnt orange, with silky black lacquer hair, and slanted eyes. Her color complexion almost matches Malik's in some respects. Finally, curiosity gets the better of Malik as he breaks the ice in Japanese.

" (***You have the Avemcernentia***)," Malik continues, "Anatahadare? (Who are you?)"

The woman briefly nods at the other two men. Both of the men bow and put their hands behind their backs. Afterwards, the woman answers Malik's questions.

" (***Greetings, Dragon Moor. My name is Himiko. I was sent on a vision to seek the one***

destined to purge the world with fire. Yes, I inherited the Avemcernentia through my people.)"

" (***Your people***?)" Malik asks, " (***No offense, but you don't look like the typical Japanese person I've seen.***)"

"(***We come from the Ainu People, Dragon Moor***)," she answers, " (***We live north of here, in an area called Hokkaido. We are a special group in our village trained to keep our people and Japan safe. We're called the Kuroikage***)"

" Kuroikage…*Black Shadow*, I see," Malik responds, "Watashinonamaeha (My name is) Malik."

"O ai dekite ureshī (Please to meet you) Malik," Himiko answers as she bows, " (***It would be our honor if we escort you. Even here, the eyes of the evil ones lurk in every corner***.)"

"(***Evil ones, you mean***…)"

"Hai (Yes)," Himiko interrupts, " (***As I looked into your eyes, I was able to grasp some of the purposes of your journey here. The pandemic is also causing trouble here in Japan, as well as those you know as the Elite 8. Only through our training of the secrets of the Kuroikage can you prevail against such a foe***."

Malik thinks about it for a moment while fully grasping the depth of the conversation. He closes his eyes and reflects on the visions as the trio waits for his decision.

"*Since she possesses the Dracocernentia, I bet you that the contaminants in the air are affecting her and her people as well. I will need their help to stop the spread here.*"

Malik opens his eyes, places his hands on his side and bows to Himiko.

" (It would be my honor if I joined you)," Malik says.

Himiko smirks as she nods to her other men. " (***These two will take your belongings***)."

Malik is a little hesitant, but realizes that he needs to conserve his energy. So he nods as the men approach him.

"(***Hideyoshi will take your bigger bag***)," Himiko says as Hideoyoshi nods at Malik while maintaining eye contact, "(***Shiori will take your backpack***) (Shiori also nods and makes eye contact with Malik), (***Come now, we will show you the city and explain the situation before getting you back to our village***)."

Afterwards, Himiko blows a layer of dark, cloudy smoke to mask their escape. Then, like ninjas, Himiko, Malik, Hideyoshi and Shiori disappear into the wind, leaving nothing to trace or follow.

Chapter 10
Burning Will
燃え上がる意志

The winds begin to blow softly. The setting sun marks the beginning of the end of the day. Standing on the top of the Tokyo Skytree, overlooking the busy city, Malik stands next to Himiko as she stares at the eternity of emptiness. Her face is soft, her eyes are damp, and her resolved stance shields an unyielding force of regret and sorrow. Malik uses prudence and caution, taking his time to inch closer while Hideyoshi and Shiori watch from a distance. The party stands in utter silence as the day whines down.

After about 10 minutes of silence, Malik gets within earshot of Himiko. He says nothing, but looks in the same direction as Himiko. Himiko breaks her silence, but avoids initial contact.

" (***It's hard to imagine that the very air we breathe is killing us),"*** Himiko continues, " (***Tell me Malik…do you ever question your purpose, your desire…your will to fight***)?"

Malik takes his time with such a damning question. His journey up to this point has given him ups and downs, highs and lows, victories and defeats. The weight of the question becomes unbearable as Malik allows himself to respond.

"(Sigh) (***When I was growing up, I didn't get the type of love from people who were supposed to be***

my parents that generates self-respect and confidence. In a twisted hand of fate, the very people, the people that I come from, the same people I'm dedicating my life to fight for…) Malik says softly, " (***Some would make fun of me, others would ignore me, very few…would even break my heart without a lick of remorse or accountability. However…)***"

Himiko pauses for a bit and looks at Malik. She notices his demeanor change: his shoulders become relaxed, his head held high, and the right side of his mouth curves upwards.

"Sorehanandesuka (What is it?) Malik-san," Himiko asks.

" (***It wasn't until I fought to learn who I am, where I come from, and even at the deathbed of my adoptive mother…that a lake cannot sustain itself without a river to feed it, a body can't live without food or water, and life can't exist without the existence of the moon, sun, and the earth***)."

Himiko's eyes widen with such a reveal. Her minute expressions give rise to a level of hope she didn't expect to have. In the distance, Hideyoshi and Shiori listen with deep intent but say nothing. Malik continues the conversation in Japanese with his revelation.

" (***What I realized is that my adopted parents understood that in order to indoctrinate and subjugate a people fully, you have to strip them of their humanity. What makes us human? What makes us a people? The connections we have, the bonds we form, and the legacies we pass down, all of it is what makes up who we are***)."

" (***So you knew…that in order to reconnect with your Fire Line, you had to seek out the people you were separated from; like a river seeking a lake or the ocean***)."

"Hai."

" (***Then we must journey back to my village. The Grand Master will teach you how to keep your will burning***)," Himiko commands while looking directly at Malik, " (***The mark chose you, and in turn your journey led you here. It is time to teach you the ways of the Kuroikage***)."

Malik nods in acknowledgement. Then the two look back at Hideyoshi and Shiori to give them the signal. The two also nod in agreement. Then, Himiko lets off a thick blanket of smoke. It covers the top of the vacant top and shrouds it with a black layer. After a minute, the smoke disappears, along with the party of four.

A few hours later, the party made their way to the ground and to the outskirts of the city. As they get into the countryside and outside of the city limits, Malik takes one good last look at the city. Himiko turns and addresses Malik.

" (***I know your power is immense, but the journey will be long),"*** she states, " (***With our speed and stealth, we should get to the village before dawn. We must go now***)."

Malik turns to Himiko and nods. Afterwards, Himiko and Malik blow another stream of black smoke. They activate their eyes in the pitch blackness of night and begin their journey to the village.

Malik and the shinobi masterfully maneuver through the brush, trees, and terrain of the countryside without detection. Himiko leads the way as Malik treads a comfortable distance behind, along with Hideyoshi and Shiori. Halfway through the journey, Malik notices green receptors coming from both escorts. Despite his reserve nature, he takes the time to converse with his companions.

“ (***I noticed that you two don’t share our powers***)”, Malik asks, “ (***Is it limited, or are there more of us back in your village***?)”

“ (***What you call the Fire Line is only reserved for the true blood of our clan,*** Malik-san)” Hideyoshi answers.

“ (***It is said that long ago, the father of shinobi possessed the all-seeing eyes and taught the commoners not worthy to be samurai how to fight in the shadows***),” Shiori adds, “ (***Today, we carry that legacy through the leadership of Himiko and the Grand Master***).”

“Sōdesu ka (I see),” Malik responds, “ (***So, does that mean that Himiko is the last of her Fire Line***)?”

Himiko begins to squint her eyes. Her body becomes more tense and anxious while overhearing the conversation. However, she takes a deep breath, gathers herself, and continues to guide the party through the countryside. The two men suddenly become reluctant to answer their questions. Malik notices their receptors turning yellow and blue, so he doesn’t press them to talk.

“*What happened, Himiko*?” Malik wonders as they continue to move on.

Suddenly, Hideyoshi opens up again and relinquishes some more intel.

“ (***About a year ago, one of our own betrayed the clan. She disclosed the secret of our village to some men, and they came with fire and blood on their minds***).”

“ (***In order to save our village and our people, Himiko’s father, Hirohito, sacrificed himself so that we may live***),” Shiori continues, “ (***However, when the attack was almost over, a strange gas came out of***

nowhere and many of our people became paralyzed.)"

"Paralyzed?!," Malik reflects, "*Is it the same chemical that kept me imprisoned in Spain?*"

" (***With the last of her strength, Himiko's mother Yasu created a warm fire like the sun to save what was left of us. After that…we never saw her again, and we escaped to a new location***)."

Malik's eyes dropped, and his heart bled with empathy. He tries desperately to maintain his composure as the story takes hold in his mind.

"I would put my entire life savings bet that the Elite 8 are behind this. That gas must be the Reintergon," Malik ponders, then he turns to Shiori, " (***I…am truly sorry for your loss. You are brave to continue to fight despite what you have lost***)."

" (***As long as the Fire Line of our clan continues to burn, the Kuroikage will survive),"*** Hideyoshi says.

"Hai!" Shiori responds.

"...Hai!" Malik follows after a brief pause.

Afterwards, the men continue to follow Himiko as they draw closer to their destination.

A few hours later, the party comes within a few feet of the village. It is surrounded by a fence made up of individual wood limbs, with two overhead rounded arches and a wooden eagle at its epicenter. At the open entrance, two shinobi guards dressed completely in black stand to patrol. Himiko cautiously walks towards the entrance with Malik behind her, as well as Hideyoshi and Shiori at the rear. The two guards walk up towards Himiko, bow, then address her.

" Meishu (Leader)," One of them says, " (***Welcome back. The Grand Master requests your audience immediately***)."

"Ryōkai shita (Understood)," Himiko responds.

Himiko begins to walk until the other guard places his hand on her chest, stopping her.

" (***Apologies, but we must ask who this outsider is)?"*** he inquires.

"(***He is who we have been seeking***)," Himiko responds again, " (***The shadow warrior from across the sea. He has the Mark of Daruma. He is known as the Shadow Warrior***)."

Himiko looks back at Malik and stands aside.

"Show them, Malik-san," she commands.

Malik closes his eyes to gather his energy. The heat from his body lights up and creates a small heat wave. His mark begins to light up, and he opens his eyes to activate the Dracocernentia. The immense power of the eyes, with the combination of the mark, creates a burst of energy that spreads throughout the village, reaching every inch of it. Some of the villagers notice the energy and begin to peek outside their wooded homes.

Convinced of Malik's power and Himiko's words, the guards step aside, bow with respect, and let them pass through the gate. Humbled, the party, including Malik, bows to the guards and continues towards the village. Afterwards, the guards resume their previous positions and guard the gate.

As the party walks by, some of the villagers are intrigued by Malik's tall stature and presence. Some stare at him like a jewel in a rockface or a beam of light in darkness. Malik feels a little unease with the amount of attention, but Himiko reassures him of his safety.

" (***You are safe at my home***), Malik-san," Himiko continues, " (***We must go to the Black Temple where the Grand Master resides***)."

"Sonogo dō naru ka (What happens then)?" Malik asks.

" (***The Grand Master will vet you. She will see within your heart, your soul, and your mind to determine if you are worthy of the secrets of the Kuroikage***)."

"Sōdesu ka (I see)," Malik responds.

" (I know that your mark is true) Malik-san," Himiko concludes, " (***However, the training to truly be Kuroikage will be difficult. Very few of us, even in our village, pass***)."

" (***Failure is not an option…)*** Himiko," Malik says.

There is a pause, as the party continues to walk. After a few tense seconds, Himiko responds.

"Hai! (***Then we must not waste any more time***)."

The small party reached the edge of the village. There lies the stronghold of the Kuroikage: a large Dojo about the size of a grocery store, painted completely black, sitting on a small hill, with a single flight of stairs with two black dragon statues at its base. The party looks up before climbing the steps. Himiko looks at Malik as he gazes upon the structure. Then she looks at Hideyoshi and Shiori, then nods to them. Both bow, put their hands together and create a ninja sign. She blows a stream of smoke at them, giving them the cover to disappear. Afterwards, she addresses Malik.

"Junbi wa deki taka (Are you ready)?" Himiko asks.

"Hai!" Malik answers while staring at the temple. Then, they both make their way up the stairs.

After a long struggle up the stairs, Malik and Himiko make it to the door of the Dojo. They take off their shoes, Himiko her socks, then enter. The inside is shrouded in darkness, lit by several rows of white candles. The area is surrounded by a squad of shinobi. At the back of the room, an elderly woman: about 65 years old, dressed in a black matanpushi with a blue fire phoenix tapestry sewn on her left side, dark olive skin, and cloudy gray eyes. Himiko and Malik take a few steps towards the middle of the room. She gets on one knee and anchors herself with her right fist. She briefly looks back at Malik to follow suit. He catches the mannerisms and gets down on one knee. Then, Himiko lowers her head.

" (***Honorable Grand Master, I humbly come before you***)," Himiko says.

The elderly woman gets up from her seated position, takes out her fan, expands it, and then waves it repeatedly. Despite her frail appearance, she commands the level of respect not even shown to the level of some kings. The room is silent, only hearing the small roars of the flames as they melt the candles. Each shinobi stands at attention, ready to move at any notice. Then, the woman graces her presence by speaking to Himiko.

" (***My child, you have return***)," she says, "(***I see that you have brought a stranger among us***)."

"Hai (***Grand Master. This is the one who bears the Mark of Daruma. The Shadow Warrior from across the sea***)."

"Sore wa hontōdesuka (Can it be true)," the Grand Master says, " (***Let me see. Step forward…Young Shadow Warrior***)."

Malik glances at Himiko. She looks back at him, nods, and faces downward. Malik slowly and reluctantly gets up and walks a few steps forward.

Keeping a safe distance, Malik begins to kneel.

“ (***There’s no need for my child***),” the Grand Master stops Malik, “***Stand before me…and open your eyes***.”

Malik says nothing and looks directly at the Grand Master. His anxiety rises like a storm. He tries to keep his nervousness at bay while keeping his eyes on her. The Grand Master, meanwhile, closes her eyes, then lets off a long breath.

“ (***There’s no need to worry. I will be able to see.)”*** she says.

“*See what*?” Malik wonders as he continues to wait.

Suddenly, the lights dim to nearly complete darkness. The Grand Master lets off one more breath. The room is still. The air is quiet. Then, after a brief moment, the Grand Master opens her eyes and transforms into the Avemcernentia. The blue light in her eyes not only fills the room with vast amounts of energy, but it re-ignites the blown candles, and it transforms Malik’s eyes back to the Dracocernentia. The mark on his chest also illuminates the room. The surge of power forces Malik into a trance with the Grand Master.

As the spiritual link between Malik and the Grand Master syncs, she begins to conjure images, memories, and beings in a white veil of nothingness.

“What…What is this?” Malik asks while in the confines of his mind and heart.

“This is the plane of consciousness beyond space and time, Dragon Moor,” the Grand Master continues, “It is a pleasure to meet you, Malik Wilson.”

The room continues to swirl with images as the Grand Master narrates through Malik’s life.

“Ah…I see. You were orphaned and taken care of by those responsible for your parents’ death,” she continues, "...You always knew that you were meant for something more than what your life provided. So you sought out your past…ah, yes, you met your grandfather, a man who disguised his blindness to see his legacy before he passed on…You continued the dying Fire Line, becoming the warrior who fights while allying himself to the Shadows."

Then, the room becomes dark. Images of pain and suffering begin to darken Malik's heart. Malik tries to quell his frustrations, but is unable to hide behind them. He sees images of Goth stabbing Audrey, the people suffering from the pandemic, and the shadowy ghosts of William Benson.

"GOTH!" Malik screams, "...and…and…I thought that I was over it. Over him."

"The pain and suffering you suffered from those who try to dominate this world by destroying it have left an imprint on you that will be difficult to erase," the Grand Master explains, "The way of the Kuroikage is to detach from this world, so that you can see how it all flows together. I do not see just the rage that you try to hide, Dragon Moor…"

Then, images of Emma pop up, along with Asir and D'Shawn.

"Your rage did not consume you. You were able to spread your love to your sister…her through another," she explains, "In order to achieve the power of Awarelessness and become the Golden Dragon, you must eradicate everything that has corrupted your way of thinking and way of being."

"Way of being?" Malik asks.

"To achieve what you seek, you must learn how to detach your mind from whatever is keeping you rooted. You must learn that one must have another: Light must have the contrast of dark to understand its effectiveness, the body must rely on the spirit, or it will crumble from the inside, and evil must be understood not to be bad, but a combination of events that collide into one. Once you realize how the thinking of connection is really about detachment, then you will achieve the power few have obtained."

After what seems like an eternity, Malik and the Grand Master break their sync, revert their eyes to normal, and return to the present plane. Malik is once again drenched in sweat as the Grand Master continues to fan herself. Then she speaks once more in Japanese.

"Hizamazuku (Kneel)...Malik-san," she commands.

Malik goes down on one knee and lowers his head.

" (***You will be trained in the ways of the Kuroikage***)," she continues, " (***The training will teach you how to not hide from your shadows, but to learn from them, ally with them, and embrace them as your burning will. These shadows will help your Fire Line, and in turn…you will help gain back the balance of the world***)."

"Hai!" Malik answers, then slowly looks up.

The Grand Master then steps towards Malik. She places her hand on his shoulder. Then she speaks to him.

" Araizu(Arise)...Malik-san. (***From this day forward, you are***…) Kuroikage!"

Afterwards, Malik stands up, bows to the Grand Master, then she returns the gesture by bowing back at him.

Chapter 11
Reveal of the Devils

The early morning gives rise to leaves rattling in the wind, birds singing in the air, and the sun rising over a quiet neighborhood. At a vacant, 2-story house with red bricks, brown shingles and large limestone boulders, a young white woman stands in front of the house. She has brown, straight hair, wearing a denim short-sleeve shirt, tight pants, and thong flip-flop sandals. Despite the vibrant colors and light of life, the young woman is droopy, sluggish, and despondent. She walks through the doors and inside of the house.

As she turns the corner, another woman with brown, streaky, curly hair, wearing a gray pant suit with black high heels, is conducting her last inspections of the house. Moments later, the woman turns her head and notices the unexpected guest.

"Oh, Renee! Good Morning," she says.

"Hey Reba, what do you think?"

"Well, the property is worth a lot, but with the housing prices and this pandemic, it'll be tough to sell," Reba explains. "Are you sure you want to sell this house? I mean…"

"(Sigh) Even though my parents left me… with all of the taxes and fees, the issues my dad tried to…" Renee hesitates before continuing, "I'm sure."

“Well, ok,” Reba responds.

Reba puts her notes and appraisal forms in her carrier. Then she begins to walk away. She turns back and addresses Renee one more time.

“Sweety, are you ok?” Reba asks, “I mean…you don’t feel like yourself?”

“It’s just…been a difficult time.”

“Oh yeah, I am so sorry about your parents.”

“Thank you, Reba.”

Both women hug each other, then Reba smiles and walks out the front door. Renee then goes to a corner, sits on the carpet and begins to sulk.

Tears begin to flow from her eyes as she tries to comfort herself. The past year has been riddled with scandal and remorse. A good chunk of Renee’s inheritance was taken for taxes, and because of her father’s suicide, the Life insurance company revoked its obligations to pay. As Renee tries to gather herself, she pulls out her cell phone and begins to scroll. After 3 simple swipes, Renee comes across a name. She presses the name, calls the number, and awaits the answer.

“RING…RING…RING…RING…RING…*He y, I’m sorry I missed your call, but if you leave a message, I’ll get back to you*, Bbbbyyyyeee! BOOOOOB”

Renee hangs up the phone and takes a deep breath. Her anxiety climbs to a new level, as her pale skin turns hot and her eyes swell with red veins surrounded by dark rings. For 2 minutes, she sits alone in a house that she’d spent most of her growing years enjoying the lavish lifestyles of the Upper Middle Class. Now she is secluded, drowned with contrition and loathing.

Suddenly, a random text message goes through her phone. Renee notices the vibration, and she reads it silently.

Whatever number comes up, answer it.

"*What the hell is this?*" Renee wonders.

Before she has time to think, her cell phone rings, showing an unknown number on her screen.

RING…RING…RING…RING…RING…

Renee feels apprehensive about the call, but decides at the last minute to pick up.

RING…(click) "Hello?"

"Renee, are you there?"

Renee begins to wipe her eyes and gather herself. Her attitude suddenly picks up, and her voice becomes clear.

"Emma? What…what the…"

"How are you, sis?" Emma asks. "Why didn't you pick up when I tried to call you?" Renee asks.

"Um…I'm sorry, Renee. There's a lot that's happened."

"No kidding, girl! I mean, we haven't spoken in about 4 months and don't get me started on Mro!"

"Yeah, that's included too…"

"Oh, wait, did he ghost you, too?"

"Not in the way you are thinking," Emma responds, "You are really emotional…are you ok?"

Renee pauses for a moment. The flow of emotion overwhelms her. Her voice begins to crack under the pressure, and she lets it all out.

"Emma, I'm just…so lonely," Renee sobs, "Ever since the death of my parents, regardless of what they did, a part of me died. Do you know…"

"Yes…I know," Emma interrupts.

Again, Renee pauses for a moment. Then, in a moment of clarity, she retraces her words and calms herself down.

"Emma, I'm so sorry. I know I can be a bitch and not think about what I'm saying."

"Renee, if anyone understands, it's Malik and 1," Emma explains, "Listen to me, ok? None of us blames you for what happened. It was the work of something bigger than yourself."

"Logically, I know that Emma…but…but…I don't…know," Renee struggles to re-gather herself, "I'm not concentrating at work, most of my inheritance is gone, and I'm forced to sell my home. The home I grew up in. I…I…"

"Renee…listen to me," Emma consoles, "You're going to be fine, Ok?"

Renee responds, ok while wiping her eyes and sniffing her nose.

"Renee, I can't say too much, but I wanted to check up on you. I also wanted to let you know that we are going through something that we can't disclose right now."

"Going through something? In this pandemic?" Renee asks.

"Sister-Girl, there's more to it than just that. All I can tell you is that Malik is taking care of some things…you know…the kind of things that happen in the shadows."

"Oh…OH!" Renee realizes, "Ok…well, if you get a chance, tell him that I'm still his (sister) too and…"

"I gotcha," Emma says, "Once all of this is over…hopefully we can…you know…"

"Right…ok."

"I gotta go…Renee…take care of yourself and be careful."

"You too…bye (CLICK)"

After the phone call, Renee puts her phone down. She then looks at her feet, then at the ceiling of the house. Then she lowers her head and closes her eyes, as she once again seeks comfort in seclusion.

On the other side of town, Reba drives up to her office in a plaza. She exits her green Lexus RC Coup, grabs her bag and walks into the building. When she walks in, she greets her receptionist. She is a short redhead, wearing a red dress with white dots, and she's sitting behind a mahogany, carved, wooden desk.

"Morning, Samantha."

"Morning…Um…There's someone…waiting in your office, Reba."

"REALLY? Huh…who is it?"

"Well, he says that he's a potential buyer for that house."

"Oh, ok. Samantha, hold my call for the next hour or two."

"Will do, Reba."

"Thanks, you're a lifesaver."

Reba clears her throat and walks calmly down the hallway. Her eyes are focused, the bounce in her step isn't as profound, and her demeanor gets defensive. She reaches for her office and slowly reaches for the doorknob. Once the hand touches the handle, she closes her eyes, takes a deep breath, and then opens the door.

When she goes into her office, there is a man, wearing a brown blazer, gray pants, with a glass of whiskey, looking at the window. He then begins to converse in a low, unassuming tone.

"You know…as industrialize advanced as America tries to present itself to be, it's nice to just look at the windows for the trees," he continues, "Hope you don't mind. I let myself in. That receptionist shouldn't be so shy."

Reba puts her bag on her desk, then puts her hand on her hip, then gives the man an annoyed look.

"Victor Goth…what are you doing here?" Reba asks, "It isn't enough that you shook up the leadership. Now you come to my area and my turf…"

"Shhhhhhhh…." Victor interrupts as he walks closer to Reba, "My dear Reba, you of all people should know that money is time, and time is something we are losing. So please, let's skip…(Victor looks Reba up and down, looks at her in the eyes, then smiles) pleasantries."

"Hmph…alright," Reba whispers while she moves closer, "What do I owe this…audience?"

Victor smiles again, then strolls towards the other side of the office to gain some distance before re-engaging in the conversation.

"So it seems that everything is going to plan. The pandemic is wreaking havoc across the globe, some of the fittest of us are enduring, and the Black problem is close to completion after nearly 600 years of planning and opportunity."

"Ok, so what does that have to do with me?" Reba asks, "With us?"

"Hm hm, hm," Victor chuckles, "As deplorable as your country, its activity leads the world. You see, America perfected the type of Racism that makes genetic genocide…acceptable…"

"Ok…" Reba responds while walking perpendicular to Victor's position, "Go on."

Victor takes one last sip of his Whiskey, then sets the glass down on a random chair. Then he fixes his hair and clears his throat.

"The house that you just appraised, the former home of our departed mentor and member, is she going to sell?"

"Without a doubt, she will, but with this market…"

"It makes no difference in the market," Goth interrupts, "We need to obtain that house to set up our operations here. That house needs to be in our hands and kept for legacy purposes."

"So what do you want me to do?" Reba asks.

"I want you to inflate the price to a ridiculous range, say about $50k more than the actual value. Then I will buy the home at a discounted rate undisclosed to everyone except for the members of Elitetion. Our banks will close the house and we'll retain our money."

Reba begins to nervously rub her left arm with her right hand. She looks down and skips a couple of breaths.

"But what about Renee? I mean, she is my…"

"You're what? Friend?"

Victor chuckles before moving closer to Reba to console her. He grabs her right hand and places it on her side. Then he touches the small of her back and smells her neck. Reba closes her eyes and breathes slowly. Then she opens them to Victor as he looks at her.

"Oh, you have so much to learn about power," Victor whispers, "Never put too much trust in your friends, Reba. Renee is a liability. Her emotional state makes her useless to us. Besides…you need to focus on…"

Reba reaches the doorknob and gracefully locks it. Then she whispers back to Victor.

"For right and reason…"

"We will fulfil…(Elitetion)" They both recite.

Afterwards, primal impulses take over. Victor and Reba forcibly take each other's blazers off. Victor rips open Reba's blouse, begins licking her chest while Reba jumps up and crosses her legs around Victor. With each passing second, both begin kissing and licking each other into audacious activities. Then Reba begins to moan into a state of sexual unconsciousness as Victor makes his presence known.

Chapter 12
Spanish Phoenix and the English Dragon

The sun is setting in the west. On the roof of the hideout, Esmeralda looks on as her curly hair blows with the wind. Finding solace in solitary, Esmeralda allows her bottled-up emotions to roll off her sleeves and travel with the wind. Her mind flushes out all of the turbidity of pain, suffering, and confusion. After a few moments of silence, a voice echoes behind her.

"You alright?" the voice asks.

Esmeralda blinks her eyes in annoyance, then turns around. She is greeted by a friendly face as his dreads blow in the wind.

"You seem a bit distracted, love. What seems to be the problem?"

"Oh…right, um…"

"Bakala," he interrupts.

"Right…Bakala. I was just unwinding up here. There's just so much to deconstruct."

"I see," Bakala says.

Esmeralda turns around and faces the setting sun over the city. Bakala keeps his distance but positions himself next to her. Esmeralda takes a deep breath, closes her eyes, then gulps in embarrassment. Bakala smirks while waiting patiently for Esmeralda to open up. As the city lights illuminate the darkening sky, Esmeralda opens her mouth.

"So Bakala…why do you do this? I mean THIS?"

"(Sigh) It's not easy protecting something that doesn't seem to give a wop about you," Bakala answers, "I thought about leaving this country. Maybe retrace my roots and go back to Africa."

Then Bakala chuckles for a few seconds. Esmeralda turns her attention to Bakala.

"What's so funny?" she asks.

"In some ways, you remind me of the Yank," Bakala answers.

"YOU MEAN…I mean…I'm…"

"Very fond of him," Bakala interrupts, "You're dealing with a Moor, and an English one at that."

"(Sigh) Fair enough."

"Like you, he thought he knew what he knew, until he came here some months back. He didn't realize the depth of our powers until I taught him a trick or two."

Bakala's demeanor switches to a serious one. Esmeralda matches the intensity by squinting her eyes slightly. She gives Bakala her undivided attention as he continues his talking points.

"However, after fighting with Malik, I learned 2 important things: that this corrupt group is global, and that because of his unique experiences, he is the only one who can cut off the head of this monster."

"You're right," Esmeralda adds, "When he told me his story and fought with him, I was able to sync with his emotions and thoughts. I thought that things were bad in Spain. Little did I realize that he grew up in the belly of the beast."

"Precisely, Love. Since he left, I've gotten certain…visions…visions that I can't explain." Bakala briefly looks away, then finishes. "These visions show of the one…who can unite our kind of people in the world. Then a large creature flashes like…the sun."

"The Golden Dragon…" Esmeralda whispers.

"Come again, love," Bakala responds.

"In your visions, did you see a large Golden Dragon?"

"As a matter of fact, in the vision, the man merges with a Golden Dragon and ignites the world. Have any idea what it means?"

Before Esmeralda could answer, another voice yelled from across the roof.

"Pequeña ave…Bakala!" Both turn their heads and face the woman.

"Eulalia? What's going on?"

"You two are needed in the conference room. We are going to need your help."

"Alright, we're right behind you," Bakala says.

Eulalia turns around and leads them to the door.

The trio walks in and down the stairway towards the first floor. The noise of steps doesn't stop Esmeralda from asking questions.

It's not easy protecting something that doesn't seem to give a wop about you. I thought about leaving this country. Maybe retrace my roots and go back to Africa.
What's so funny?
In some ways, you remind me of the Yank.
YOU MEAN...
I mean...I'm...
Very fond of him. You're dealing with a Moor, and an English one at that.

"So what kind of help is needed?"

"We were able to locate the buildings that Goth owns, but we don't know where the secret facility is that holds the containers of the Pustula virus strain."

"So, this is a reconnaissance mission?" Bakala asks.

"I believe it's more to that young man," Eulalia continues, "Black Tiger will explain once we get to the conference room."

The trio makes it to the floor. They begin to walk towards the conference room. Eulalia continues to finish her point as Esmeralda and Bakala look at each other with a level of confusion and anxiety.

"Regardless, this mission is essential to our fight against the Elite 8." Eulalia stops in front of the door to the conference room, turns around and concludes her advice, "My advice to you and especially you, Pequeña ave, listen carefully and do your best."

Bakala nods, then glances at Esmeralda. Esmeralda closes her eyes for a second, gulps, then nods. Eulalia nods and smirks, turns around, and opens the door.

The conference room has Terrance, Mason at the center of the table with 8 militia surrounding the walls. Terrance looks up and greets the trio.

"Glad you all came to the planning party," Terrance says, "Alright, let's get to it."

The trio nods, then Terrance briefs them on the upcoming mission.

"So we decided that we are going to push our plans for Operation Liberation back until we can get the best reliable intel," he continues, "We can't afford to attack a stronghold without refutable evidence of the manufacturing center."

"We know that the virus that causes the Pustula Flu is being engineered in London or the surrounding areas," Mason adds, "but we don't know where."

"So, that's where we come in, ya?" Bakala asks.

"Yes, but there's more." Terrance responds, "Because we don't want the Royal Armies or Scotland Yard to get involved, we can't afford to expose ourselves yet."

"So in other words, once we find it, we're on our own?" Bakala asks, "Well, that's just a kick in the balls, ya."

Mason looks up at Bakala and Esmeralda. He moves around the table and stands a few feet away from them. His stance is firm, his gaze is focused, and his posture commands respect. Esmeralda knows the look, so she glances at Bakala and gives him a serious look. Bakala takes the hint, then redirects his attention back to Mason.

"Listen, you two, I can't tell you how many men you will encounter. Remember that the flu is attacking our very bodies as we speak. We are still trying to produce enough herbs to make the vaccines, but until we can supply all of OBR, we can't afford to unnecessarily send men."

"So, you are banking on the fact that our combine powers can quell the effects long enough for us to take it out, right, Señor Mason?" Esmeralda asks.

"That's right, Lass," Terrance responds.

" Well…I (she nervously looks at Bakala, then continues with her thoughts), Bakala and I have yet to fully get acquainted with our combine powers. In the texts of old, it took months, even years to…"

"At best, you two have an hour," Mason interrupts.

"Don't worry, Esmeralda," Bakala reassures, "Our powers are on par with one another. We will have to force the issue."

"I agree," Eulalia says.

Eulalia looks at Esmeralda in her brown eyes. She rubs her arms and gets her focused.

" Es hora de dejar de huir de tus emociones y usarlas Pajarito (It's time to stop running away from your emotions, and to use them Little Bird)."

" Si…" Esmeralda responds softly.

"Nosotros... NOSOTROS... somos la Sombra del Fénix. Somos poderosos, somos fuertes y somos versátiles. Estarás bien (We…WE…are the Shadow of the Phoenix. We are powerful, we are strong, and we are versatile. You will be fine)."

With that moment, Esmeralda regains her conviction and confidence. She briefly closes her eyes, then activates the Avemcernentia. She looks directly at Bakala, forcing his eyes to transform into the Dracocernentia. The flow of energy creates a silhouette of a blue phoenix around Esmeralda's body and a red dragon on Bakala. After the display, Esmeralda and Bakala power down, much to the amazement of the room.

"We're ready," Esmeralda exclaims.

"DAMN RIGHT WE ARE!" Bakala adds on.

Mason looks back at Terrance. Both smile at each other before the men give out their objectives.

"Then get ready to go. Bakala's smoke technique can keep you two hidden between the city streets on your way to Goth's facility," Terrance says.

"The combine power should help regenerate your powers long enough to scout out the place. We'll have secret surveillance through our network of city cameras to keep you in view," Mason says while patting Bakala's and Esmeralda's shoulders, "Good luck, you too. If you feel like your powers are weakening, make sure you recharge before engaging the enemy."

Bakala and Esmeralda nod, then Mason removes his hands.

Afterwards, Bakala and Esmeralda turn around and walk out of the conference room. Mason folds his arms as Terrance clasps his hands behind his back. He walks around towards his friend and begins to speak his mind.

"They're powerful. Very powerful," Terrance reflects, "But what's to keep them from not getting overconfident? I mean, one of them…"

"Yes, Terrance, the stakes are high," Eulalia interrupts as she walks towards Mason and Terrance, " but we can't afford to coddle them."

"She's right, Terrance," Mason adds, "I wish we could help them (and that I was 20 years younger), but too many eyes are on our people. We don't have an adequate force and quite frankly, I don't think we ever will."

"But Mason, you and I both know it doesn't take an incredible force," Eulalia says, "We're American, Foundational Black Americans to be exact. Yes, one side of my family dates back to the Moors who settled before Jamestown…and yes, regrettably, my family tried to erase that side and reside themselves to the same people who have devastated this world. However, I know that my ancestors, as well as yours, only needed enough dedicated people to overthrow their oppressors."

Mason looks at Terrance and nods. He rubs his beard and closes his eyes as Eulalia finishes her point.

"I know that our parents and grandparents messed up…I know that our generation found out too late about their mistakes. I wish that Esmeralda's generation didn't have to fight what should've been…"

"But they're stronger and more resourceful than us, Eulalia," Mason says, "Our work in the FBI proved that. I think it is time to take the training wheels off and let them fly (thinking about Malik and his exploits). I've seen firsthand what they can do. It's time to trust them."

"Right on, mate," Terrance ends, "In the meantime, their meditation allowed some of the herbs to grow faster. I suggest that they meditate for about an hour before they head out. That way, they'll leave this mission on full power while we get to work with the vaccines."

The 3 elders all nod to each other in agreement. Eulalia walks out of the conference room to look for the Young Adult Moors. Afterwards, Mason pulls out a phone from his pocket. He turns it on, scrolls down, and begins to text.

Over in the OBR facility in Florida, Asir is sleeping in his bed. He begins to toss and turn, sweating profusely as he tries to comprehend the amount of imagery plaguing his mind. As he is dreaming, he sees images of his ancestor Chittoluthphwa, war, and death.

"No…no…sharp…slafkaw (knife)..." Asir mumbles, "...Hul-wah (Bad)...chatolaswaw (tongue)....soletawa…soletawa!…SOLETAWA (WAR)! AAARRRRGGGGHHHH!"

Asir wakes up screaming before letting out a fire blast. The flow of energy is so powerful that Emma and D'Shawn rush towards Asir.

D'Shawn opens the door while Emma stands behind. Asir's eyes are fully activated, he is breathing hard, and he can't control himself.

"Asir…ASIR…SON" D'Shawn yells.

Then, D'Shawn activates his eyes, grabs Asir, and uses his Fire Line to counteract and disturb the flow of energy in Asir.

Asir controls his breathing, deactivates his eyes, and then calms down.

"Asir, are you alright?" D'Shawn asks.

"(Huff HUFF Huff Huff) yeah, I'm good now…" Asir answers.

Emma keeps her arms folded and slowly walks in. She keeps her distance while D'Shawn ascertains the situation.

"Did you have a nightmare, son?"

"I…I…kept seeing visions…of our ancestor…of a person," Asir continues, "Someone called…Sharp Knife…"

"*Sharp Knife?*" Emma asks.

"Sharp Knife…can you tell me what he looks like?" D'Shawn asks.

"He…was an old man with gray hair. I've seen him on…money before…"

"Money…wait?!" D'Shawn pulls out a $20 bill from his pocket, "Him?"

"Yeah, that's him. Our ancestor kept saying that his tongue is bad. Dad, I saw what this man did to the ancestors. I saw fighting, blood, and…and…"

"Listen, Asir, I know that you are afraid, but…I won't let anything happen to you, Ok?"

"Alright, Dad," Asir says, "I want to try to go back to sleep."

"Good idea, son. What you saw is something you'll meditate on in the morning. Get some rest now."

"Alright, Dad."

D'Shawn gets up and leaves Asir. Asir lays back down and tries to go back to sleep. When D'Shawn walks down the hallway, Emma follows next to him. She treads lightly as she attempts to ask D'Shawn.

"What happened to Asir?"

"Exactly what I was afraid of," D'Shawn continues, "It's one thing to train for something, it's another to be in actual battle. The ancestors know the fight to come."

"What do you mean?" Emma asks.

"Are you familiar with our family history? With what happened to the Blacks and Native Americans in this region?" D'Shawn asks.

"Unfortunately, that kind of history was hidden from me growing up."

"I see."

D'Shawn stops in the middle of the hallway and looks at Emma intensely. His eyes are sharp and his mouth is tense. Emma calmly gives him her full attention.

"Asir saw Andrew Jackson. The Seminoles called him Sharp Knife…he called us…ALL OF US NIGGERS!" D'Shawn continued, "When Jackson became president, he enacted the Indian Removal Act to force Native Americans and Blacks out of their lands…"

"Wait a minute…the Trail of Tears…"

"Exactly," D'Shawn responds, "What Asir saw is parallel to what is going on now. You and I both know that this pandemic has the same function Jackson had for the Seminoles nearly 200 years ago…(sighs) I don't know if I can let Asir go through this."

"D'Shawn, Asir is stronger than you know. It's up to you to teach him…but it's also up to his ancestors."

"What are you saying?"

"I think Asir is old enough to allow his ancestors to help him," Emma suggests, "Just like they helped us. The ancestor that he's comfortable with."

"You mean Chittoluthphwa."

"D'Shawn, maybe he needs this to learn how to deal with this. There is no perfect way, but maybe if his ancestor can allow Asir to see, learn, and know how to cope…"

"I understand," D'Shawn says before patting Emma on the shoulder, "Go get some sleep. We'll talk more about this in the morning."

D'Shawn nods and walks down the hall.

Emma looks back at the room of Asir, then she looks at D'Shawn walks away. She continues to fold her arms, then leans on the wall. Her sense of duty has blurred the lines within her. The feeling of holding back is countered by the importance of rekindling a once broken relationship.

"*I know that D'Shawn has a lot on his plate right now*," Emma reflects, "*Leading a revolution and learning how to be a father is a difficult task…* (looks back at the outside of Asir's room) *It can't be easy for Asir either. To become a teenager with unresolved emotions and learning to trust his dad…*"

Emma clears her throat and closes her eyes. She takes a deep breath, holds it in for 3 seconds, and blows out. She stays silent for a brief moment to recollect her thoughts and to put things in their proper perspective.

"*I now understand my role. I have to support them both…and despite D'Shawn not being in Asir's life, allow him to go through the trials of being a parent.* I need to go back to bed."

Emma unfolds her arms, gives one more look at Asir's door, then walks down the hall towards her sleeping room.

Chapter 13
Shinobi of the Shadows

The sun rises above the mountains and volcanoes that border the village. As the morning takes form and lights the skies, Malik wakes up from his wooden floor bed to greet the day. He stretches his arms and back, then leans forward. Afterwards, he stares at the village from a window in his sleeping room.

As he glances, he takes note of the people going around with their day: some are gathering wood for fires, others are preparing to fish at the nearby river, and some are planting rice in nearby pools. Malik takes a deep breath and says nothing. He allows himself to clear his mind of any distractions.

Suddenly, a knock on the door interrupts his peace. The door slides open, and Malik turns around. Himiko walks in with a set of black clothing in her hands. Malik looks at it for a second and notices a small emblem on the top left side. It is an oval with black clouds, an outline of a red dragon on the left side and the blue phoenix on the other. Then stitched is the distinctive gold and blue that represents the eyes of each. Overwhelmed by the coincidence of the uniform and its logo, Malik redirects his attention to Himiko.

"Malik-san," she announces, "It is almost time for your training. The Grand Master will be waiting. Please accept this."

"It looks like the suits you wear."

"Yes, we call it yoroi. It will honor us if you wear this for your training."

Malik slowly places his hands underneath the clothes, then bows in acceptance. Himiko gives the clothes to Malik, then walks out to give him some privacy. Afterwards, Malik thinks to himself and smiles.

"*Why does this seem so familiar, yet so foreign?*"

Malik places the clothes on his bed, takes his night clothes off and gets dressed.

Ten minutes later, Himiko is standing guard outside the building where Malik spent the night. Hideyoshi and Shiori appear in front of Himiko to report to her in Japanese.

" (***Have you figured out the whereabouts of her***?)"

" (***No, I'm afraid we haven't seen any activity yet***)," Shiori responds.

" (***However, we noticed that something strange is happening with the local Yakuza clans***)," Hideyoshi adds.

"Kimyōna… dono yō ni (Strange…How)?" Himiko presses.

" (***Seems that there is a turf war that is on the rise, but none of the leaders that we know of is the clear instigator***)," Hideyoshi explains.

"(***It's as if someone else is pulling the strings***…)" Shiori concludes.

" *Odd*…hmmm," Himiko thinks, " (***Go back to Tokyo and continue to search for clues. We need to stop the Elite 8 and bring her to justice***)."

"HAI!" Hideyoshi and Shiori yell, then they make their hand signs and disappear in the wind.

Moments later, Malik walks out of the building fully dressed in his shinobi wear, only exposing his head. Himiko turns around and looks with admiration. She inspects the fit from afar, then speaks when Malik walks next to her.

"I hope the fit is right," Himiko says.

"It's a little tight, but I will get use to it," Malik says.

"Then we must be off," Himiko commands, "But I must show you something first."

Malik remains silent as he pays attention to Himiko. She puts her hands together, bending her last 2 smallest fingers together while straightening the first two upwards.

"With your Dracocernentia, you are able to move at incredible speed," Himiko explains, "But you must learn how to move with the wind. When you put your hands together like this, it balances the light and the dark so that your power can be like the wind."

Malik mirrors the gesture and forms the same stance with his hands. Himiko nods in acknowledgement as she continues.

"Now, with the power of smoke, we will mask our escape and move like the wind. Like so…"

Himiko closes her eyes. She lets off a flow of smoke from her lips and allows it to cover herself and Malik. Once they are fully covered, Himiko activates her Avemcernentia, causing Malik to activate his eyes. The energy from their combine powers becomes so intense that Malik struggles to maintain the fire burning inside him.

"Do not fight your power, Malik-san," Himiko explains, "Find your balance, then your power will explode into the wind, transferring you through great distances in a short time."

Malik heeds the words of Himiko and begins to breathe softly. As he finds his center, he is able to control his Fire Line: focusing all of his energy on one point in his body. Himiko then matches her energy then nods to Malik.

Afterwards, a burst of energy pushes Malik and Himiko through the air as the smoke disappears. Despite moving at top speed, Malik is able to see the movements and distance at a slower rate due to his Dracocernentia.

"*Wow…it's almost like I'm moving through my visions. I can't believe I still haven't hit the pinnacle of my powers yet*," Malik reflects.

Himiko smirks but maintains her focus as they approach the dojo.

Two seconds later, from the initial spot in front of the building where Malik slept, Himiko and Malik seemingly teleport in front of the Grand Master inside the dojo. With little time to react, Malik takes two steps in front of Himiko. Both face the Grand Master, then kneel as they await instruction from the Grand Master.

The Grand Master takes her time to greet Malik. She waves her fan with a steady rate as Malik patiently awaits her. She remains stoic and non-wavering. The room is silent, except for the roar of flames lighting the candles. The room is once again surrounded by ninja as the room sits still.

After a minute of waiting, the Grand Master gets up and continues to fan herself. She walks closer towards Malik. Malik senses her presence and looks up at her with prudence. Despite his Dracocernentia, Malik cannot see the receptors in the Grand Master. Her power has clouded her receptors, making it difficult for Malik to get an accurate read. Despite this, he looks at her with the respect she commands.

" Kyō(Today), Malik-san, (***You will start your training as Kuroikage. To achieve this, you must control the shadows that linger in your heart. You***

must confront the rage that lays dormant inside you. Then you must learn how to ally with them to create your Burning Will.)"

Malik gulps a little, then responds softly in Japanese.

" (***Grand Master, I have trained to achieve the Invisible Ember. I have purged my inner demons to clear my path to my Fire Line***)."

Suddenly, the Grand Master smirks and chuckles. She places her hand on Malik's left shoulder. Malik lowers his head. Then she rises and paces as she continues her explanation.

" (***I am aware of the 10 trials of the Moors***) Malik-san," she continues, " (***That training was to unclog the pipeline that feeds your fire. However, to control fire is an illusion and cannot be controlled or contained. The purpose isn't to limit your Fire Line, but to accept it***."

Malik looks up in confusion as the Grand Master continues her explanation.

" (***In all of us, we have the capacity to go from one path to another. We can live our lives to do good or live our lives to do evil. But there are times that to do evil means to ensure good people survive, or doing good and letting evil win. We have emotions: love, hate, sorrow, and***…"

" Ikari (Anger…)" Malik jumps in, " (***I understand now…I still feel it in me***)."

" (***Because a person, who conceded to their fate was brutally murdered in front of your eyes. You still feel responsible but have yet to realize the flaw and truth in this world***)," the Grand Master concludes, " (***This exercise will teach you how to ally with your emotions and direct them, just like the lava that flows towards the ocean to create new ground***

for life to appear, or how the eagle catches the fish, robbing it's life to ensure life for it's chicks)."

The Grand Master then activates her Avemcernentia. She creates a windy gust of smoke so powerful that it blows the flames out of the candles, then covers the room in shrouded darkness. Then she claps twice now and yells, " Hajimeru (BEGIN)!"

Malik suddenly gets up and looks around. His Dracocernentia is clouded, and he tenses up.

"*This is almost like that time I first met Bakala*," Malik reflects, "*I just need to calm down and relax. Remember, learn to ally yourself with the shadows.*"

Malik calms down, puts his hood and mask on. He notices that the smoke emits a level of heat that can aid him in this training. Then he adjusts the power in his eyes so that he can conserve energy and focus better. The Grand Master nods her head while internalizing her thoughts as she continues to blow smoke.

" (*He is beginning to understand. Now, can you rely on your abilities to pass through this training*?)"

As the smoke thickens, Malik is moving in a small circle. Suddenly, he feels a hit in his back.

"*Ouch...*" Malik grunts, then he swings his arms.

Feeling frustrated, Malik continues to maintain his nerve while awaiting the next hit. A few seconds later, a sudden kick slaps the side of his left cheek. Malik is briefly knocked partially to the ground.

"*Alright...It seems that I can't just rely on my eyes...but wait a minute...*"

Malik gets up, adjusts the power of his eyes, and makes them cloudy. The frequency omitted allows Malik to see in a lighter, more distorted frame of vision. Despite not seeing what appears to be sharp, precise objects, Malik can now see something else: vibrations, heat, wind and air direction.

So, when another random ninja tries to sneak up behind him, with another kick, Malik is able to see the air vibration distort the field, and he reacts. He blocks the kick, then throws a punch. The ninja counters with several punches, which Malik blocks. Afterwards, Malik ignites his right foot with a flame and tries a spinning jump kick. The ninja dodges by performing a back flip, then seemingly disappears from view.

Malik is puzzled by this display of inconsistency. He continues to keep his body on guard while trying to comprehend the training.

" *I don't get how I can see the movements but not the receptors*," Malik ponders, " *What is it that the Grand Master is trying to teach me?*"

Suddenly, Malik hears a barrage of rings fill the air. The smoke still fills the dojo as the Grand Master continues to blow. Her eyes illuminate to a brighter blue, the smoke gets thicker, and Malik finds himself struggling to breathe. His eyes begin to water, his heart begins to race, and he begins to panic under the stress.

"*Wow…this smoke is thicker than anything Bakala created. The Grand Master sure is powerful*."

SLASH! "UGH!"

Malik yells in pain as a sword slashes through his back. He briefly stumbles before getting his footing back. The Grand Master then stopped blowing smoke and clasped her hands behind her back. She continues to watch without making any facial expressions or showing concern. She continues to process this challenge under the gaze of her wise eyes.

"Ima (Now) Malik-san, (***Will you allow your anger to consume you, or will you learn to embrace all as one***?)"

Malik closes his eyes and tries to remember how to find his attackers. He then changes the intensity of his eyes to see the vibrations in the air.

However, moments later…SLASH!.

"ARGH!" Malik yells in agony as his leg is slashed.

The blood he feels leaking out of his body adds to the frustration of feeling helpless.

" Why in the hell can't I find anyone?!"

Then, Malik's irritation starts to get the better of him. His eyes start to turn red, the field of vision transforms red, and his patience wears thin. Malik drops his guard and becomes consumed with frustration and rage. The room turns hot to the point where some of the candles begin to melt. All Malik can do is breathe heavily as the predator eye takes hold of his senses.

In a split moment, another ninja cuts Malik, this time on his left arm.

SLASH!

Malik falls to his knees and holds his left arm in agony. Blood leaks through his fingers and clothes. Not knowing what to do or how to proceed, Malik lets off a roar that generates a heat wave.

"AGHHHHH!" he roars, but to no avail.

The power he emitted not only caused the smoke to get thicker, but Malik wasted precious energy and is quickly losing his strength. Afterwards, Malik slinks his head down in apparent defeat.

As Malik keeps his head down, his eyes go from red to golden brown. As the flow of energy begins to leave him, he notices his other senses sharpening.

DRIP…DRIP…DRIP…

Malik pauses for a moment. He takes the time to reflect on the events and how to pass this test.

"I used up a lot of energy trying to find my attackers," Malik realizes, "Getting angry didn't help my cause, but now that I'm calm, I can hear the blood dripping out of my body. I can feel the heat that surrounds me…wait a minute!"

Malik closes his eyes. He puts his bloody hands together in the hand sign position that Himiko taught him. Instead of trying to bottle his anger, he uses it to absorb the heat from the smoke.

Another ninja tries to go through the smoke and slice Malik. The shinobi gets closer and closer.

Finally, at the last minute, WHISH…the ninja swings his sword, but Malik dodges it effortlessly. The ninja disappears, but Malik doesn't relinquish his nerves.

Malik gets up, takes a deep breath and closes his eyes. The Grand Master watches in anticipation. Malik begins to move. His rhythmic moves and martial art techniques begin to rejuvenate him. With each move, his wounds begin to heal, the mist gets clearer, and Malik becomes more focused. Another ninja tries to attack Malik by swinging his sword. Malik graciously avoids the series of swings from the ninja. After 5 seconds, the ninja disappears.

Afterwards, the Mark of Bodhidharma illuminates and transforms the smoke from black to a lighter gray. Still thick and hard to see, Malik stands in place and remains calm. His eyes are still closed, but his senses allow him to pick up anything that would trigger a response. Seeing this, the Grand Master nods at three different shinobi from different positions to attack Malik.

Slowly, the warriors move without making a sound. CREEP…CREEP…CREEP, the shinobi get closer and closer. Malik still doesn't make a move or show any signs of anxiety.

After standing still for 5 seconds, 2 of the shinobi attack by swinging their swords. The first shinobi nearly makes contact with Malik, but he dodges in a fraction of a second. The shinobi tries to kick Malik, but Malik blocks it. Like a symphony, the fighters all engage in sequence, hitting and dodging. The ninja tries desperately to hit Malik, but Malik moves with the grace of wind and the efficiency of water. As he continues to move, the heat from his Fire Line creates enough power that when the shinobi think they have Malik cornered, Malik lets off a stream of smoke that darkens the dojo. Then, in the cover of darkness, Malik disappears.

Silence fills the air once more. The disoriented ninja go back to their corners, leaving the Grand Master to remain in her stoic stance. As the smoke gets darker, the last shinobi quickly heads towards the Grand Master and draws their sword. As the warrior inches closer, something unsheathes at the edge of the smoke and blocks the attack. The smoke clears, and the ninja's sword is blocked by a flaming katana.

Malik generated a sword from his hands while having another flaming sword pointed at the Grand Master. As the eyes of the Dracocernentia illuminate, the smoke is blown away, the eyes of the ninja and the Grand Master transform into the Avemcernentia and the room is filled with a volley of gasps.

The ninja lowers their mask and smiles at Malik. Malik is shocked at who it is and immediately responds to it.

"Himiko…it was you?"

Himiko nods as Malik turns towards the Grand Master. She nods as Malik gathers himself to realize what he's done. From out of nowhere, two flaming swords appear in his hands.

"How…did I…" Malik wonders.

" Subarashī (Well done) Malik-san," the Grand Master congratulates, (***In apparent defeat, you found the will burning inside of you. When you commit yourself to your convictions, then the power we possess can create something out of nothing***)."

When Malik begins to understand, the swords disappear. Malik and Himiko stand in front of the Grand Master and kneel. The Grand Master continues with her instruction and the purpose of the exercise.

"(***As Kuroikage, we are bound to protect our people and Japan in the shadows. In every battle, you will not always have the advantage, see very clearly, or be in the best of shape***)," she continues, " Malik-san, (***this is but the first of many tests, lessons, and trials to truly fight to your fullest potential as Kuroikage. Himiko will help you learn the ways of being a true shadow warrior. When you are ready, you will test your new skills in actual combat. Now, I command you to get some rest. You have many moons ahead of you***)."

"HAI!" Malik responds.

The Grand Master turns around, walks towards her mounted chair and sits down. Afterwards, Himiko and Malik get up, bow, then, with the technique learned earlier, generate smoke from their mouths before disappearing.

Moments pass by when an advisor walks behind the Grand Master. He is a scrawny, tall man wearing a black kimono wearing a hat, with sandals. He is also anxious and begins to nervously address the Grand Master in Japanese.

“ (***Grand Master, we have reports that the people responsible for spreading the virus are planning on sending a stronger form directly towards us***),” he nags, “ (***How can anyone know of our village***)?”

“ (***It matters not***),” the Grand Master responds, “(***Right now, we must have our shinobi ready to hit them before they come here***).”

“ (***Should I inform Himiko***?)”

“ (***No. Training with Malik needs to continue. He will prove a powerful ally against whoever I think is behind this***).”

“ Kono ushiro? Dare? (Behind this? Who?”

“ (***It concerns you not. Make sure that Himiko trains him well***).”

The man bows and walks away. After the man is beyond visibility, the Grand Master closes her eyes. She takes a deep breath, then activates her Avemcernentia. The flow of power creates a heat wave that re-lights all of the candles. Once the display is orchestrated, the Grand Master takes out her fan, waves, and stares into infinity.

Chapter 14
Shadows and the Light

The next morning, Himiko is walking towards the building where Malik sleeps. She greets some of the villagers as they go on with their business. The morning breeze cools any assemblage of rage, discontent, or vile intent. The village is calm and peaceful, as Himiko embraces the flow that gives her strength.

Upon reaching the building, she looks up at the window and stares for a while. She smiles and closes her eyes. Another cool breeze flows within her. After standing for a few moments, Himiko opens her eyes, walks up the stairs, takes off her sandals, and enters the building. She turns left and walks down the hallway. She reaches the door outside his room and knocks on the door.

KNOCK KNOCK, "Malik-san…Malik-san…"

No one answers.

She slowly opens the door and calls out to him.

"Malik-san…"

She walks in to see that no one is in the room. The bed is made, Malik's normal clothes are folded, and his shinobi gear is missing.

" Kare wa dekimashita ka(*Where can he be)*?" Himiko wonders.

Then, Himiko closes her eyes. She takes in several slow, deep breaths. She remains motionless as she gathers power from within her Fire Line.

After the 6th breath, Himiko opens and activates the Avemcernentia. She scans the village and surrounding areas, trying to pinpoint any receptors that resemble the training hero.

After moving her head, she notices a set of reddish-orange receptors by the lake 3 miles away, facing the volcano ranges. Meanwhile, Malik's eyes brighten and alert him that he's been detected, but it doesn't allow it to distract him from what he was doing.

" Wa… naruhodo (I…I see)...Malik-san," Himiko deduces.

Himiko deactivates her eyes, blows a stream of dark smoke. After covering the room, she disappears, clearing the smoke in her absence.

Three miles away from the village, Malik is standing shin deep in the cold mountain waters. His stance is rigid, his heart is empty, and his mind his focused. He activates the Dracocernentia and allows his Fire Line to create small ripples in the water. He stares at nothing as he faces the mountain ranges. He begins to take slow, deep breaths as he tries to meditate through his struggles.

"(SIGH)...(SIGH)...(SIGH)...I can feel myself in turmoil, like a storm brewing inside of me," Malik reflects, "What if I can't get over my rage…what if I allow my guilt to ruin everything that I've fought for? (SIGH)"

Suddenly, a voice breaks his concentration by uttering words of encouragement in Japanese.

" (***Whether it be Shinobi or Samurai, Bushido dictates that a warrior must accept what they cannot change***)."

Malik deactivates his eyes, then turns around. Himiko stands as the winds blow her long hair into the wind. Malik stands speechless and motionless, as Himiko continues with her words.

" Malik-san, (***the Grand Master has seen this in you. I've seen it as well. Let me tell you a story***)."

Himiko walks towards Malik and into the lake. Despite the cold water, she stands in front of him and pats him on the shoulder. Malik remains silent, but pays attention to Himiko. Himiko's dark brown eyes glimmer as she continues to tell her story.

" (***Long ago, before I was born, 2 brothers were destined to lead the Kuroi Kage. Their father was getting older and felt that younger leadership was needed to push the clan towards the future***)," Himiko continued, " (***The brothers had different ideologies on how we needed to run the Kuroikage: the older brother believed that strength came from unification, working together, and making every one equally strong, the other believed in pure strength and discipline. So on the next day, the brothers were matched together to fight for the right to rule***)."

" (***Wow, I didn't know the Kuroi Kage had such a custom)," Malik responds, " (What happened next***)?"

" (Sigh) (***So the battle commenced, and each brother was equally skilled. No clear winner could be decided…until the younger brother tried to temporarily blind the older by blowing flames in his eyes. Although the fire didn't hurt the elder brother, the temporary distraction gave the younger brother the advantage, and he began beating the opponent to the ground. The elder brother was beaten badly, but he would not concede defeat. He instead closed his eyes. The younger brother yelled, demanding that the match be decided; however, the father refused to acknowledge the winner. Soon afterwards, the older brother got up with his eyes closed and stood in front***

of his younger brother. Enraged, the younger brother tries once again to attack, but the older brother continues to dodge his attacks. As the younger brother got weaker, the elder generated power from within, yet no one watching could see it. As a final desperate attack, the younger brother raged towards the older brother. Still, when the older brother opened his eyes, they showed not the original color, but a color of purity. With one swift and untraceable attack, the younger brother was knocked to the ground unconscious for a few minutes."

Malik takes in this story with the seriousness and intensity it deserves. He mentally tries to correlate the story with his understanding of his journey.

" *Is this…the power of Awarelessness that Bodhidharma and Muqadas alluded to*?"

Himiko turns away, then finishes the story.

" (***After the fight, the right to rule the Kuroi Kage was passed down to the elder brother. Because of the act of dishonor, the father wanted to banish his younger son for his insolence. However, the elder brother pleaded with his father and wanted to forgive his brother***."

" Nanto iu jihi to meiyo (What compassion and honor)," Malik responds, " (***Even after that, he didn't allow his anger to dictate his decisions).***"

" (***Indeed, but it came at a cost. Later that night, bells rang of danger. The older brother woke up and jumped out of bed. The village was burning, and people were found dead in the streets. This enraged the brother, but he wanted to know what was causing this destruction. So he rushed to find his father. Then…when he reached his father's room, there was a stream of blood that flowed on the floor. The elder brother feared the worst, and when he stepped in, he saw his father's lifeless body on the***

ground, his mother cowering by the corner with a shinobi with a black flamed sword about to strike his mother. The elder brother yelled to stop and face him. When the shinobi did, the elder brother was horrified by the sight of the shinobi. He removed his mask and revealed himself to be the younger brother, so full of rage that his eyes transformed to blackish red. The younger brother laughs, creates a smoke screen from his lips, and disappears, leaving his brother and mother scarred for the rest of their days."

Malik could hardly believe the outcome of the story. Himiko continues to look down at the water to dwell in the depths of the story. Malik remains speechless as Himiko glances at him one last time.

"Malik-san, there will be a time when you will have to make such a difficult decision," Himiko warns, " What would you have done? Would you kill someone who shows you that they are dishonorable? How much is your honor to you?"

Then, Himiko walks up to Malik to conclude her message, "Your struggle isn't a unique one, Malik-san, but you must allow the Kuroikage to teach you the essence of balance and sacrifice, when to do it, and how to live with the consequences."

Himiko puts her hair in a bun, puts her hood and mask on, then instructs Malik. " Come, and follow me."

"Where are you taking me?" Malik asks.

"You will see, as we go…Malik-san."

Malik wipes his forehead, then closes his eyes for a brief moment. Then he relinquishes his stubbornness, puts on his hood and mask, then walks up to Himiko.

As they draw close together, Himiko and Malik perform their hand signs, blow out a stream of black smoke, and disappear into the wind.

The duo runs through the forests to take in the serenity of the land. Malik finds himself at a calm that allows him to feed from the energy of nature. Himiko continues to lead Malik as they approach the range of mountains.

A few minutes later, Himiko and Malik stop at a cliffside overlooking a range. They stand there in silence as the whistling of the wind blows through their ears. Feeling a sense of harmony, Malik loosens his shoulders, removes his hood and mask, then relaxes his head downward. Himiko, too, removes her mask, walks over to Malik and taps him on his right shoulder.

"I understand the burden you feel, Malik-san," Himiko says, "Look…over there."

Malik lifts his head and sees smoke coming from the mountain top. He squints his eyes to focus on the brewing volcano. Himiko faces the same direction, then continues her explanation.

"You see, Malik-san, the volcano represents fire, death, and destruction when it erupts. But as the lava cools, it creates more land and nutrients for life to thrive," Himiko draws Malik's attention as she concludes her wisdom, "As Kuroikage, you must accept what was once was and how people decide their fate. You will see that not everyone can be saved. My people once roamed all of Japan…and now, we reside here. Do not allow your misjudgment of this truth to bring you calamity and shame."

Malik nods, then looks at the volcano as it continues to fill the skies with smoke, pyroclastics, and gas.

"Hai," Malik says silently.

Himiko grabs Malik's arms, places her head on Malik's shoulder, and briefly embraces him. Malik feels a sudden warm, tingling feeling in his body, then looks at Himiko.

Malik and Himiko look at each other's brown eyes. The tension between them can crash air into powder. Before either one could act on their innermost thoughts, Himiko's eyes light up, causing Malik's to do so in the process.

A lone shinobi appears from the shadows and kneels before Himiko. Himiko walks away from Malik and steps towards the kneeling ninja.

" ***(Excuse the intrusion, Leader, you are needed back at the village)."***

" Kore wa dōiu imidesu ka(What is the meaning of this)?" Himiko asks.

"(***Hideyoshi and Shiori have been captured. The traitor sent a message to the Grand Master***)," the shinobi responds.

" Fukanō…(Impossible…)," Himiko exclaims silently as she looks away.

Malik walks over and inquires about the situation.

" Dō shita no (What's going on)?"

"Ayaka…" Himiko says silently, " (***We need to go now***) Malik-san. (***All will be explained when we address the Grand Master***.)"

The shinobi stands up and nods at the same time as Malik. Himiko and Malik put on their hoods and masks. Then quickly make their way towards the village.

The squad of ninjas circles the floor of the dojo as the candles continue to burn. The Grand Master sits patiently, waving her fan as the room remains silent. She says nothing and shows no level of concern or doubt. Her presence continues to evoke respect as the Kuroikage remain steadfast and prepared.

A few moments later, a stream of smoke blankets the floor in front of the Grand Master. As the smoke clears, Malik and Himiko appear to be kneeling on one knee. Both have their masks and hoods taken off as they await instruction from the Grand Master. Her voice rises as her compliments lead to her commands.

" (***I see that your training has progressed far,*** Malik-san."

" (***You honor me with your confidence, Grand Master***)," Malik says humbly.

" (***And now, it is time to put your skills to the test***)."

" (***Grand Master, what of Hideyoshi and Shiori?)"*** Himiko asks.

The Grand Master looks to her left and nods. A servant girl appears with a laptop and a flash drive. Then she presents it to the Grand Master. The Grand Master nods as the servant opens the laptop, starts it up, and inserts the flash drive.

" (***This was delivered this morning***...)" the Grand Master says.

When the drive is inserted, a video appears. It shows a hideout filled with chemicals, men in white suits, Hideyoshi and Shiori with arms hanging by wall chains and a woman wearing a white blazer, grey blouse, white knee-high skirt, a pair of red-bottom black pumps, with a light olive complexion, shoulder-length straight hair, and a demonic disposition. She cracks a smile while showing her purplish blue eyes.

"Ayaka..." Himiko growls.

Malik briefly looks at Himiko, then returns his attention to the laptop as the video continues to play.

Moments later, Ayaka begins to list her demands in Japanese.

"Kuroikage, (***I have here your poor excuses of shinobi to send you a message. You have one chance to save your village and clan. Relinquish your rule, Grand Master, to me, the rightful heir to the Kuroi Kage. If you refuse, then***…"

"(***We…will…never…surrender***)," Hideyoshi wheezingly interrupts.

"Hee hee hee," Ayaka squeals, "So sorry…"

Ayaka then turns around and looks at one of the men, " (**Can you bring me a cup, please**)? Hee hee hee."

A man brings a cup and stands next to Hideyoshi. Then Ayaka walks over, continues to chuckle like a little girl.

Suddenly, her eyes illuminate into a dark purplish-blue color, she generates a black flame sword and with one motion.

SWIPE…an eerie silence is followed by a collected gasp. She slits Hideyoshi's throat. As his eyes roll back and he gurgles the last remnants of his life, Ayaka prompts the man to fill the cup with Hideyoshi's blood.

As the cup fills, Himiko's anger bleeds through as her teeth begin to grit and her eyes slightly turn purple from the red mixing with the blue. Malik is horrified at such a psychopathic, sadistic act of cruelty. When Hideyoshi's head slinks downward, Ayaka takes the cup, skips towards the front of the camera, and then takes a sip of the blood. After chuckling, she throws the cup down and re-engages the camera.

" (***I will take pleasure in drowning your whole damn village with your blood. You have 24 hours to***

***surrender or…you will wish your lives would end quickly when I'm done with you*).”

Then the video stops.

Himiko closes her eyes and sheds a tear. Malik feels a sense of helplessness as Himiko struggles to regain control of her emotions. Himiko takes 2 harsh, heavy breaths before calming herself down. Then the Grand Master expresses her thoughts again.

“ (***This act of treacherous murder will not go unpunished***),” she says, “ (***I will send Himiko and Malik-san to deal with her, and to stop the virus from spreading. Do not take her life if you can. Ayaka must be brought back and face Kuroikage justice. Is this understood***?)”

“HAI!” Malik and Himiko respond in unison.

“ Himiko…Malik-san, (***You bear the pride and honor of the Kuroikage. Rescue Shiori, end this evil, and fight what we stand for***).”

Malik and Himiko stand before the Grand Master. She stands up, prompting the surrounding ninja to shout out their collective war cry. Malik and Himiko close their eyes, put on their masks and hoods. The Grand Master activates the Avemcernentia, generating the power to activate Malik and Himiko's eyes in a display of solidarity. As the power of the Kuroikage flows through the dojo and through the village, Malik's eyes glow brighter as he does a series of hand signs, then, with Himiko, disappears in an instant cloud of smoke.

Chapter 15 Complete Elitetion

Victor Goth is sitting in his secluded hotel room in Greensboro, North Carolina. He greets the morning by buttoning his gray striped shirt, putting on his brown blazer, and fixing his hair. He goes to the small refrigerator, grabs a bottle of gin, and then sets it on the table. Afterwards, he grabs a glass cup and puts some ice cubes in it. Suddenly, something vibrates in his pocket. Victor reaches into his pocket, looks at the screen and then swipes sideways.

"Good Morning," Victor answers.

" Good Morning, Mr. Goth. I was calling to let you know that I have appraised the house as you wanted. The property is now up to $3 million on the market."

"Good job, Reba. Have you had any more contact with Renee?"

"Nope. As a matter of fact, I haven't talked to her in a day or two."

"Allow her to drown in her sorrow. The stress of maintaining the house will be overwhelming. Show the appraisal to one of our operatives at the tax office. With the property taxes mounting, she will have no choice but to sell the house short."

"Understood, Victor," Reba responds, "But won't someone suspect?"

"Don't be ridiculous. With the pandemic in full swing and the amount of currency depleted, too many people will be trying to prioritize the economic crash to even notice the discrepancy. Trust the process."

"Understood", Reba responds, "For right and reason…"

"We will fulfill Elitetion," both say in unison.

Victor hangs up the phone, inserts it back in his pocket, then goes back to the table. He grabs the bottle of gin, pours it into the glass cup, then puts the bottle back inside the refrigerator. As he grabs the glass, he takes a sip of gin while contemplating the plans brewing in action.

"*Soon, the house will be ours for the taking*," he revisits, "*Then we can fulfill the dreams William couldn't*. (Sip) Shame he couldn't live to see this triumph."

Victor opens the drapes and looks out at the window. He smiles as he continues to enjoy his morning drink.

A few seconds later, a few knocks interrupt the silence that Victor is enjoying.

KNOCK KNOCK KNOCK.

Victor turns around and puts his glass on the table. Then he walks towards the door and opens it. A man in a black suit, white shirt, and sunglasses stands with his hands crossed downward.

"Sir…it is time," he says in a stoic, non-emotional tone.

"Indeed, it is", Victor responds pleasantly as he walks out of the room.

The man then escorts Victor down the hallway.

As the men walk towards the elevator, Victor checks his watch and chuckles. They reach the elevator, the man pushes the down button and stands by waiting. After a few seconds, a ding sound signals the arrival of the elevator. Both Victor and the man walk in as the doors close in front of them.

"So, have we secured the facility on the east side of town?" Victor asks.

"Yes, sir", the man answers while looking forward, "As instructed, I'm going to escort you there."

"Excellent. It's almost time to converse with our New World Order."

The door opens, and the man escorts Victor out. They walk past the lobby towards the door. Awaiting outside is a Black GMC Yukon on a 2" lift and 22" black rims. Another man, wearing a black suit and black sunglasses, holds the door open for Goth. Once Victor approaches the SUV, he looks at the man, nods, then enters the back seat, followed by his escort. The other man shuts the door, walks towards the driver's side, and enters the Yukon.

"You know where to go," Victor reminds, "Get us there quickly." The man nods, buckles his seatbelt, and drives off the loop way.

While driving towards the secret location, the escort informs Goth of his itinerary.

"Sir, we have several meetings with the local Pharmaceutical companies. On top of that, we are supposed to go to the capital to discuss the mandates imposed by the pandemic."

Goth chuckles, grabs a cigar from his pocket, and his cutters. He moves his cigar to the small space by the door, then cuts the tip of it, allowing it to land in the small compartment. Then he smells the cigar and closes his eyes.

His escort remains speechless while awaiting Goth's response. Goth pays no attention to anyone or anything around him. He smells the cigar, then slowly takes out his pocket of matches. The scent of the freshly cut cigar fills the inside with a cloudy mist of sweet, dry aroma of tobacco. Goth then lights it, takes a long, sensation-filled puff, then looks at the lit cigar.

"(Blowing out smoke)...This is good, so good," Goth says while looking at his cigar, "You know…it's little wonder that in a world of instant gratification, few take pleasure in simple patience."

Goth takes another puff of his cigar, blows the smoke out, then clears his throat.

"The Governor can wait," Goth continues, "Right now, we need to solidify our ranks around the world. So this meeting is paramount to that goal. Once the new council has fulfilled its obligations, then we will make our way to Raleigh."

"Understood, sir," the escort responds.

The SUV continues to drive to the secret location.

Fifteen minutes later, the SUV pulls up to a building on the west side of town. The building is about 2 stories high, with lightly colored cement and 2 floors. The SUV pulls up towards the front of the building. The driver puts the Yukon in park, unbuckles his seatbelt, then gets out to let Goth out of the truck. Goth unbuckles his seat belt, brushes the ashes off his clothes, walks out of the truck, and awaits his escort to accompany him. Then, Goth, along with the escort, walks inside the building.

When Goth walks in the door, he is greeted by a woman with brown hair, light makeup, wearing a blue dress and dark blue high-heeled shoes. Goth looks around as the woman addresses Goth.

"Good Morning, Mr. Goth," she says.

"Oh, hey there Heather," he responds, "Can you take this (cigar) for me please?"

"W…why sure, Mr. Goth," she responds.

Then Goth leans closer to her, gives her his cigar, then whispers maliciously.

"Thank you, sweetheart. You are a…(muah) darling, love."

Heather nervously smiles back, takes the cigar, and then turns around. Then Victor taps his hand on her behind. Heather tries to keep her composure as she desperately tries to smile in compliance before walking off. Goth smirks, then addresses his escort.

"So…shall we be off?"

The escort then nods and walks Goth towards the stairway.

Victor and his escort make it to the second floor. They walk down the hallway towards the last door on the left side of the floor. Victor stands in front of the door. The escort walks around Goth, opens the door, and then allows Victor to walk through. Inside is a laboratory with different sets of chemicals, scientists with clear white coveralls, masks, and biohazardous Personal protective gear. There is also a machine built against one of the walls with a huge vent that leads outside. Mounted in the middle of the machine is a magnificent golden sword. The sword's energy fuels the machine, pumping vast amounts of heat while altering the compounds of the chemicals the scientists pour into it.

"Grab me my glass at once." Goth orders.

The escort turns around and finds his alcohol. Then, Goth walks up to the machine.

"*It's…beautiful,*" Goth ponders, "*I can feel its power. Who would've thought that the same power that slew my ancestors would eventually help slay the very people whose ancestors forged the sword? I love irony when it favors me…*"

The escort returns with a glass of Cognac with 4 ice cubes. Goth looks at the escort, then grabs the drink.

"Excellent!" Goth commands, "Now get the screens up. The meeting will start in 3 minutes."

Saying nothing, the escort nods, then walks towards the back of the room to sync the 7 screens. As the escort is setting up, Goth revels in his apparent victory as he looks at the sword while sipping his alcohol.

A few minutes later, Goth makes his way towards the loading screens. As the buffering ends, the screens clear up, showing members from England, Japan, Russia, Australia, Brazil, Dubai, and Canada. Goth smiles as the member gives him their undivided attention.

"Welcome, council members. We're here to discuss the effects of the Shroud as well as the productions of the vaccines," Goth continues, "What news do you bring?"

"Well, the cold weather here has elevated the effects on our non white populations," the Canadian council member states, "However, no cases of deaths from our white populations have been recorded."

"Good." Victor responds, "What about the Middle East?"

"We still control the commerce and the resources," the Dubai member states, "Some of the prominent oil tycoons have fallen ill due to the pandemic, and if their health fails, it will be easier to seize some of the wells."

"Same here," the Russian member adds, "We are beginning to monitor production of our wells to drive up the worldwide gas prices. It'll cause chaos in much of areas that need fuel."

“A necessary but control type of Chaos,” Goth explains, “Ladies and Gentlemen, we are at the cusp of world dominations from the shadows. This is the time we take what we can and give nothing back.”

Goth turns his attention to the monitor with the English flag. On the screen is a dark, brown haired fellow with a thin mustache and beard. His name is Nathan. He has beady, brown eyes, a gray collar shirt, and a skittish personality. Goth smiles at the screen before engaging with him.

“What about the vaccines, Mr. Goth?” Nathan asks, “We’ve had to limit our operations because of our problems.”

“Please elaborate, Nathaniel,” Goth responds with a snarky tone. “There is a group that has been gathering resources and people to fight back. Also, there is a dark skin bloke with dreadlocks and these…crazy eyes who’s apparently teamed up with them.”

Victor raises one eyebrow, then takes another sip from his cup before re-engaging the conversation.

“Crazy eyes? Do they resemble what I think they resemble?”

“They look like that of a bloody dragon,” the frightened council member responds. “The Reintergon should…”

“We are running out of resources to produce the chemical. Perhaps if we had the sword…”

“ENOUGH!” Goth interrupts.

Then, he fixes his hair, clears his throat and takes another sip of his alcohol.

“Ladies and Gentlemen, there will always be small insurrections that try to challenge absolute power,” Goth continues, “But rest assured, the Pustula virus will cover this globe like a blanket, shrouding it in the kind of darkness we were unfortunate to succumb to during the Dark Ages. Yes, I'm aware that there are a few of those…who possess those unobtainable powers. Let us not forget that our late mentor, William Benson, tried and failed to find the genes necessary to obtain this power. So I say to you all, stay the course. They will be dealt with soon enough."

"Understood, Goth," Nathan responds. Goth then raises his glass then makes a toast.

"Ladies and Gentlemen, let us not forget that we hold the destiny of men. Destiny cannot be denied, so neither shall we…FOR RIGHT OR REASON…"

"WE WILL FULFILL ELITETION!" they all recite. "Ladies and Gentlemen, until we meet again," Victor concludes.

All of the monitors turn off while Victor sips the last of his cup. When he looks up, he notices that one screen is up. The woman looks at Goth with concerned and focused eyes. Victor puts his glass down on the table and addresses the lone screen.

"Ayaka…my sweet Ayaka," Victor says softly, "What is the matter?"

Ayaka points to the wall where Hideyoshi's lifeless body remains. Goth chuckles, grabs the bottle of Cognac, and fills his empty glass. Then he whispers to himself as he puts the bottle down.

"This is going to be interesting."

Goth picks up the glass, takes a sip, then clears his throat.

"So…you had to kill an intruder, yes?"

"One of many, in order to please the council…and to you," Ayaka responds, " That is not what troubles me, Mr. Goth."

"Please," Goth opens up, "go and explain your troubles to me."

Ayaka pulls up a laptop and scrolls through the screens. She brings it up for Goth to see. Goth begins to walk closer to the screen to get a better view.

"I threaten the group known as the Ainu, our version of the dark people who, for centuries, have protected Japan from the likes of us."

"Us?" Goth chuckles, "Ok, so what is the issue?"

"This is what our cameras capture during the exchange…"

Goth looks up and sees a familiar face. Cloaked in the ninja garb with the Kuroikage seal, the black man stirs up emotions that Goth has a hard time repressing. His teeth begin to grit, his pores begin to sweat, and his face turns red. Then Goth closes his eyes, turns around for a moment, and fixes his hair. He takes another sip of his glass, calms himself down, and turns around to face Ayaka.

"My dear, in you runs the blood of warriors," Goth inspires, "There's an old saying: the only one who can defeat a dragon…"

Ayaka briefly closes her eyes. Then she tenses her muscles, balls her fist, then activates her Avemcernentia. The small wave of black flames surrounds her body as Goth smiles in approval.

" (***The dragon shall die by the dark phoenix. They will all die***…)," Ayaka growls in Japanese, " Kenri to riyū no tame ni (For right and reason…)"

" Erīto-ka o jitsugen shimasu (We will fulfill Elitetion…)" Victor whispers, " Sā… meiyo o motte tatakai ni ikou (Now…go fight with honor.)"

Ayaka bows, then turns her camera off. Goth then walks around while looking at his glass. Then he looks up while contemplating his goals for the next phase of his plans.

"I have to get the Shroud to its peak potential. Only then can I finally rid this world of his infection."

Afterwards, Goth takes his last sips of Cognac before setting it on the table. Then he begins to walk out towards the door with the escort.

"Come now, let's not keep the Governor waiting."

Goth and the escort exit the room.

In the OBR base in Florida, Asir is walking down the hallway. Suddenly, a sharp pain hits the left side of his head. He hits the floor screaming while holding his head, twisting his body from side to side, and some of the members hear him screaming. They rush to help the teenager as he is agonizing in pain.

One of them reaches Asir while placing his hand on him.

"Asir…ASIR?!!!" he yells.

Asir doesn't hear the screams. Voices ring in his head as Asir struggles to regain control.

"Asir…Asir…ASIR…"

The voices continue. Suddenly, the pain becomes less intense. Asir sits up and leans against the wall. The members of OBR continue to reach out to him.

"Asir, are you ok?"

Another man asks, as Asir continues to hold his head.

"Someone get Snake Sight…NOW!" the man commands as 2 members run down the hall, "Asir, you're going to be ok…"

"Sharp…sharp…slafkaw (knife)..." Asir mumbles, "...Hul-wah (Bad)...chatolaswaw (tongue)....soletawa (war)…soletawa (war)!"

"Soletawa?" the man asks.

Asir continues not to hear anything but the voices in his head.

" Soletawa...soletawa!" the voices say.

Asir then responds to the voices.

"Ch...Ch...Chittoluthphwa?" Asir whispers.

Then, a silhouette of his ancestor appears in his mind like a light in the darkness. Asir's Dracocernentia activates and ignites his body. The OBR member scoots back to avoid the flames covering Asir's body.

Moments later, D'Shawn runs through with King Cobra and the other 2 members. Asir stands motionless as his eyes and body burn like a flashlight. D'Shawn tries to calm Asir down.

"Asir...son...can you hear me?" D'Shawn asks.

Asir turns around and says nothing. He looks up at his father and puts his palm up. Then the combination of voices echoes out of Asir's lips.

" Soletawa...soletawa!"

King Cobra looks at D'Shawn in a confuse state.

"Soleta...what? What is he saying?"

D'Shawn squints his eyes, then he recognizes the voice.

"Chittoluthphwa..."

D'Shawn then activates his Dracocernentia and addresses King Cobra.

"Soletawa means war in Seminole. Asir is getting a vision from our ancestor."

"What does that mean?"

"If I'm thinking right, we may be in the same position our ancestors were in. Tell everybody to get ready as I try to ascertain this vision."

"Right," King Cobra responds, "You three, gather the OBR and mobilize. LETS GO!"

King Cobra and the other members run down the hall. D'Shawn walks towards Asir. He continues to look as Asir's hand is still up in the air. D'Shawn briefly looks down and whispers to himself.

"(Sigh)...Ok, show me what you want me to see."

D'Shawn puts his hand up. He places his palm against Asir's. The combination of power creates an energy wave that flows across the whole base. Then both Asir and D'Shawn go through the vortex of their own minds, as they once again dive deep within their genetic past.

Chapter 16
The Start of the Never-Ending War

As the recurring transport of flashing lights comes to a close, the father and son reunite with their long-passed ancestor on the cusp of another genetic memory. Like before, despite not having the ability to speak, they remain conscious and aware of the scenes they are about to experience.

The year is 1837. As the crickets and frogs sing throughout the night, a lone plantation becomes the epicenter of a theater of brutality and dehumanization. Surrounded by a lone squadron of soldiers, a group of overseers surrounds 20 enslaved people as a demonic old slave orders two slave overseers to tie up a black slave to a wooden post. The man, about 55 years old, with a dirty salt and pepper beard, looks at all of his slaves as he embarks on a rant of supremacy.

"Some of you think you have rights. Some of you think you are human…" he screeches, "BUT LET ME TELL YOU THAT YOU NIGGERS ARE NOTHING MORE THAN ANIMALS TO ME! THIS BASTARD THOUGHT THAT HE WAS DIFFERENT! HE THOUGHT…THAT HE WAS A MAN LIKE ME!"

Then, the old slave master begins to unzip his pants. He begins to show his crooked, diseased ridden teeth, then softly concludes his speech. As the surrounding slaves whimper and sob for the dastardly deed to be done, the slave master's steps are interrupted.

Out of the shadows of the night, a lowly howl in the air spooks the people in the plantation. The few soldiers begin to draw their weapons and scout the area. As some of the soldiers begin to walk in the thicket, one is struck in the head with a tomahawk. UGH, the sound alerts another soldier. He turns towards the direction of the sound. He slowly walks closely.

As he slowly walks, a maroon warrior stalks the lowly soldier by crouching in the brush behind the soldier. When the soldier stops, the maroon swiftly runs behind him, covers his mouth, and then slits his throat. The maroon keeps his hand on his mouth as the soldier helplessly feels the blood flowing out of his neck. After a few seconds of wiggling, the arms slink down, and the maroon tosses the lifeless body to the ground.

Again, the howl raises eyebrows and suspicions about the plantation. The slave master zips his pants and looks around. His fear is shrouded with blunt statements of condescension and irritability.

"What in the hell is all of that racket?!" he yells, "And where are my protection soldiers?"

One of the overseers looks around and shrugs his shoulders. The deranged master grits his teeth, then orders the overseer to find the soldiers.

"Go out there and look for my soldiers! Something isn't right here."

The man walks towards the outskirts of the plantation as the other overseers corral the slaves closer together.

Waiting in the brush, Huncelahtotika stays low as the overseer draws closer to his sight. Camouflaged in black fur, the only thing that gives him away is the glowing reflection of light piercing out of his eyes. His superb night vision allows him to carefully stalk his prey.

As the lonely overseer gets closer, he notices something thumping against his boot. He crouches down to inspect the object. He places his hand and rubs it around. Suddenly, he feels something wet and distinct. He lifts his hands and discovers a stinky red substance covering his hand. His eyes widen, and his throat becomes dry. Before he could yell, the swiftness of the wolf closed the distance and grabbed the overseer by the arm. The overseer begins to yell in horror as he is getting mauled by the vengeful wolf.

"AGH ARGH ARGH GET OFF ME!" he yells.

The screams carry over towards the slaves and slavers. The slaves begin to caress each other as the Slave Master hopelessly looks around. His cowardice takes hold as the overseers begin to step away, hoping to get a head start to run away.

Then, several screams and yells begin to surround the plantation. Suddenly, a series of gunshots light up the air, as several overseers are struck, leaving only the Slave master and 2 other slavers upright.

Out of the brush, several Maroons, ex slaves, and some Seminole warriors walk towards the slaves and their owners. The remaining overseers run away from the Slave Master. The Slave Master becomes petrified with fear: the sweat from his face goes uncontested down his neck, his eyes widen to expose his hazel eyes, and his mouth curves downward. When the slavers try to run, one is immediately shot in the head by a Maroon with a flintlock pistol. The other runs towards the brush.

As the overseer runs towards the brush, a sudden ball of fire intercepts his course and engulfs the man, burning him instantly to death. The horror of the screams further solidifies the Slave Master's anxiety. After a minute, the ball burns out, leaving only a charred husk of a skeleton. Out of the shadows and smoke, a lone warrior with the green tint of the Dracocernentia graces the presence with his majesty.

Chittoluthphwa slowly walks closer as the Slave Master looks on, consumed with the same type of fear he tried to inspire towards his slaves. He gathers enough nerve to attempt to run the other direction.

However, when the Slave Master takes 3 steps, he is blocked off by Huncelahtotika. The war-tested old wolf tuffs his ears back and shows his blood-stained teeth. The wolf growls with intimidation and resolve as the trapped Slave Master is forced to confront his eventual fate.

"You seem to have no place to run, coward!" Chittoluthphwa scolds, as the Slave Master turns around, "You say that we are nothing more than animals…Yet we continue to stand while your comrades lie dead, giving the earth back the blood they have stolen."

The Slave Master falls on his knees and clasps his hands together. He begins to shed tears and pleads for his life.

"Whatever you are, please…please (sobbing)," he continues, "If you let me go, I will let all of the slaves go. They will be free…PLEASE, I BEG YOU!"

Chittoluthphwa's eyes illuminate. He sees the red and yellow receptors flowing in the Slave Master's body. His eyes squint further, then he walks closer to the pleading man.

"Free…free…," Chittoluthphwa continues, "Our people, my people, are already free. I will not make deals with men who try to take away the freedom of my people to satisfy their unending bowl of greed. You shall die…(Chittoluthphwa lights up his tomahawk with fire) like the animal you claim we are."

The Slave Master holds up his hands and begins to yell.

"No…NOOOO!"

Chittoluthphwa lifts his hands and raises his lighted tomahawk. His shriek echoes across the land as the tomahawk blade lands right in the middle of the Slave Master's skull. Chittoluthphwa hacks at the body 5 times before he lets his rage cool down.

Covered in blood, Chittoluthphwa turns around and walks towards the bound slave. The other Maroons cut him loose and set him free. The fortunate slave rubs his wrists, then faces Chittoluthphwa, thanking him for the rescue.

"So you must be the one they call Snake Eyes," the slave says, "I's thank you. I thought that…"

"No worries, my friend, " Chittoluthphwa interrupts, "You and the rest will settle in our camp. We have food and shelter."

"What about the whites?" he asks, "They'll try to snatch us again and put us back in the fields."

"Not while I'm still breathing fire," Chittoluthphwa responds, "Now follow the rest of my men as I ensure no one will catch you."

The slave nods, then prompts the other slaves to follow the maroons. Chittoluthphwa looks at the plantation building and stares. Huncelahtotika walks next to him as Chittoluthphwa pets him. The loyal wolf whines as Chittoluthphwa laments his same concerns.

"You're right, my friend," he continues, "You have been fighting since I was a boy. There's only so much fight we have, no matter the desire."

Chittoluthphwa gets up and walks towards the main house of the plantation. He closes his eyes and takes several deep breaths. With each breath, his body intensifies as covering his body with flames. Chittoluthphwa continues to generate power as Huncelahtotika looks on at a safe distance.

After several breaths, Chittoluthphwa opens his eyes, flashes the Dracocernentia, then blows a huge volley of flames from his lips. The greenish, yellow flames consume the house until the entire structure is completely ensnared in burning destruction. Once the plantation is engaging in the dance of death, Chittoluthphwa stops blowing and stares at the glowing flames. The wolf slowly walks next to him. Both look on with a sense of uncertainty as the crackling of wood evaporates along with the smoke in the air. Chittoluthphwa nods his head and looks down at Huncelahtotika.

"Let's go, my friend," Chittoluthphwa says.

He and Huncelahtotika turn around and make their way towards the thicket, leaving the remains of the plantation to burn into oblivion.

A few hours later, the maroons led the newly freed slaves into the strategic encampment surrounded by the swamps. As the slaves get acclimated to their newfound freedom, a circle of war chiefs looks on with hesitation and concern. Standing up first is Osceola, whispering to himself his thoughts.

"*Where is Chittoluthphwa?*" he wonders as he walks towards the edge of the camp.

He is followed by an escort: a slender man with dark brown skin, short curly hair with buckskin clothes and a long-barreled rifle.

Osceola continues to maneuver through the camp until he reaches the edge. He stares at the thicket and stays silent. His eyes scrunch downward with despair and disappointment. The man next to him stands a few feet behind him. The eerie sound of silence is muffled by the whistling of trees blowing in the wind. After a deep breath, the sound of panting alerts Osceola and the man. The man begins to load his rifle and aim at the dark thicket.

A tense moment of rustling keeps the men on guard.

"Do you have any idea what that is?" the man whispers.

"With most of the game driven out by war, we can't be too sure," Osceola responds.

A few moments that seem to last an eternity end when a shadowy figure appears out of the thicket. The old wolf comes out of hiding. His eyes not only shine in the darkness, but also shine a small smile on both men.

"Still a warrior at your age, my friend," Osceola smirks.

The man disengages his rifle and slowly walks up behind Osceola. Osceola bends down and pets the black wolf and smiles again.

"What of your master, Huncelahtotika?" Osceola asks.

Then a voice echoes through the brush.

"His master is alive and well…"

Osceola and the man look up at the thicket. As Osceola stands up, a pair of greenish gold eyes appear through the thicket. Chittoluthphwa appears to face the duo; battle-hardened, filled with sweat, grit, and burdened with exhaustion. Osceola and the man walk up to greet their friend.

"Welcome back, my friend," Osceola greets, " Hie la! Ay-it-liepts-e-chez (Ah! How is your health?)

" Mathint-a-mas-tshay (It is well)," Chittoluthphwa responds, " The plantation… Souks-cha (It is all gone)."

"I see…hmm, come, let us eat and welcome our new friends at arms," Osceola instructs.

Osceola turns around and walks towards the camp. Chittoluthphwa and the man walk side by side as they converse. Eager to hear about the exploits, the man begins to speak his mind.

"It is good to see you again, Chittoluthphwa," he says. "As I am to see you, John. How has the fighting been with you?"

" The whites are relentless, but so are we. Every day we fight, we free more of the slaves. They, in turn, help our small numbers and prove to be our best fighters."

"Fighters…I see…"

Chittoluthphwa begins to lower his head. Huncelahtotika whines while walking alongside the duo. Concerned with the silence of his friend, John tries to ascertain the flow of emotions that cloud Chittoluthphwa's mind.

" Estomah (What's the matter), Chittoluthphwa?"

Chittoluthphwa takes a deep breath and looks up at the sky. The winds blow but do little to quell the spiritual pain that flows in his body. The same sense that he thought once alluded to him now resurfaces through the events he experienced in the last raid. After a few moments, Chittoluthphwa stops and faces John.

"John, you were born a slave, yes?"

John mounts his musket on his back and crosses his arms. He briefly looks down, nods his head, then faces Chittoluthphwa.

"My mother was born a slave. She told me stories of how the white men would do all sorts of things to them. She risked her life to flee and met my father in these lands."

"As was my mother," Chittoluthphwa responds, "I remember the last time I saw her. She risked her life to save me. She too told me stories when I was young. She was a courageous and powerful woman."

Chittoluthphwa shifts his weight and glances away for a moment. John is growing increasingly concerned but says nothing. After another deep breath, Chittoluthphwa finishes processing his trouble mind.

"What I saw was unspeakable. The white man tied one of the slaves to a post facing backwards. The slaver attempted to…," he stutters, then re-gathers himself, "Had I not killed them and burned their plantation to the ground…"

John takes his time to collect his thoughts. Then he encourages Chittoluthphwa with words that slightly lift his spirits.

"What you did is save the legacies of our mother while fighting to preserve the legacies of our fathers, my ahessi (friend)," John says with a smile, " These white men call us savages, yet their brutality to their fellow man and the land knows no ending."

"You are right, John," Chittoluthphwa says, "I will continue to fight until our land is secured and the slavery that caused our mothers pain ends in tootkah (fire). Come, let us go to the fire."

The men continue to trek through the encampment with Huncelahtotika.

When the duo reaches the council fire, Osceola begins to address the circle of Maroon and Seminole war officers and chiefs. He looks at a note given by one of the scouts. His eyes are heavy, his throat is dry, and his stance is slightly slumped. Chittoluthphwa disengages the Dracocernentia to regain his strength while paying attention to the body language of his comrades.

"I have received this note stating the white men want a truce under a white flag…"

The council all murmur amongst themselves. John and Chittoluthphwa remain silent as Osceola continues to address his plans.

"Tomorrow, I, with a select few, will meet the white men and speak, to end the fighting and to allow us to live in peace."

Several men begin to yell and talk in disagreement.

Some yell, " Esticha-bucke-nawhansle (Bad people)!"

Others yell, "They are liars! They have no honor!"

After a few moments, Osceola holds his hand up and addresses the crowd.

"Wy-kass-tchay (Be Still)," he commands, " The white men are many, but we are only a few. The game is nearly gone, and the land that we stand on isn't good for crops. We cannot allow our people to starve."

"With respect, Osceola," John interrupts, as he walks towards Osceola, "I do not trust these white men. Their tongues are painted with blood and lies."

"Indeed, but they, too, have suffered so much bloodshed and will continue to come."

"Then I should go with you," John says. Osceola crumbles the note and smiles. He walks towards John and places his hand on his left shoulder.

"You are a good friend…and a mighty warrior. If what you say is true, then they will need your strength and leadership."

John gulps, then whimpers. He gathers himself and nods, not saying a word. Afterwards, the council disperses, and Osceola begins to walk away from John.

As Chittoluthphwa continues to watch, Osceola notices him and stops in front of Chittoluthphwa. Still weakened by his exploits, Chittoluthphwa looks at Osceola with deep brown eyes.

"...Git-lo-sthah (I do not understand) Osceola," Chittoluthphwa says, "We have been fighting these white men for 2 growing seasons. We have seen what they do to our people. I have burned plantations and put many under my knife. Why?"

Osceola smiles and faces down. He looks around the whistling trees, the blowing grass and the purple, black skies. As the winds continue the blow, so do Osceola's words.

"An hisseh elittal mas cheh (I am your friend) Chittoluthphwa. We have fought with honor and for the legacy of our people. Through the times, we have come together: former slaves, runaways, broken men, and fatherless women. As I look at the white men, infecting this land and making her sick, I must find a way to heal her. Make no mistake, the whites will continue to come. Their greed knows no boundary, for even the waters won't fill their bellies."

"Then why risk your life? I should…"

Osceola places his hand on Chittoluthphwa's shoulder. His smile gives Chittoluthphwa the kind of warmth 10 suns couldn't match. His confidence and assurance in himself begin to transfer to Chittoluthphwa. Chittoluthphwa begins to look at Osceola in a different light as he concludes his message.

"John will need you. You are what keeps our people from dying, my friend. I must do what's best for our people. You must do the same. You must rest… goodbye…warrior with Snake Eyes."

Afterwards, Osceola lets go of Chittoluthphwa's shoulder and walks away. Chittoluthphwa, filled with a tsunami of uncertainty and grief, anticipating the events that may unfold yet unable to change the course of the river of inevitability, looks on as Osceola walks as if he is about to fade into history. Then the memory becomes fuzzy and fades to white. The lights flash through a tunnel of time that leads back to the present plane. After a few moments, Asir and D'Shawn awaken from their long, enlightening meditation.

Chapter 17
Welcome Home

Asir and D'Shawn awaken from their long, detailed mental vision. The sweat from their skin flows out of their pores like facets. The heavy breathing echoes throughout the hallways. Suddenly, Asir crouches down to regather his strength as D'Shawn towers over him.

"I…I'm still not used to the flow of power yet," Asir says, "Do you think my head hurts bad because our ancestor is trying to tell us something?"

D'Shawn takes a deep breath. He clears his throat and nods his head.

"When we are in tuned with our purpose and our convictions, they become a conduit for our ancestors to communicate with," D'Shawn explains, "To answer your question, Asir, I think it's that and more. It'll be up to you to figure it out."

D'Shawn extends his hand to Asir. Asir looks up and sees D'Shawn smirk, nodding him to grab his hand. Asir takes the hand and allows D'Shawn to pull him up. D'Shawn pats Asir on his shoulder.

"You are getting stronger every day, son. Do not rush towards strength. Allow yourself to build it up, and in time, you'll be able to use it to help our people."

Asir nods with conviction and smiles.

Suddenly, steps echo through the hallways. They get louder and louder. When the person finally shows up, she immediately stops in front of D'Shawn.

"Ms. Emma, what's wrong?" Asir asks.

Emma continues to pant until she catches her breath. She looks at Asir with concerned, wet eyes. Then, she looks at D'Shawn.

"You two are going to want to see this in the conference room."

"Alright," D'Shawn answers, "Come on, son, let's go."

The trio makes their way towards the conference room. Their pace is urgent and motivated. They race towards the room until finally, they are greeted by a room of dedicated OBR militants. All of them look at the flat screen TV showing images of riots and police. King Cobra walks up to D'Shawn, Emma, and Asir.

"What's going on?" D'Shawn demands.

"It's bad Snake Sight. An officer gunned down an unarmed 19-year-old during an unjustly traffic stop," King Cobra explains, "The people have been up in arms ever since."

"We just saw a task force throwing tear gas and other projectiles at the citizens," Emma adds, "We need to do something."

Meanwhile, Asir stares at the screen. His eyes pay attention to the minute details of the shots. As his awareness draws nears, he is suddenly overwhelmed with an infusion of emotion and realization.

"WHAT A MINUTE! LOOK! IT'S IT'S…"

"What is it, lil man?" King Cobra asks.

Emma looks at the screen and notices the buildings. She immediately deduces why Asir is up in arms.

"*Oh my god…It's his…*"

Unable to control his rage, Asir erupts by transforming his eyes into the Dracocernentia and facing D'Shawn.

"WE NEED TO GO NOW! THAT IS MY HOME! WHAT ABOUT MOM?! WHAT ABOUT GRAMMY?!"

As the heat emanates from Asir's rising power, Emma and King Cobra gaze at him with a confuse and startled look. D'Shawn, meanwhile, maintains his poise and looks Asir directly in his eyes.

"We'll send out a squad to intercept the Race Soldiers Asir," D'Shawn says, "But…I can't have you come with us in that state. You need to control your emotions."

Asir begins to growl and grit his teeth. He gives D'Shawn another look, and small flames begin to consume his body. D'Shawn says nothing, but continues to look Asir in the eyes.

Suddenly, a pat on Asir's left shoulder briefly calms the teenager down. He looks towards his left and sees King Cobra. His brown eyes soften, his shoulders are relaxed, and the words that follow give a calm recollection that breeds competent advice.

"Lil man…Asir," King Cobra says, "When I was a little older than you, I lost my older brother to the police, who shot him because the pig claimed he was robbing cars. Despite the evidence that my brother was innocent, the jury found the cop not guilty."

Asir sees the light blue, red, and gray receptors in the King Cobra. The subtle touch of his shoulder diffuses the flames Asir generated as King Cobra continues his speech.

"I felt exactly what you felt, Lil man. Unlike you, I didn't have powers, resources, or a family to help me deal with the pain. But your dad is right. We need you in your right mind so that more of our people don't get hurt."

"That's right, son," D'Shawn adds, "Absolute power corrupts absolutely. We're not immune to this.

The best way to help your mom and grandmother is to make sure these Race Soldiers don't try to overuse their power."

Despite her impulses, Emma chooses to say nothing. Her innate sense of order and compliance allows the men to redirect Asir's focus to where it needs to be. Then Asir deactivates his Dracocernentia.

"Dad, I think what you're trying to tell me is…I can't just throw out fires because I can burn people important to me just as easily as our enemies."

"Exactly," D'Shawn responds while King Cobra nods in confirmation.

Then, Asir faces King Cobra and performs their signature handshake. D'Shawn states his commands.

"King Cobra, mobilize a unit of 25 men. We will focus on protecting the people and avoiding bloodshed unless necessary."

King Cobra salutes, then begins to gather the crowd.

"Asir, go with Emma and meet the squad in the loading lot."

"Ok, Dad."

Asir begins to walk away, then Emma grabs D'Shawn's arm.

"D'Shawn," Emma whispers, "This isn't training. This is…"

"Exactly what Asir needs. He's getting older, and part of being a man is being tested. I know this isn't exactly what you envisioned…"

"But you also know that he has to understand his role in the community. I don't entirely agree, but I will not begrudge you of your decision. I will do my best to…"

"I know…" D'Shawn finishes.

"Are you coming, Ms. Emma?"

Asir asks. Emma remains silent and nods. Then she looks back at D'Shawn for a brief moment. As their eyes meet, Emma senses a man masking his emotions with commanding resolve and prophetic insight. Then she releases her grip, turns around, and walks with Asir. D'Shawn looks at them as they walk out of the conference room and then gets his squad ready.

Thirty minutes later, two carrier trucks are loaded and filled with the chosen squad members. In the first transit are D'Shawn, King Cobra, and half of the chosen forces. Armed with battle gear, masks, and guns, OBR prepares for the fight as the large truck starts the ignition and drives out of the location. As the truck makes its way towards the projects, King Cobra is the last to put on his mask. He then looks down at his gun then begins to question D'Shawn.

"Snake Sight, our forces are stretch thin. How do you expect us to fight to the full force while this pandemic has compromised our ranks?"

"At this point, we don't have a choice," D'Shawn states, "If we wait any longer, the White Supremacist machine will justify gunning us down as insubordination. The effects of the Shroud have elevated their Anti-Black racism to the degree that we have to fight."

King Cobra nods and waits to respond. He clears his mind, checks his gun one last time, then faces D'Shawn.

"You…know…we are with you. I…am with you."

D'Shawn nods as King Cobra puts on his mask.

In the other truck, Emma and Asir sit quietly as the 2nd squad prepares for the engagement. Emma looks at Asir as he sits, eyes curved downward, while breeding discontent with the impending circumstances. Emma uses prudence to slowly place her hand on Asir's back. She rubs it softly, applying a nurturing energy that calms Asir down enough to engage with her.

"Ms. Emma, I don't want my mom to get hurt…or worse."

Emma takes a deep breath and sighs for a moment. She continues to rub his back until she grabs his attention.

"Asir, look at me," she commands.

Asir raises his head and looks at her. He gives her his undivided attention as Emma relays her story.

"Asir…I grew up not knowing my parents. My mother died sometime after I was born. I was raised by a man who led me to believe that she'd abandoned me. As I grew up, I became consumed with anger and rage."

"Why were you so mad, Ms. Emma?"

Emma pauses for a bit. Despite the redeeming events, some of the traumatic memories still linger like mold in a kitchen sink. The stench of regret is still present. Determined to make peace with who she used to be, she continues to relay her honesty to Asir in an attempt to help him convey his emotions.

"Asir, do you know what it feels like not to like yourself?"

"Like me, like think that you're weird, no one will like you?"

"That's exactly what I mean," Emma responds, "Well, because I believed that no one would love me, I began hating the world. I would hate black people, and sometimes the people who were taking care of me."

"Wow…so, how did you get over it?" Asir asks.

"I had love…from my brother, and my grandparents. My brother didn't give up when my emotions almost led me down that dark path when I confron…confronted…"

Asir waits as Emma begins to sulk again. She sniffs the air, then clears her throat. She closes her eyes, then wipes her eyes with her hands.

"I saw my father…my real father."

"What was he like?"

"He…was an evil man who used my mother and caused her to go into a deep depression. He allowed her to kill herself while at the same time abusing my brother. When I saw him, I thought for a moment he would hold himself accountable, even…even love me."

Asir looks at Emma with soft, innocent eyes. Then, he slowly speaks again.

"What happened afterwards?"

"Well…when he refused even to acknowledge me, his daughter, it took my brother's words of love and encouragement to bring me back. I guess what I'm trying to tell you is…is…"

Emma struggles to find the words. Her voice gets choked up, and she becomes completely vulnerable. Then, Asir does something unexpected. He wraps his arms around Emma and squeezes the insecurities out of her. Emma, initially dumbfounded, returns the gesture. She embraces Asir and closes her eyes. Tears of validation and resolution leak out of her eyes; for a brief moment, both are lost in the warmth of love.

Once they release their grip, Emma waves her hand to dry her eyes. Asir smiles, then activates his Dracocernentia.

"I sense that we're close to my home," he says.

Emma sniffs her nose and gathers herself. Noticing that the carrier truck is slowing down, she concludes that Asir is perceptive in his analysis of the situation.

"You're right, Asir," Emma responds while transforming her eyes, "Are you ready?"

Asir nods, then fixes his face to intensify his focus.

The convoy made it to the housing projects. Upon arrival, there is a layer of squad cars blocking the other side of the area. A single line of Anti-Riot unit stands at the ready as several black protestors yell, scream, and hold up their signs.

As D'Shawn, King Cobra, Emma, and Asir, along with the rest of OBR, exit, a command is given to strategically position the men near the protestors.

"King Cobra, take a squad of ten men and center the defenses," D'Shawn orders, "Quickly hand-pick each member to flank opposite sides of the projects. We don't want to show the full force yet."

"Understood!" King Cobra says.

"Emma and Asir, I need you near me. We will blend in with the crowd. The fact that we are not carrying guns should divert attention away from us."

Emma and Asir nod in acknowledgement. King Cobra then selects 2 men and organizes them into 2 fifteen-man squads. The remaining men stay behind to guard the vehicles and provide escape if needed. After a few minutes of deliberation, the squads position themselves on the outer borders. King Cobra marches his group in two columns towards the epicenter of the rioters while D'Shawn, Emma, and Asir make their way through the crowds.

The riot intensifies tenfold. Several black protestors yell and scream at the cops to not only mourn the death of the young black man, but to seek justice. A police sergeant uses the LRAD (long-range acoustic device) to address the disgruntled crowd.

"Attention, stop what you are doing, and please return to your homes! Failure to comply, we will fire upon you, and if caught, you will be arrested for disorderly conduct!"

The demands further infuriate the masses. Chants of "HELL NO, WE WON'T GO!" drown out the air like a cloud, spreading across the area. The sergeant looks around and sees that no one is budging. A nearby officer consults the sergeant when he sees the inevitable.

"Hey, Sarge, these protestors aren't moving," he says.

"Then, you know what to do next. Give them the tear gases."

The officer nods, then runs towards his Anti-Riot ranks.

King Cobra, from a distance, glances at some of the officers getting cannisters from their squad cars.

"*Oh no*," he concludes, "*I know what this means...*"

Suddenly, King Cobra gives out the order to his squads.

"Put on your gas masks now! Make sure when they throw the gases, we protect the citizens. Do not fire unless fire upon!"

"YES, SIR!" they collectively yell.

The squad quickly put on their masks and got their rifles ready.

Disguising themselves in the crowd, D'Shawn, Emma, and Asir notice the receptors of both the rioters and the police. Asir notices the shift of red and yellow receptors from the squad. He quickly deduces the energy, then addresses his father and Emma.

"Dad! KC and OBR sense something is wrong. Do you see it?"

D'Shawn focuses his attention on their position. Then he focuses on the police and notices their receptors turning blue collectively. D'Shawn understands, then responds to Asir.

"Asir, you and Emma will have to help some of the people who will get caught up in this," D'Shawn continues, "You two need to be careful not to hurt the people if you have to defend yourselves."

"D'Shawn, what's going on?" Emma asks.

"They're about to gas the rioters, then…"

"Then…wh…"

D'Shawn gives Emma a look that signifies impending strife. Emma is taken aback, then quickly understands the situation. She then looks at Asir.

"Let's go, kiddo!"

Asir nods as they sneak towards the center of the crowd. D'Shawn strategically remains hidden while building up his power.

The Anti-Riot group stands still as the rioters continue to hurl their insults at the police. The dastardly race soldiers then unleashed a volley of gas containers by hurling them towards the crowd. Initially, the crowd shows little regard for the flown objects. Suddenly, a stream of white, powdery gas ignites and spreads all over the crowd. The conglomerate of coughing and confusion creates a maelstrom of calamity and disorder. Many flee backwards to avoid the smoke as the Anti-Riot group begins to march upon the unarmed citizens.

Once the field is covered with tear gas, a few officers begin chasing after the rioter with their clubs. Some stragglers are caught in the crossfire, while most retreat towards the rear of the commotion. The Anti-Riot group then began to march towards the field. The group remains unmatched for a few steps. Each straggler is rounded up and handcuffed by some of the policemen.

Meanwhile, Emma and Asir use their eyes to maneuver through the crowd of rioters and a few policemen. Despite the mixture of smoke and the shroud from the pandemic, their internal heat sources allow them to weather the storm while surveying the chaos.

"Ms Emma, this is crazy. I can see some of the police up front, but I can't get to them."

"I know, Asir, but we need to focus on the ones we can protect."

"I understand, but..."

"But what..."

Asir's focus has him geared towards a series of yellow receptors. When he looks to his right, he sees a policeman harassing a woman. She's yelling at the policeman as 2 other men back him up. He suddenly runs in that direction while Emma yells at him.

"Asir...ASIR! WAIT!"

The woman continues to stand her ground as the policeman threatens her with commands.

"You need to go back to your home, or else you will be arrested," the officer scolds.

"THIS IS MY HOUSE AND I HAVE MY RIGHTS!" the woman yells, "YA'LL NEED TO GET OUT OF MY PROPERTY!"

"Negro please," the cop retorts, "Ok, so you want to do this the hard way, huh?!"

Suddenly, the cop grabs the woman and wrestles the woman towards the ground. As she continues to fight, she yells in desperation.

"HELP! HELP ME! HELP!"

"SHUT YOUR MOUTH! YOU'RE UNDER ARREST! PUT YOUR HANDS BEHIND YOUR

BACK!" the officer yells as the others try to help restrain her.

With little hope of escape, a yell carries across the street and hits the officers like a hurricane.

"LEAVE MY MOM ALONE!"

Not showing much concern, the officer looks in the direction of the yell and gives a command.

"You need to stay back if…"

Suddenly, a fire wave knocks the officer back towards the brick of the project housing. Partially burned and unconscious, the officer alerts his peers to the presence of a highly pissed off teenager.

As the woman looks up, she sees the majesty of the Dracocernentia coming from someone she hasn't seen in nearly a year. Her surprise is only met with a slight measure of relief.

"A…Asir?" she whispers as Asir engages the cops.

The officers look up and see Asir. Then they try to bully him into submission.

"Look, you need to back away. I don't give a damn…"

Asir interrupts the cops by manifesting his energy in the form of a giant flame dragon.

"Holy…shit…" the cop whispers as they attempt to draw out their guns.

When the woman sees it, she begins to yell in horror.

"NO! ASIR!"

Before the cops could aim, a single flaming tomahawk strikes the backup cop in the forehead. The lifeless body falls as fast as his morals, as the lone, initiating cop is left, surrounded by the results of his incompetent bigotry.

As the smoke clears, D'Shawn, followed by Emma, walks behind Asir to calm him down. The touch from her allows Asir to control his power and dissipate the silhouette.

D'Shawn walks slowly towards the lone cop and gives him an alternative.

"So, the way I see it, you have 2 choices: either you take your comrade and get out of here…or you end up at the end of my blade. Which will it be?"

Shaken by the power of D'Shawn while force to concede to his cowardice, the other officer picks up his unconscious comrade, wakes him up and starts to leave. Then, D'Shawn removes the tomahawk from his forehead and addresses the cop again.

"Hey, it's rude to leave trash on someone else's yard…"

D'Shawn lights up his tomahawk with flames, as the two cops reluctantly and with prudence, drag the body out of the yard.

Asir then runs towards his mother and hugs her.

"Asir, where in the hell have you…Baby, where were you all of this time?" she asks.

After a short embrace, he picks her up and responds.

"I've missed you, Mom. I'm sorry I didn't come home. A lot has happened, and…"

"And what?"

Asir looks towards his right as D'Shawn walks towards the two. Then the woman's face turns from joy to scorn: her eyes scrunch down, her face tenses up, and her pores expose more sweat.

"Tameka…" D'Shawn says in a soft voice.

"D'SHAWN!" she responds, before attempting to calm herself down.

After the small exchange, Emma shows up as Tameka quickly recognizes her.

"So, you were in this as well? How could you…"

"Mom, Ms Emma saved me from W.A.V.E. They were putting poison in me and made me sick."

"I don't give a damn!" Tameka responds, "You are MY CHILD! And…"

"You need to take it easy on Asir, Tameka," D'Shawn interjects.

Realizing that Tameka was saved and the rest of OBR is controlling the situation, Tameka reluctantly keeps quiet for the time being. Then, she brushes herself off and walks back into the house with Asir. Emma walks next to D'Shawn before they follow in.

"Are you ok?" she asks.

"You should ask that of Asir. I sense that this won't be a warm reunion. So, whatever is going to be said, please…let it go."

Emma nods at D'Shawn, then follows them into the house.

Chapter 18
Shutting the Valve

The dim lights of the day recede towards the horizon. The echoes of the night resume their ritual of filling the skies with noise. As darkness overshadows the skies, Bakala and Esmeralda perch on top of one of the buildings of London's skyline. The winds of change blow as softly as a summer breeze. As Esmeralda looks on, Bakala lightens the mood to ease the tension of the impending mission.

"Enjoying the sights from above, love?" Bakala asks, while smirking at Esmeralda.

"Huh…oh, I'm sorry. I was just thinking."

"Thinking of who, might I ask?"

Esmeralda hesitates to let her emotions go. He tucks her head down and closes her eyes. The ever-flowing breeze of the English skies prevents her from evading the question. Then, Esmeralda gathers herself, opens her eyes, and addresses Bakala.

"I…miss…Triana," she admits, "The last time I did a mission like this, I lost her because we underestimated the effects of the gases. I…just…"

"Don't want to lose anybody else," Bakala adds, "Quite understandable love. Truly, I'm sorry for your loss. Just remember, we're stronger together than apart. Don't be afraid that your emotions make you weak."

"Heh heh heh," Esmeralda chuckles, "You sound just like Malik er…Shadowmoor."

"Well, the Yank is capable of learning, I'll give him that," Bakala chuckles as they both smile at each other.

Then, complete darkness overtakes the skies as they look onward towards their destination.

"It's time," Bakala reminds.

Esmeralda nods, then both descend down the building and move into the shadows of the streets to reach their goal.

Meanwhile, back in the OBR hideout, Terrance and Mason look at the secret surveillance cameras to monitor the progress of their operation. Behind them is Eulalia with her Avemcernentia activated. Mason glances back briefly, looking at her eyes before redirecting his attention to the screen.

"I can never get use to those eyes," he says, "No matter how much I see them."

"It's never easy to unsee something that has been deliberately hidden from you, Mason," Eulalia responds, "Still, it's kind of refreshing to believe what our ancestors originally made instead of the lies our former employer tries to hide."

"Fair point." Mason agrees.

"Well, based on the cameras, our troops are in position to overtake the building," Terrance mentions, "All we need now are our secret weapons. Are you sure the Lass is ready for this?"

" Pequeña ave is very strong and brave, but sometimes will allow her emotions to block her power," Eulalia explains.

"But I believe Bakala will keep her honest," Mason adds, "From what I've learned through experience (thinking about Malik and Emma), they represent two objects that balance each other out."

“Well, I just hope they can pull off this mission,” Terrance concludes, “The fate of our people, and the whole world, depends on this.”

The trio continues to look on as they anticipate the moment OBR attacks the building.

Minutes later, members of OBR gather around the building and crouch down in the surrounding brush. Among those leading the squad is Lionel. He keeps his eyes open for the moment while contemplating the details of the mission.

“*Well, this is a bit of a mix-up,*” he ponders, “*I wonder how much longer we need to wait? I hope they show up soon.*”

Bakala and Esmeralda show up at the rear of the troops. Not wanting to alert their presence, Bakala and Esmeralda link up with their eyes to communicate with one another. As the Dracocernentia and Avemcernentia intensify, both talk to each other telepathically.

“Alright, love, this is it. We need to create a diversion so that we can sneak and outflank the blokes.” Bakala states.

“So, before we do this, should I amplify my power to aid you when you create the smoke?”

“No love, we’ll need to conserve as much strength as possible. We don’t know the extent of the gases or the Shroud. The troops will need our Fire Line to aid them in this fight.”

Esmeralda agrees, then disengages the link.

Afterwards, Bakala takes a deep breath and closes his eyes. Esmeralda keeps her composure and waits for the moment to engage in the infiltration. After three long breaths, Bakala reactivates his Dracocernentia, circles his lips, and blows out a deep, dark smoke.

As the smoke percolates through the ranks, Lionel recognizes it and gives out a hand signal to alert the troops. Each of the members put on their masks and infrared googles. When the entire perimeter of the building is covered in smoke, the OBR members get out of hiding, slowly walk towards the door, and barricade the entrance with little ease.

Inside the building, members of the Elite 8 are organizing their chemicals while monitoring the machine pumping out infected particles in the air. One of the members, a man named Nathan, is overseeing the project. His shrew, timid, and anxious demeanor does little to distract the other members as he paces back and forth in the small confine space.

While contemplating the prudence of their actions, a lowly member wearing an all white, containment-secured suit walks up to Nathan to give him some news of their developments.

"Council Leader," he says, " I have the results of the Pustula Virial mutation."

Nathan pulls out a rag from his pocket. He wipes his head, ridding it of sweat, then addresses the man.

"Is it worse than we suspected?"

"I'm afraid so. Even though the spread is potent, it does not differentiate between hosts. Even the effects of the Reintergon can't sustain its mutation."

"So what are you saying?" Nathan anxiously asks.

"Without the sword's power…the virus will soon target and produce the same sick symptoms on us as well."

"Is it taking care of the "targeted" group?"

"Well…(sigh), even though the reports still suggest they are mostly affected, it's only because of the worldwide emboldened activity against them. As far as the sickness, fewer of them are dying than before."

Nathan nods his head and turns away. He continues to shake his head while trying to think of solutions. The lowly member waits for a response while looking at the security cameras. Then, after a few seconds of internal deliberation, Nathan faces the man and instructs him on the next steps.

"Continue to experiment with our captors in the cellar. If you see any abnormalities or any resistance, report it to me immediately," Nathan concludes, "We have to make sure the virus can counteract any antibiotic out there."

The man nods, then walks away.

Nathan furiously turns to the security cameras as he ponders to himself. His skin turns red. His sweat continues to overflow his confidence while drenching his skin with the putrid aroma of guilt and shame.

"*How in the hell does Mr. Goth think we can keep this up*?" he contemplates, "*Despite our best attempts, their) Immune systems are better equipped than ours. It's only a matter of...*"

Suddenly, alarms set off in the workroom. Startled, Nathan looks around, seeing flashing red lights and horns blowing from speakers. When he glances at the screens, he sees the images filled with black smoke. Then, one of the leaders of the building's security system approaches Nathan.

"Sir…we've been breached! We don't have a visual of who's in the building."

"Inject yourselves with a super shot of Reintergon and intercept them," Nathan commands, "They must not reach this area! If they do…"

"Understood, sir."

The man turns away and mobilizes the resistance groups. Nathan crosses his arms and paces back and forth while other members begin to evacuate the area.

"*Damn it...*"

Then Nathan turns around and leans on a desk. His anxiety takes hold. He balls up his fist, violently slams it on the desk, and yells from the top of his lungs.

"DAMN IT!!!!"

As the security forces move up towards the bottom floors, they are met by a thick area of smoke. Weary with their guns cocked and loaded, the leader slowly scans the scene while remaining visible to his squad members. An eerie silence fills as fast as the blackened smoke. Not a sound or a mark to signal the presence of friend or foe.

All of a sudden, POW…

A single bullet from a .45 mm gun strikes the forehead of the security lead man. As his corpse falls backwards, a barrage of machine gun fire upon the Elite 8 security members as both sides exchange bullets in a smoke-filled battle zone.

At the rear of the lines, Bakala and Esmeralda match their combine powers to blow enough smoke to engulf most of the buildings. Meanwhile, Lionel is taking cover while using hand signals to direct different members of OBR to maneuver through the battle. After a series of signals, Lionel looks at the Moors and yells at them.

"We got it from here," he reminds them, "We'll provide the distraction while infiltrating the building and destroying the machine."

Both Bakala and Esmerald stop blowing. Then Bakala sees red, gray, and yellow receptors coming from beneath the building. After a split second, he addresses Esmeralda about the change of plans.

"Esmeralda, you need to get to the basement of this building."

"But, I'm supposed to fight with you! How can you change the plan like that?!"

"If you calm yourself and take a look-see, you'll understand," Bakala retorts,

"THEY…are the priority right now. As soon as they're secure, then you can assist me."

"If you two are done arguing like a couple," Lionel interrupts, "YOU BEST BE GOING!"

Esmeralda looks at Bakala. Bakala smirks and winks at Esmeralda. At this moment, Esmeralda, too, sees glimpses of the receptor fields that come from the bottom and understands.

"Don't worry, Love, I'll be alright." Bakala reassures, "Best be off."

Esmeralda nods and goes in another direction. She generates a fire shield to guard herself from any ricochet bullets. Bakala does the same, as he ventures towards the other direction. After the Moors exit the scene, Lionel and the remaining OBR members continue to trade blows with blows, bullets with bullets, death with death.

Nathan continues to nervously pace the small space while looking at the security cameras. Despite being surrounded by a small force of security men wearing black suits, white shirts, black ties, with sunglasses, Nathan loses more confidence with each passing second.

"Sir," one of the bodyguards says while attempting to comfort the distraught leader, "They have suffered some casualties and we're holding. We can beat them back."

Nathan looks at the bodyguard through his shades and smiles. Then his sarcasm responds with an extra spice of pessimism.

"Apparently, you don't play chess much…I'm not worried about the pons, I'm worried about the king and queen."

Nathan steps away while shaking his head. Then he addresses the bodyguard with words of discontent and hopelessness.

"It took me a while, but I know who created that smoke. He's been a pain in our arse as far as we can remember. He'll be here soon, and when he does…"

"We'll protect you, sir," the bodyguard finishes.

Nathan smirks again, puts his hands behind his back and responds.

"Fools…the lot of you. Even our fearless Leader will learn soon enough."

Esmeralda reaches the bottom of the building. There is a door that has a metal handle and a digital combination lock. Esmeralda scans around to see any other ways to enter with no avail.

"UGH…no tengo tiempo para esto(I don't have time for this)," Esmeralda complains, "Supongo que solo hay una manera de hacer esto (Guess there's only one way to do this)." Esmeralda closes her eyes and focuses her energy. As the heat forms on her right fist, the energy erupts into a flaming, blue fire. Once the flames get to about the size of a basketball, Esmeralda opens her eyes. The glory of the Avemcernentia amplifies her power, and Esmeralda lets out a glorious yell as she punches the door handle.

After partially melting the door handle, Esmeralda slowly opens the doors. As she enters, she notices a dungeon-like setting: several cages with drugged-out African immigrant victims, old clothing, and two Elite 8 members trying to have their way with one of the victims. As they turn around, they see Esmeralda glowing with blue fury. The young lady they were attempting to defile suddenly crouches, anticipating a violent liberation.

When Esmeralda sees the receptors of the 2 men turning from blue to yellow, they hold their hands up, begging for mercy. Esmeralda's eyes intensify, her fist ball up into flames, and her eerie voice echoes through the chamber.

"Bastardos... han causado tanto dolor y muerte. Ya es hora de que experimentes lo que creaste (You bastards…have caused so much pain and death. It's about time you experienced what you created)," she whispers, "*This…is for you…Triana!*"

With a flash, Esmeralda seemingly teleports towards one of the men and punches him in the gut. Flames explode through his back, and what little blood exiting from his mouth evaporates in the heat. Esmeralda grits her teeth as the moisture from her body burns, leaving a charred, blackish husk of a body behind to tumble towards the ground.

Before the other man can let out a yell for no, Esmeralda condenses her lips, creates a small opening, and blows a huge, blue fireball at the man. When the ball hits the man, it instantly sets the man on fire. His screams echo across the chambers, awakening the victims as his arms wave violently in the air in a feeble attempt to stop the burning.

After a minute of the main, the body collapses on the ground as the flames continue to consume the lifeless body. Esmeralda calms down and looks at the woman she just saved. Shedding tears of joy, the immigrant gets up and places her hand on Esmeralda's arm.

"Thank you...for saving me," she says.

"I need to get you and the rest of the girls out of here," Esmeralda says, "after that, I will lead you out of the building. We must do this quickly."

"Yes, I agree. I will help you."

Afterwards, Esmeralda and the young woman opened all of the cages, unshackled the victims, and led them out of the chamber, towards the back of the building, and through the outside towards the back to avoid the conflict ensuing in the building.

Nathan continues to pace back and forth in the laboratory. He continues to wait for the inevitable as the squad of security valiantly holds their perimeter. Suddenly, black smoke begins to form out of nowhere and fill the room. The lead bodyguard quickly mobilizes his force while instructing Nathan.

"SIR, I need you to stay in the middle of us. We will protect you."

Nathan stands still as he allows himself to be surrounded by the remaining security.

As the smoke thickens, Nathan cowers on the ground while covering his head. The security force has its guns ready, awaiting a sound or move. On the left side of the room, a sound resembling a pebble sets off the guards. They begin shooting in that direction. They do not hit anything but glass and other objects. Then, a similar sound comes from the other side of the room. Again, the guards fire in that direction.

"Hold your fire, men," the lead bodyguard commands.

Then, the same eerie silence appears as the smoke gets thicker and thicker.

In a flash, a large string of fire quickly engulfs and burns the guards, encircling Nathan in a trap of burning security members. As the screams of the men begin to fade, the smoke clears up, leaving Nathan to nervously gasp at the pile of ashes that was once his last form of defense. As he slowly gazes up, he looks to his right and sees a cocky Moor with dreads.

"Seems you turned up the heat a bit, eh?" he says.

Nathan looks at him with a confused glance. Then he stutters with a response.

"Eh..eh…excuse me? I don't quite follow."

"I wasn't talking about you, mate." Bakala sarcastically says as Nathan anxiously turns the other direction.

When he sees that he's been surrounded by a beautiful, battle-tested woman with the Avemcernentia, he looks back at Bakala with sad, defeated eyes.

"Yes, I gave those bastards a sun tan of their lives. Too bad it took their lives." Esmeralda says.

"Well, maybe they shouldn't cook in the kitchen if they can't handle the heat," Bakala says as the Moors walk towards Nathan.

When they reach Nathan, Bakala smiles and relaxes his body to ease the tension. Then he softly asks Nathan questions.

"Alright mate, it's going to be ok," Bakala says, "just point to the direction of the machine and we'll be on our way. If you don't, then (he looks at Esmeralda, prompting Nathan to do the same)..."

When Nathan looks at Esmeralda, she puts up a fist, then ignites it with blue flames. The terrified Council member then looks at Bakala, then slowly points his head towards the machine. Esmeralda and Bakala follow his head to the other side of the room, then look back at Nathan.

"Much thanks to you, mate," Bakala says.

Nathan looks at Esmeralda as she diffuses her fists, then blows a kiss for good measure.

Thirty minutes later, Terrance and Mason await word from their forces. Terrance looks downward while Mason puts his hands on his back. Mason nods his head and smiles. Terrance notices his mannerisms and engages in conversation.

"You seem overly confident, mate," he states, "Are you sure that they will complete this mission?"

"I have no doubt in my mind, my friend," Mason retorts, "You have yet to see these wonderful young people in action. I promise you they will not disappoint."

"Heh heh heh, If only I had your confiden…"

Suddenly, a radio signal interrupts the conversation. Terrance quickly picks up the radio and pushes the button.

"This is Black Tiger here."

"Black Tiger, this is Barbary Lion here to report to you."

(Sigh) Terrance breathes a sigh of relief as he looks at a smiling Mason. Then he responds to Lionel.

"What is the status of the mission?"

"Mission is a success. We took heavy casualties, but we destroyed the machine and…"

"And what, mate?"

"We discovered that they had hostages beneath the building. The secret weapons were able to quickly seek them out and escort them to safety."

"Understood, what of the leader?"

"As you suspected, Goth isn't here, but they let the one in charge go."

"That is unaccept…"

Mason interrupts Terrance by putting his hand on his shoulder.

"Terrance, the main objective is that machine. The Elite 8 are known for cutting loose ends. He's a dead man anyway."

Terrance reluctantly nods his head and gives out his last commands.

"Alright, Barbary Lion, set bombs around the building and blow it up. Then take the remaining men and report back to base."

"Affirmative Black Tiger, Over and out."

Terrance takes the radio and taps it on his head. Then he looks up and sees Mason gathering his things. Terrance suddenly puts his radio down and addresses his comrade.

"What's the meaning of this?" Terrance asks.

"The mission is over, my friend," Mason responds, "It's time for me to pack and get to the airport." "But, your experience, your knowledge…you could be a big help…"

"Back home, Terrance. You have two new allies who will help with the operations here in Europe. I need to help the main weapon against this worldwide oppression so that he can reunite our people."

"Do you think he's ready for that, Mason?"

"That's why I need to catch up with him to find out."

"Well then (Both hug each other), there's no stopping you. It was good working with you again. I'll see to it that we get you there."

"No doubt, my friend."

Afterwards, Mason walks out of the office, towards his chambers, and begins to pack his belongings.

Chapter 19 Dark Light vs Bright Shadow Part 1

The sun begins to set beyond the horizon. The barrage of crickets and other insects begins to orchestrate their voices in the pure, purple night. Malik sits in the dojo, devoid of another presence as he contemplates the upcoming mission ahead of him. The stillness of his mind and determination fight against the rushing anxiety of the impending choice he may be forced to make.

Slowly, he closes his eyes and begins to take long, drawn-out breaths. His power grows, yet he tempers the inner flames by calming his mind and utilizing the teachings of the Kuorikage.

Suddenly, a rush of feminine energy graces Malik's presence. Malik opens his eyes but remains seated in place. As the person walks by him, he briefly closes his eyes and takes one last deep breath. A comforting voice begins to ease his concerns while implanting final words of wisdom in Japanese.

"(***It seems that on the eve of battle, there is a calm before the storm)"*** she says.

" Hai. Dōi shimasu (I agree)," Malik answers while facing the Grandmaster, " (***I've seen this type of evil before. More specifically, the ones responsible for it are the reason why I am in this journey to begin with***)."

The Grandmaster takes out her fan, unfolds it, and then waves it to create air towards her face. Her face remains stoic and unanimated; however, the words that exit her mouth contradict her outer appearance.

"(***You underestimate your purpose, and the purpose of your journey***)," she continues, " (***The true enemy is not in front of you, but inside you. What you call the enemy is nothing more than the reflection of the internal demons that plague all men. Evil men are a conduit to the repressed issues they refuse to deal with***."

" (***Even so, how do I stop these men without going into a rage that can't be controlled***)," Malik asks, " (***If I go over the edge, important people can get hurt or even***…)"

" (***You have trained well in our ways***) Malik-san," the Grandmaster compliments.

Taken aback by this sudden shift in the conversation, Malik faces the Grandmaster. Her eyes continue to glow blue, but her admiration and pride shine brighter than the full moon migrating towards the middle of the sky. A slight smirk precedes the lasting words to lead Malik on his treacherous mission.

"Anata wa pawafurudesu (You are powerful)... Shadowmoor. (***You have mastered many of our techniques and have exceeded your own expectations. When you find yourself in a place where your honor will come into questioned, remember your training, remember your ancestors…and remember yourself. The flames of your power…will always reside in the same place every man has access to, but few have the courage to engage***."

Moved by the powerful words, Malik gets up from his seated position. Himiko walks in and gives reverence to the Grandmaster by bowing her head. Malik looks at the Grandmaster in the eyes. The wetness and genuine gestures speak volumes as both he and the old woman express their farewell without saying a word. After a brief moment of silence, Malik looks at Himiko as they put on their hoods and masks. Then, both perform their sequence of hand signs before creating a layer of smoke. At this moment, the grandmaster states her final words to them.

"(***Remember…light cannot prevail without darkness. Darkness is neither evil or good, but it is an ally. Never forget…the Kuroikage way***)."

Both Malik and Himiko nod as they disappear in the blanket of smoke. After the smoke clears, the Grandmaster walks towards the entrance of the door and watches the night overtake the skies.

As the two shinobi race through the forests towards the city at high speeds, Himiko takes the lead as Malik follows close by. The flow of power transmits emotions and mental complex thoughts, enough for Himiko to engage in a brief conversation with Malik.

" I briefly saw…that you had words with the Grandmaster. What troubles you?"

Malik takes his time to answer, knowing that he must be in his right mind to prevail in the upcoming showdown. Nonetheless, he tries to tell the truth while remaining cryptic.

"It's not what troubles me, it's how I overcome when facing our enemies."

"There's only one way to win, Malik-san. There is only victory or defeat."

"What do you consider victory? Destroying an enemy? Killing them?"

"Would you prefer dying?"

"Depends on what you call death, Himiko."

Himiko and Malik make it through a vast countryside in a matter of minutes, then stop when they reach within 30 miles of Tokyo. They decide to recuperate their strength while continuing their earlier conversation in Japanese.

" (***In my…our clan, we are taught that death is a way to not only meet our ancestors, but to weigh the value of our lives***)," Himiko continues, "(***You're worth isn't always easily seen, even with our eyes***)."

" (***And that's what I'm beginning to learn. It seems that this journey is more than just getting over my grief, my insecurities of losing***…)," Malik responds.

" (***The ancestors led you here***) Malik-san," Himiko faces Malik while activating the Avemcernentia, " Now is the time to confront the fear of failure…by learning to keep going."

Malik nods in response as the transformation activates his Dracocernentia. After reviving each other's powers, both shinobi look on with Tokyo in sight to rescue their comrade while taking down one of the major players of the newly formed Elitetion.

In the Elitetion building, Shirori continues to fight, losing consciousness as Ayaka paces back and forth. Her girly demeanor does little to mask her demented, demonic sense of humor as she continues to torture her battered victim. Wearing a white karate-style top, purple outlines, with the Elitetion sign imprinted on her left chest, a black belt, and black hakama pants, Ayaka walks around with a pair of wooden Geta. She looks at Shiori, giggling with each word of taunting.

" Hee hee hee hee hee, (***How are you feeling***?)," she asks, " (***Are you***…) (Ayaka cocks her right hand backwards, then with a force of thunder smacks Shiori in the face) Daijōbu(alright)?!"

A stream of blood enters the air as it migrates from his mouth. Ayaka continues to giggle while covering her mouth with three of her fingers. Then she walks up to him and whispers in his ear.

" (***Oh, does your stomach hurt? Let me help you fix that***)."

Ayaka then punches his stomach.

"GWAH!" Shiori yelps as Ayaka punches his stomach 3 more times, slow but hard times.

Ayaka relieves the tension in her hands by wiggling them in the air. Shiori's blood begins to drip to the ground as Ayaka looks down at the stains. Her eyes begin to turn slightly black, and she begins to grit her teeth. Afterwards, she takes a deep breath and closes her eyes. She looks up at Shiori and smiles. She takes off her Getas and walks closer to Shiori.

" (***Don't you like my new pedicure***?)" Ayaka asks.

She wiggles her toes while bragging about the black nail polish. Shirori looks down at her toes, then looks back at her. He briefly spits out blood from his mouth in an attempt to spit at Ayaka. Ayaka gets irritated but keeps her composure.

" (***Perhaps, you didn't get a good look at them***)," she says.

Then, Ayaka twists her body, lifts her leg, and lets out a yell before performing a roundhouse kick to Shiori's face. Her face shows maniacal intent as the pain begins to overtake Shirori. Ayaka continues to mock him as he struggles to remain conscious.

" (***Maybe you need another look. I think I can do that for you***)."

After a demonic smile, Ayaka once again yells before performing three, simultaneous spinning hook kicks to Shiori's face. The blunt force of her foot knocks Shiori out with the third kick.

As Shiori's head slinks down, Ayaka stares at Shiori while one of the accomplices of the building, dressed in all white, walks behind Ayaka. Without moving her head, Ayaka notices the presence and immediately gives commands.

" (***I need a towel for my pretty feet***)," she commands, " (***And keep our security systems active***)."

" (***As you command***)," the accomplice responds while giving her a towel.

Ayaka takes the towel and wipes the blood off her feet. She then smiles at the unconscious ninja as she continues to pace around the laboratory.

One hour later, Himiko and Malik keep to the shadows a block away from the facility. As they scan the building, Himiko and Malik notice key receptor fields while trying to formulate a plan of action.

" I can see Shiori on the bottom floor of the building," Malik says, "He's in bad shape."

"Must be due to the torturing he's force to endure," Himiko responds, "If we storm the building, Ayaka will probably…"

"We can't let that happen," Malik interrupts, "I think I know a way to get in and at least buy some time."

Himiko nods and faces Malik as he explains his plan.

"There's bound to be cameras everywhere. It'll take too much time and power to try to find them all. I propose that we blow black smoke and surround the area. I will rescue Shiori…"

"...And I'll deal with Ayaka."

"Are you sure you can…"

"Malik-san," Himiko interrupts, "Ayaka is drunk with blood, and by only killing me and taking over the Kuorikage will quench it. This ends now."

"I can't let you fight her alone," Malik contests, then finishing his thoughts in Japanese, "(***Shiori is more important. Remember who we are and what the Grandmaster said***)."

As Malik looks in Himiko's eyes, her determination and resolve speak louder than words. Her eyes glow blue, and the power of her Fire Line flows high enough that small heat waves surround her body. Malik briefly closes his eyes and takes a breath. Afterwards, he relinquishes his position on the matter, then responds to Himiko.

" (***I…understand. I'll rescue Shiori…and let you balance your debts***)."

As both nod to each other, they manifest their power and clasp their hands together. Both take a deep breath, meditate for a few seconds, then blow a deep, black, suffocating stream of smoke from their mouths.

The smoke engulfs the perimeter of the building and covers all of the lenses. Meanwhile, the security forces of the building are viewing the screens. One of the guards began to notice that the images were covered with smoke. Another guard is confused and begins to question the visuals.

"Nani ga okotte iru (What is going on)?" he asks, " Soto hi wa arimasu ka (Is there an outside fire)?"

Before the main guard can answer, the sound of clacking flip flops interrupts the brief exchange. Ayaka walks in and sees the smoke. She says nothing for a few seconds as she views all of the video feeds from the cameras. The main security guard cautiously asks Ayaka about her thoughts.

" (***Mentor, what are you doing here***?)"

" (***Doing what you are being overpaid to do inadequately, spot and anticipate danger***)," Ayaka scolds, " (***This is no outside fire. This is a fire that will consume us from within. Sound the alarm***)!"

Immediately, the guard pushes the button to sound the alarm. A low bell alerts all of the occupants to assume their stations while Ayaka slowly walks out of the room. The guard then questions her one last time.

" (***Where will you be, Mentor***?)"

Ayaka's eyes glow blue with a layer of black at the rim. She slowly responds with evil intent as she smiles.

" (***The time has come to shine a light on this darkness, and blow out the flames***)."

Afterwards, Ayaka puts out her right hand, generates power from within her body, and generates a black flaming sword.

The smoke has covered the whole facility. Himiko and Malik come out of the shadows of the alleys and move in unison towards the building. Then, Himiko and Malik solidify their plans while wishing luck to each other.

"Are you sure you can handle Ayaka, Himiko?"

"Shiori's well-being is our main concern, Malik-san," Himiko responds, "Be careful."

"Anata mo (You as well)," Malik says before heading towards the back of the building. Himiko reactivates her Avemcernentia and breaches the front door.

The chaos ensues as the smoke masks the intrusion of the building. Malik sneaks through the back way. The door is locked. Knowing that the alarms are already set, Malik focuses his power by formulating flames in his fists. With one swift, accurate strike, Malik punches the door and melts the handle. He slowly opens the door and slips right in.

With discretion and prudence, Malik makes his way towards the stairway. With each step, Malik amplifies his eyes and ears for any impending danger. His previous run-ins with the enemy have given Malik enough foresight not to let his guard down.

"This seems...too easy", Malik ponders, *"I would expect even someone to be down here guarding the doors."*

Malik continues to make his way down the stairs, keeping his head on a swivel while picking up the receptors of his comrade.

"At any rate, I can see that Shiori is fading fast. I must hurry."

Moments later, Malik makes it towards the double doors of the laboratory. Still wary of unexpected traps or triggers, Malik makes one more scan of the area. He amplifies his Dracocernentia to look at the ceilings, walls, and corners.

"So far, so good," he says.

Afterwards, he slowly opens the laboratory doors.

Malik enters the laboratory and looks around. The area is vacant and sloppy. Empty bottles of chemicals, flasks, and instruments scatter around the tables while unfinished projects are left on the computer screens. Suddenly, a noise interrupts Malik's viewing of the mess.

"Ugh…UGH…"

The moaning echoes across the laboratory. Malik suddenly looks up and sees across the area. He sees Shiori, handing on chains slowly coming out of unconsciousness.

"Shiori!" Malik yells as he rushes towards the fallen shinobi. Malik reaches Shiori and pats him on the shoulders.

"Shiori, Shiori! Daijōbudesuka, Tomoyo (Are you alright, my friend?)"

Shiori slowly opens his eyes and looks up. He begins to sigh as his mouth curves slightly upwards in relief.

"Mal…Malik-san…" he slurs.

" (***Hang on. I'm going to get you out of this***)."

Malik balls up his fist, ignites it with flames and precisely punches the chains and shackles. The metal partially melts, but Malik removes them before burning Shiori's skin. Once freed, Shiori leans his weakened body towards Malik. Malik quickly catches him and helps him towards the floor.

"Watashi wa… arigatō (I…I thank you)," Shiori says.

" (***Save your strength. I'll heal you and***…)"

" Jikanganai (There's no time) Malik-san," Shiori interrupts, " (***Ayaka anticipated your arrival and is planning on using the same paralyzing gas she used on me***)."

"Mahi gasu (Paralyzing gas)?" Malik responds, " *It's probably the newer version of the Reintergon. That means…*"

" (***You must reach Himiko…and save her***)."

" (***What about you***)?"

Shiori smiles, sits in easy pose and puts his palms together.

" (***Do not worry. We have a secret healing technique***)," Shiori reassures with a smile, " (***Go now. You are Kourikage. We must protect your own***)."

Malik stands up and briefly looks down. Shiori bows his head and smiles again. As Shiori performs several hand signs, his wounds slowly begin to heal.

Meanwhile, Malik looks away and faces towards the entrance. He slowly walks away as he contemplates the battle ahead. He closes his eyes and breathes slowly. Each breath becomes louder and louder. He senses dull out every outside distraction. The fuel of his Invisible Ember generates a fire that can't be extinguished or sensed. Learning from the defeat in Spain, Malik makes sure that this time, the gas will not defeat his Fire Line.

The smoke continues to blind the men of the building. Himiko walks through the smoke with her Avemcernentia glowing like a lighthouse. As some of the men desperately try to approach her, she cuts them down effortlessly with her flame katana.

SLASH…SLASH…SLASH…The sound of yells and screams suddenly succumbs to deathly silence as each enemy crashes to the ground like dead leaves in the fall. The rage within Himiko begins to transform the outer layers of her eyes. The predator eye that exists in every Moor begins to take hold in Himiko. The red mixes with the blue, creating a purple hue that surrounds the outer layer of her eyes.

"(***WHERE THE HELL ARE YOU, TRAITOR***)," she yells, " (***COME OUT! AND FACE KUORI KAGE JUSTICE***)!

Moments later, the lights begin to dim. Himiko stops to look around. Several valves on the walls begin to open. Himiko begins to worry as she looks around to ascertain the meaning of these valves.

"(***What are you planning, Ayaka***?)" she wonders as she puts her sword close to her body.

Then, a strange gas begins to shoot out of the valves. It mixes with the smoke, but Himiko becomes affected. She begins to cough and crash towards the ground.

"COUGH COUGH COUGH, (***What matter of treachery is this***?)" Himiko wonders, " Ugokemasen (I can't move)."

Shortly afterwards, a flush of wind reaches Himiko, followed by a punch in the gut.

"GWUAH!" Himiko yelps.

Then, she is punched in the stomach, jabbed in the face, right hooked on her left cheek, and then reversed kicked towards the floor.

Partially bloodied and caught off guard, Himiko's flame sword disappears as a cocky warrior keeps her dirty sole up in the air in a kicking pose. Ayaka then chuckles in Japanese as she slowly puts her foot down.

" Hee hee hee, (***So you thought that I would just…allow you to take me back to the village? The same village that denied my father of his rightful birthright***)?" she continues, "(***The village, which has abandoned our tradition of strength and power? Are you that stupid…cousin***)?"

Himiko struggles to regain her balance as she slowly gets up. She looks up at Ayaka and responds to her claims.

" (***You are as twisted as ever, cousin***)," Himiko responds, " (***Strength is useless without purpose and foresight. You have forsaken our ancestors and sided with the same enemies who will see Japan destroyed for nothing***)."

" Nashi, NASHI (Nothing? NOTHING?) hee hee hee (Ayaka kicks Himiko towards the floor again), (***Oh, little cousin, you are still a fool***)."

Ayaka puts out her hand. She transforms her eyes to the Avemcernentia; the eyes contain a blackish outer layer with a blue core. Then she generates a black flame sword and points it at Himiko. Then she begins to chuckle again.

" (***In this world, fools are the first to die. So prepare for your gift…little cousin***)."

As Ayaka raises her sword, Himiko closes her eyes and smiles. She resolves herself and does what she can to stay strong while refusing to plead for her life. Ayaka begins to swipe her sword.

Suddenly, a firewave blows the Reintergon gas and smoke away. The intense heat takes Ayaka by surprise while healing Himiko of her paralysis. Ayaka squints her eyes as Himiko looks back. A shadowy figure slowly walks down the corridor. The rage on Ayaka alerts Himiko to someone who has joined the battle of the Moors.

" So…You must be the famous Shadowmoor," Ayaka says with a smug sarcasm. Malik walks up with his hood and mask on. His Dracocernentia burns high, and his confidence begins to trigger Ayaka.

"What a waste…and an dishonorable way to engage your opponent," Malik says.

"Honor…HONOR?!" Ayaka retorts, "You are just as foolish as my little cousin. I guess I will have the pleasure of killing two fools tonight."

" (***What makes you think I'm the fool? You're the one who's outnumbered and without your gas to back you up***)," Malik retorts in Japanese, " (**Let's settle this, like true warriors: the Dark Light versus the Bright Shadow**)?"

"Kyōmibukai teian (An interesting proposition)," Ayaka responds, " (***I accept. Your head will be most pleasing to my master***)."

Himiko stands up next to Malik while both look at Ayaka.

" (***Are you fit to fight***)?" Malik asks.

Himiko reactivates her Avemcernentia, holds her hand out, and generates another flame sword.

" (***It is past time to settle this***)," Himiko whispers, " As you Americans say…Let's get it on!"

Malik looks at Himiko. Himiko returns with a smile. Afterwards, all combatants begin to stare at each other, as the flames of conflict begin to inch towards a dilapidation of pride and glory.

Chapter 20
Dark Light vs Bright Shadow
Part 2

A light gust blows between the combatants. Each warrior stares at their opponents like the first gaze of men to the stars. The devilish, killer intent pours out as Ayaka's blue eyes turn purple to black on the outer edges. Himiko's eyes scrunch downward, barely revealing her blue eyes, as she watches her cousin transform into her true nature.

Meanwhile, Malik slowly moves around to surround Ayaka in the confined hallway. Ayaka keeps her eye on Malik and smirks. The eyes of the Dracocernentia reveal the blood red, blue, and purple receptors. They also see a dark, flaming silhouette of a phoenix purging its power in her veins. Malik briefly relaxes his mind and muscles as he ascertains the upcoming battle.

"*I know this power*," Malik reflects, "*It's similar to what Emma possessed when we first met. However, due to her proficiency in her martial arts, her control of her power is more potent...I can't underestimate her*."

Feeling imprudent and overconfident, Ayaka speaks in Japanese with a condescending and audacious way.

" (***Trying to read your opponent, are we***…) Shadowmoor," Ayaka squeals, " (***Let me put it in a way that you two will understand***…) hee hee hee (Ayaka ignites a black flame sword from each of her hands and amplifies its powers) I am going to kill her! And then I am going to let you watch her blood flow out of her body… and then…Well, I might have fun with you before I chop off your dick and choke you with it!"

"Anata no satsujin shōfu (YOU MURDEROUS WHORE)!" Himiko yells before igniting her flame sword.

Let's settle this, like true warriors. The Dark Light versus the Bight Shadow!
Kyōmibukai teian (An interesting proposition).

WOOSH
WOOSH
I accept. Your head will be most pleasing to my master.

Malik says nothing, ignites the light in his eyes, and joins suit by creating a flame katana.

As they get into fighting positions, Malik notices the look that Himiko and Ayaka share. He becomes nervous about the growing tension and anger between the two of them.

"*I just hope she doesn't allow herself to be clouded with rage, that it blinds her*," Malik worries, as he gets ready for the clash of flaming blades.

After a brief standoff of silence and another brief gust of wind, Himiko and Ayaka seemingly teleport towards each other with the speed and force of a bomb as they charge. The clash of swords creates a heat wave that ignites the whole building. Due to the heat, some of the rooms begin to catch on fire.

Himiko starts to swing her sword up and down. Ayaka counters by blocking the sword, then attempts to hit Himiko by doing a reverse back kick. Himiko dodges by doing a backflip. Malik takes the chance to jump in by rushing in to swing his sword.

Ayaka glances behind her and, at the last second, uses her other sword to block Malik's attack. Malik and Ayaka look at each other as each tries to gain the upper hand. Ayaka smirks, then blows a kiss. Malik tries not to be distracted by her pseudo advances. Himiko recovers and charges towards Ayaka and Malik.

Once engaged, the Moors continue their barrage of swings, kicks, counters and dodges. The battle rages for several minutes, with no one gaining or losing ground. Ayaka's precise skill with two flame blades and her Avemcernentia, she begins to emit a layer of black flames around her body. Himiko is taken aback by this surge of power. Malik remains calm and poised; however, sensing that the display is intimidating her opponent, Ayaka smirks again in her arrogance.

" (***You seem surprised, little cousin***)," Ayaka whispers, " (***Did you think you are fit to lead the Kuori Kage***)?"

Himiko scrunches her eyes, lets out a yell, and then charges towards Ayaka.

" HIMIKO, WAIT!" Malik yells as he tries to rein Himiko in, "She is trying to goat you into…"

Ayaka squints her eyes and smiles.

Himiko swings her sword at Ayaka. Ayaka dodges and moves sideways. Himiko swings again. Ayaka does the same, goading Himiko again by laughing at her. Himiko yells again and attempts to thrust her sword towards Ayaka. Ayaka then smiles, moves out of the way towards her right, and with the sword in her right hand, slashes Himiko's wrists.

Himiko screams with pain as the blow ignites black flames on her wrists. In an attempt to stop the flames, her sword disappears, leaving Himiko vulnerable.

"NO! HIMIKO!" Malik yells.

Malik rushes in to try to help Himiko. Ayaka turns her attention towards Malik and begins to laugh maniacally.

As Malik gets closer, Ayaka blows a stream of black smoke at Malik. Once the smoke encases Malik, she then positions her swords parallel to each other, and with one swift, violent swipe, creates two massive fire air blades that knock Malik 40 feet across the hallway, slamming against the locked door.

Malik hits the door and slinks towards the ground. Blood violently blots out of his mouth as he tries to figure out what happened to him.

"What…COUGH COUGH COUGH force…" Malik stutters, "How…can…she…"

Then, Malik briefly slips into unconsciousness as Ayaka laughs and returns to Himiko.

Ayaka allows her swords to disappear in her hands as she walks towards Himiko. Himiko is still trying to stop the pain from her slit wrists. She looks up as Ayaka continues to walk towards her. She continues to laugh as Himiko is consumed with anguish and pain.

" (***I told you…little cousin***)," Ayaka gloats, " (***You…are too weak to lead***) hee hee hee."

Himiko violently erupts from the floor and tries to punch Ayaka with her good hand.

Ayaka dodges it, kicks her in her stomach. Himiko is caught off guard. Ayaka then punches Himiko in her stomach. She flexes her palm flat and hits Himiko on the nose. As blood flows out of her nose, Himiko becomes disoriented and stumbles back.

In this moment, Ayaka begins her barrage of attacks on Himiko. She jabs Himiko with two punches to the face. Then she hits her with a left hook, then a right. As Himiko struggles to maintain her balance, Ayaka laughs maniacally again as she prepares for her most devastating attacks. She wiggles her toes, blows a kiss, then mocks Himiko one last time.

"Amai yume no chīsana itoko (Sweet dreams, little cousin)".

Ayaka does a reverse back kick and hits Himiko. Himiko yelps after the initial contact.

Then Ayaka repeats the motion with another reverse back kick. As all hope begins to leave Himiko, Ayake ignites her feet with black flames and, with a loud, convincing yell, does a jump spinning back kick. The force of her kick crashes into the cheek of Himiko and knocks her to the ground.

As Malik slips deeper into unconsciousness, the mark of Bodhidharma begins to ignite. The flow of energy transports Malik into a familiar veil in his mind. The walls are surrounded by the color of nothing, white as the purest snow, with a flame in the middle of the room. As Malik walks around the small flame, a voice echoes into the veil.

"Greetings…Dragon Moor." The voices echo.

Malik looks around and tries to find the source of the voices.

"Hello, is there anyone there?"

"Yes, we are in you. And around you. We are your past, your present, and your future."

As Malik begins to understand slowly, he sits in front of the flame and allows his mind to clear.

Malik sits in an easy pose. As his mind becomes open, the flame begins to grow, and the voices continue to instruct.

"In the midst of battle, one assumes that it is between themselves and the enemy outside. However, the enemy outside is a reflection of the enemy inside of you," the voice states.

Malik closes his eyes and absorbs the instruction. With 2 slow, controlled breaths, he engages in conversation with voices with prudence and conviction.

"I know that anger will not win every fight, because it eventually destroys both inward and outward. So how do I defeat this type of anger?"

"As you learned from your experiences, anger isn't just a single entity, but a collective that builds reality," the voices continue, "The flame is the combination of heat, fuel, and air. Take away one component and the flame ceases to exist. When we detach ourselves from the confines of single components, we allow ourselves to see ourselves as a whole. Each component works in unison to make reality."

Malik takes his time to contemplate the messaging. His body becomes relaxed, his breathing becomes rhythmic, and his understanding becomes clearer.

"So, in other words, this isn't just about fighting an enemy. This is about understanding the circumstances and the root of…"

At that moment, Malik begins to reach a revelation. When he entered the Dragon Temple, he reflected on the moment he understood the source of not only his suffering, but the suffering of Audrey. At this point, the voices convey and solidify what Malik has realized as well.

" When you allow yourself to acknowledge the presence of such pain and anger, then detach from it, you will be able to judge it for what it is, and then shine a light on it. When we ally ourselves with the darkness, it is not to allow it to taint ourselves; it is a means to acknowledge and embrace the irrefutable fact…that it too is the part of the whole. Light cannot exist without darkness, water cannot be contained and directed without land, and air must be separated from the ground. Use this as a moment to unleash the dormant power…within you."

As the voices disappear, Malik's understanding allows the flame to grow. As the flame grows beyond the space of the veil, Malik wakes up. He sees Himiko on the ground, unconscious, and Ayaka walking towards her. Malik begins to groan and tries to reach out to Himiko.

Then, Malik closes his eyes, sits in easy pose and relaxes. Still shrouded with smoke, with the building burning, Malik closes his mind to all thoughts and sounds. He takes slow breaths and maintains his composure. As the heat in the smoke intensifies, he uses it to heal his wounds and gather his strength.

A few seconds later, he performs the hand signs that Himiko taught him. The immense power within begins to grow as Malik's body begins to glow.

Ayaka senses the power and immediately turns away from Himiko. The black smoke that she generated has transformed into something that she can no longer see.

" Kanjiru kono chikara wa nanidarou (What is this power that I'm sensing)," Ayaka ponders as she begins to walk towards the smoke.

As she draws closer and closer to the smoke, suddenly, a pair of fire waves clear the smoke and rush towards Ayaka. Ayaka quickly exposes her hands, ignites her black flame swords, and cuts the fire waves while clearing a path towards the source of the surge. The remnants reach Himiko and temporarily heal her back to consciousness.

Then the hall clears, and Ayaka sees Malik standing up with his head down. Ayaka's Avemcernentia sees the invisible flames manifesting into a dragon through a different plane of existence. Ayaka's once cocky attitude now turns to concern, as this influx of power raises the stakes.

" (*His power is immense, and his control is extraordinary*)," Ayaka concludes, "Yudan dekinai (*I can't let my guard down*)."

After 3 seconds of clearing the air, Malik raises his head but keeps his eyes closed. Suddenly, Malik moves like a flash and punches Ayaka in the stomach with a flame fist.

GWAK!

Ayaka yelps as she stumbles backwards to regain her footing.

Malik keeps his eyes closed, widens his stance, then positions his arms in a stance with his hands flattened. Ayaka growls with disgust, then lunges forward at Malik.

Ayaka swings her flame swords up and down. Malik dodges the attacks but refuses to counter. Himiko slowly gets up from the ground and watches from a distance. Ayaka again swings her swords from side to side. Malik remains motionless until the swords get within micrometers of him. Then, with grace, Malik dodges by rotating his body and forcing Ayaka's inertia to switch places.

As Himiko watches, she begins to ponder to herself to better understand the circumstances of the fight.

" Yatta… kare wa sore o yatta (Has…he done it)?" she wonders, " Did he achieve the power of Awarelessness?"

Moments later, Ayaka begins to pant profusely. Her stamina has been drained, but her frustration is tenfold. The rings around her eyes get darker and darker, as her eyes become more possessed with killer intent.

" (***You…you will not make a fool of me, you black son of a bitch***)!"

Malik remains voiceless and poised. His eyes stay closed, and he remains in his stance.

The intense rage and frustration reach their boiling point.

Ayaka, fueled by Malik's apparent nonchalant attitude, charges recklessly towards Malik.

Himiko, nearly healed enough to stand up straight, continues to spectate the final moments of the climactic battle.

“(***What will you do now***)?” Himiko wonders.

Ayaka lets off a yell with her swords raised in the air. Each of her footsteps and vibrations is picked up by Malik's senses. Everything moves into slow motion, as each closer step gets louder and louder, Malik gets ready for the moment.

When Ayaka reaches a striking distance, Malik maneuvers his body downward, punches Ayaka in the gut. The force knocks the wind out of her lungs, and she loses her swords.

After a moment, a golden flaming sword shoots out of Malik’s hand, through Ayaka’s stomach and protrudes out of her back. Ayaka screams while blood flows out of her mouth, then her body crashes to the ground. Malik walks away and towards Himiko.

Himiko runs up to Malik. Malik begins to open his eyes. Himiko notices that his eyes subtlety change from a strange, clear, tan color to the brownish orange of the Dracocernentia.

“ Daijōbu (Are you alright)?” Himiko asks.

“Hai! I’m O…”

POW!

The door at the end of the hallway explodes, and the fires continue to consume the building. From the other side of the hallway, Shiori yells to get Malik and Himiko's attention.

"HIMIKO! MALIK-SAN! (***The fire will consume this building. We must go now***!"

" (***Wait! Ayaka must be taken back to face trial***)," Himiko responds.

"GWAH GWAH (spits), (***I would rather die here than face her in disgrace, little cousin***)," Ayaka slurs.

Himiko starts to move towards Ayaka before Malik grabs her arm. He nods no, then speaks.

"There's no time, Himiko. We have to go now," Malik states, then looks at Ayaka, "She's…accepted her fate, it's time to decide ours."

Himiko looks on with sad, wet eyes. Before she can let out a tear, she wipes her eyes, looks at Malik, and then nods.

Shiori runs towards Himiko and Malik. In unison, each performs their hand signs while the building around them is engulfed in flames. After the procedure, Malik and Himiko reactivate their eyes, blow smoke from their mouths, and disappear.

Ayaka, refusing to mend her ways and heal herself, laughs with her blood-stained teeth. Then whispers, " Kenri to riyū no tame ni (For…right and reason…)"

After the trio makes their way out, the building explodes and completely covers the infrastructure. As the sirens ring through the city streets, the local fire departments rush to contain the fire caused by the fight. From several blocks away, the trio stands on top of a nearby building and watches as the building disappears in a sea of flames.

" (***You have done well***)...Malik-san," Himiko says.

"(***I'm…sorry Himiko. I know that she was your***…),"

"Bangō (No)," Himiko interrupts, " (***I allowed my feelings for her to cloud my judgement. I almost got us killed because of my inability to separate my frustration from what's right***)."

Malik glances down at Himiko as she is still weak and hanging off Malik's shoulder. Then she smiles and finishes her thought.

" (***At the end, she went down like a shinobi***)."

" (***It is nearly dawn***)," Shiori says, "(***We must return to the village and relay this news to the Grand Master***)."

Himiko and Malik nod. With one last look, the trio then creates another smoke ball, disappears into the wind, and leaves the city.

One hour later, the trio makes it back to the village. Tired, weary of battle, and bloodied, the shinobi make their way towards the back of the village to the temple. Waiting with anticipation, the Grand Master is seated, waving her fan.

A ball of smoke is created in the middle of the dojo. Once the smoke disappears, the three shinobi kneel in front of the elderly leader. She waits about ten seconds before she engages with the three.

“ (***I see that your mission was a success***),” the Grand Master says, “ Shiori-san, o genki-sōdesu ne (Shiori, you appear to be in good health).”

“Hai!” Shiori responds.

“(***Where is Ayaka to face trial for her crimes***)?”

Himiko hesitates for a moment. Malik senses it and starts to respond to the Grand Master.

“Grand Master, we…”

“No…Malik-san,” Himiko interrupts, “ (***I allowed my anger to consume me, and was soundly defeated by Ayaka. Before she could strike the killing blow, Malik awakened the inner power and defeated her***).”

“Dono yō ni (How)?” the Grand Master asks.

“(***With an invisible, flaming blade Grand Master***),” Himiko answered, “(***Somehow, she could not escape nor heal her wound***).”

“ Uchinaru Seigi (Inner Justice)!” the Grand Master uttered, “ (***A blade that is forged for the purpose to inflict the inner wounds that bind the hatred and suffering to their opponents…only the one could master such a technique without instruction***).”

“ (***Which is why we need him back home***),” A voice echoes from across the dojo.

Malik recognizes the deep voice and looks around. As he peers towards the side of the Grand Master, a man slowly walks out. Malik’s gaze turns into surprise as a friendly face graces him with its presence.

"Hey, Malik." Mason says, "Seems your training here is complete."

The Grand Master nods in acknowledgement as Mason continues.

"Are you ready to come home?"

"Really, but how? I mean?" Malik asks as he and the others get up.

Then, Himiko looks at Malik.

" You have trained and fought with honor. There is nothing more for you here."

"But, Himiko, I…"

Himiko puts her finger on Malik's mouth and hushes him. Then she leans up, kisses him on the cheek and smiles.

"Go…and fulfill your destiny."

As Malik looks at the Grand Master, she stands up, prompting all of the shinobi to stand up.

As Malik looks around, everyone, including the Grand Master and Masons, bows to Malik. Shiori and Himiko smile as they rise.

Afterwards, Mason walks down towards Malik and pats him on the shoulder.

"Come on, son, let's get packed up."

As the two men walk out of the dojo, Himiko looks on as the Grand Master walks next to her. She continues to wave her fan with her right hand and uses her left hand to caress Himiko.

Which is why we need him back home!
Uchinaru Seigi (Inner Justice)! A blade that is forged for the purpose to inflict the inner wounds that bound the hatred and suffering to their opponents Only the one could master such a technique without instruction.
Hey Malik. Seems your training here is complete.

Chapter 21 R.O.O.F.S (Return Of Our Former Selves)

The next morning, Malik is packing his meager belongings in his bag. Time seems to run in slow motion as he takes in the amount of experience from his journey. As the winds of change blow outside of his room, Malik takes the time to reflect on his thoughts while meandering through his emotions.

"Seems like only yesterday that I decided to partake in a quest for Audrey," he laments, "Since then, I've encountered a new face of an old enemy, new allies, and the realization that I know nothing in the bigger scheme of things. (Sigh) So what now?"

Suddenly, a knock outside his door interrupts his pondering.

KNOCK KNOCK.

Malik turns his head and sees Mason crossing his arms. With a grin on his face and his grayish beard shining through treads of black, Malik asks Mason a series of questions.

"Mason…how did you know to find me here? And how did you know about the Kuorikage?"

" Heh Heh Heh, I've had a life before you were even born, young blood," Mason chuckles as he walks into his room, " Remember when I told you that I was tasked with finding people with special lineages?" Malik nods before Mason continues his explanation.

"About 25 years ago, the FBI and the CIA did a joint investigation of some of the soldiers mysteriously disappearing from the local bases in Japan. I went undercover and discovered that a man with certain powers was behind recruiting prostitutes to lure the men into these undisclosed locations."

"That's interesting, but how does this tie in with Kuorikage?"

"The man I was after was Kaito, and he had the power to manipulate men just by looking at them."

"So! He had the Dracocernentia?!" Malik responds.

Mason nods his head, puts his hands behind his back, and circles around before reengaging the conversation. His mood shifts a tad, as he coverts his tone to a more serious and empathetic tone.

"While I was scooping some of the hideouts, I was approached by a shinobi. A woman and her son came out of nowhere in a ball of smoke."

"So, the Kuorikage found you first," Malik deduces, "then what happened next?"

"They looked at me, but at the time, I didn't know the significance. The woman had eyes as pure as water. Her son had eyes as bright as flames. Both looked at me as if they were looking deep within my soul."

Malik is startled by the revelation. Once he grasps the significance of the reveal, he whispers to himself, "The Grand Master…and Himiko's father…"

"That's right, Malik," Mason continues, "Once they deemed me worthy, I was able to use my skills as a detective to find out Kaito's hideout. With the help of some of the locals who were not bought off, the CIA/FBI task force, and the Kuorikage, we cornered Kaito." Mason wipes the sweat from his head and shakes his head. "We…lost so many men that day. I never thought that I would be in a shootout like that," Mason says. "Meanwhile, when the Grand Master and Hirohito fought Kaito, Hirohito defeated him but tried to spare his life. When Hirohito turned his back, Kaito ignited a flame sword from thin air and tried to kill his brother. Before Hirohito could turn his head, who you know as the Grand Master now, intercepted Kaito, and did something that I still cannot explain."

"What exactly?" Malik pushes.

"It…it was as if she'd stabbed Kaito, but it wasn't until he fell to the ground that some invisible sword ignited into flames."

"Just like what I did to Ayaka," Malik pieces together, "I overheard the Grand Master say something… Uchinaru Seigi (Inner Justice)"

"Well, when I walked in and saw his body, a little girl was shivering in the corner. She was maybe 5 years old, and the horror in her face was something I will never forget for the rest of my life."

"A little girl? Could that've been Ayaka?"

"Yes, but because of the crimes committed by her father, she was taken by the Japanese Government and placed in the system. The Kuorikage have a strict code, and her presence, they believed, would've tainted their honor."

"So they abandoned her…" Malik deduces, "No wonder she sought revenge. Something tells me that Himiko never knew this side of the story."

Mason grabs Malik's attention, pats him on the shoulder and sighs. He nods his head, smiles, and then instructs him on the complexities of life.

"You know, young man, there is so much that our children won't know about. Yes, they'll know about the key events in Slavery, Jim Crow, Civil Rights, etc," Mason states, " but very few times will they know about the difficult decisions that separate morality from a means to an end. Sometimes, you have to separate morality to get the job done."

"So…do you regret it? After knowing what happened to Ayaka?" Malik asks.

Mason ponders the question and says nothing. He removes his hand and begins to walk out of the room.

"You'd better finish packing, the plane is going to leave in a few hours. We don't want to miss our flight."

Malik watches Mason as he walks out of the room and out of the building. Malik ponders why

Mason didn't answer the question, but chooses to trust his mentor. He goes back to finishing his packing.

Twenty minutes later, Malik walks out of the building and down the stairs. At the bottom, he is greeted by Mason, Himiko, Shiori, the Grand Master and her bodyguards. When he reaches towards the bottom, Himiko and Shiori step in front of him. With a concerning look, Malik puts his bags down and addresses Himiko.

"What do you have in your back?" Malik asks. Himiko and Shiori look at each other. Then, Himiko takes something from her back and, with two hands, presents it to Malik.

"You will need this…" Malik looks at it and is surprised at the presentation.

"It's my…leather jacket…" he responds.

"It's more than that, Malik-san," Shiori states. "Use your eyes," Himiko commands.

Malik places his hands underneath the folded jacket. He glances at Mason. Mason winks at him. Then, Malik reverts his attention to the jacket. He takes a deep breath, closes his eyes, then activates the Dracocernentia.

As the eyes awaken, the flow of energy ignites the jacket, showing a Fire Line that runs up the middle of the jacket, then branches on each side: the left side with the outline of the mark of Bodhidharma and on the right side, the outline of the Kuroikage emblem. Amazed, Malik looks back at a smiling Shiori and Himiko as they step aside. The Grand Master walks up to Malik. She continues to wave her fan while Malik bows in reverence.

"Grand Master…" Malik says softly.

" (***You have done well in your time here),*** Malik-san. (***Take this as your reminder of who you are, where you come from, and where you will go***)," She states in Japanese.

Then, in a remarkable turn of events, she smiles then concludes her speech.

"Now go forth, and forge your destiny with your Fire Line!"

Shocked by how she expresses her words of encouragement, Malik's eyes begin to water as they share a last bow. Malik wipes his eyes, then walks out of the village with Mason. As they trek out of the village, a row of villagers on each side bows in appreciation for Malik's heroic deeds. Mason also notices the celebrity but keeps Malik grounded.

"This is all too much for me to absorb," Malik says, "Still, I'm going to miss this place."

"It's never easy when you are a hero, especially when you're actually appreciated," Mason responds, "It's not easy to remember that every action affects other people that you may or may not know. Just know that your deeds will not go unappreciated."

"So that leads to the task of going home."

"Yes, home…we'll talk about that later. Right now, we need to get to the airport."

Malik nods as they exit the village and enter the black BMW 8 Series sedan.

Moments later, Mason is driving down the road towards Tokyo. Malik looks out the window and sees the landscape. Mason notices his mind wandering, so he decides to spark up a conversation.

"Beautiful, isn't it?" Mason asks. Malik stumbles a bit before answering Mason.

"Yeah, it is. For a moment, I was actually at peace. It was as if I had nearly forgotten about everything that brought me pain. I don't know how to explain it."

"I think that this journey taught you more than you realized," Mason continues, "I think that the loss of that young lady hit you hard because it was someone who refused to be saved. Malik, you will have to realize that not everyone in our community wants to be liberated. When you think about all of the slaves in those plantations, I think only 1 in 10 actually had the nerve to run away or fight back."

"Yeah, I hear you, but why would so many just…just…"

"Because most of us either don't know who we truly are, or refuse to acknowledge who we truly are," Mason concludes, "Think about it this way. Before you became aware of your powers, was it easier to believe that you were nothing but a nigger OR that your ancestors rode dragons and conquered half a continent?"

Malik takes the time to reflect on his life and journey. When he briefly remembers the moments with his adoptive family, as well as his experiences with his ancestors, he acknowledges the truth behind Mason's words.

"You're right, Mason," Malik states, "It's funny how dark the world is, when you realize that nearly everything we have today was derived from a black mind: from the concept of math and science, to agriculture, to sea bearing, hell even some of our legends. If someone had told me 4 years ago that dragons existed and that black people controlled them, I would've called the Psych-ward on them."

"And this is what you are fighting, Malik," Mason says, "This is why my father tried to teach us about our real history, so that we could be empowered. This is why the Black Panthers made it mandatory for each of their members to know what they were fighting for, why they were fighting, and how to maintain that fight. It'll be up to you to rejuvenate that passion back to the people, Malik."

Malik nods as Mason continues to drive toward the Airport.

Meanwhile, in Jacksonville, Asir is sitting next to his grandmother in her bed. Her condition is getting worse, and Asir feels a level of hopelessness. Tameka glances at Asir while Emma sits on the couch. D'Shawn leans against the wall while he looks out the window of the door. After a few moments of watching, Tameka walks towards the living room and sits in front of Emma.

She awkwardly looks at Emma and says nothing. The tension in the room remains thick and heavy. Neither person says a word nor makes a move. The dead silence goes on for at least 5 minutes.

Afterwards, Emma begins to breaks the silence and gets up.

"I think I'm going to..."

"What did you do to my son, D'Shawn?" Tameka erupts.

D'Shawn takes a deep breath through his nose while Emma desperately tries to leave the room. Again, Tameka asks with a smug attitude.

"You don't need to go anywhere, Miss Thang. NOW D'SHAWN, WHAT THE HELL HAS HAPPENED TO ASIR?!"

Before Emma can answer, D'Shawn decides to speak while focusing his attention outside.

"Asir has the Fire Line, which he inherited from me."

"Fire Line? FIRE LINE?" Tameka responds, "Do you think I'm Boo BOO DA Fool you BASTARD?! YOU GOT ASIR...Asir is different. He's not the same boy I raised by myself."

"No, he's not a boy anymore, and you just saw, just a small portion of his power," D'Shawn continues as he turns around to face Tameka, "Tameka, it wasn't until after Asir was born that I realized that our ancestors once had the power of dragons. You saw him burst into flames, but he didn't burn."

"Ok, then how come I haven't heard of... whatever the hell you are talking about?" Tameka asks.

"Because it was purposely hidden to control our people and subjugate them," Emma adds.

"Oh, so that must mean that you have it too, right?" Tameka asks.

Emma nods. Tameka then sighs while putting her hand over her head.

She gets up and walks in front of D'Shawn. D'Shawn looks her in her eyes and says nothing. Then, after a brief standoff, she violently slaps him. Emma begins to get up, but D'Shawn holds his hand, prompting her not to interfere. Then Tameka slaps him again, then bangs his chest. Finally, when her energy is exhausted, she begins crying. Her tough exterior melts away as the tears finally reveal a vulnerable side. She leans towards his chest and continues to cry. Feeling apprehensive, yet responsible, D'Shawn slowly puts his right arm around Tameka and embraces her. He continues to say nothing as Emma sits there, now understanding why it was essential for her to stand down.

Tameka gathers herself, wipes her eyes, then addresses D'Shawn.

"It's…it's late. I need to put Asir to bed. I don't care how old he is, he needs to let my mom rest…and he needs his as well."

D'Shawn nods as Tameka walks into the room.

Emma gets up and walks next to D'Shawn.

"What was that all about?" Emma whispers.

"The funny thing about pain is it doesn't discern what caused it, it only reacts," D'Shawn answers, “Despite what she did to me or our actions, no mother (or woman for that matter) wants to confront their mistakes.”

“But she shouldn’t have…”

“Have you ever felt so much pain that you just wanted to let it go?” D’Shawn asks.

Emma looks at D’Shawn after the question and sees the seriousness in his eyes. At that moment, Emma reflects on the same feeling she once had with Malik and William. Her eyes begin to water, and her nose begins to get stuffy.

Then she wipes her eyes, sniffs her nose, then nods, “Point taken.”

Then, a notification on D’Shawn’s phone buzzes and lights up. He reaches into his pocket, taps the phone and looks at the message. Emma looks at D’Shawn while he’s reading the message.

“What is it?” Emma asks.

“It’s Mason, he’s got your brother and they’re coming home.”

“Home?! Is Malik ok?”

“Yes, seems that he thwarted an Elite 8 scheme in Japan and weakened the effects of the spread. However, with all of the surveillance going around, it might bring too much attention to Malik.”

“But Malik can handle himself,” Emma responds, “Surely he can…”

"We can't afford that type of attention, not now. I'm going to pick them up at the Airport. King Cobra will stay here and patrol the projects."

"But D'Shawn…"

"I need you…," D'Shawn interrupts, "to stay here and watch over Asir, Tameka, and his grandmother."

Emma is taken aback by this responsibility. Tameka walks in at the end of the conversation.

"What's going on?" Tameka asks.

"I have to go. Asir can stay here for a while."

"Go…GO?! So you're just going to run…"

"I don't have time for this, Tameka." D'Shawn scolds. "The hell you…"

D'Shawn's temper briefly gets the better of him. He interrupts Tameka by activating the Dracocernentia and looking directly in Tameka's eyes. She controls her actions while controlling the shock of the reveal.

"Who…what are you?" she silently asks.

D'Shawn then closes his eyes, reverts them to it's normal brown hue, then continues with his explanation.

"Emma will stay here to protect you, Tameka," D'Shawn says, "Tell Asir when he wakes up that I'll be back soon."

"And why should I do that?" Tameka scolds.

"Because, D'Shawn loves Asir very much," Emma adds in softly, "That you can't deny, as much as you want to."

Tameka snaps her head towards Emma, but surprisingly says nothing. Emma continues to mediate and console while amplifying D'Shawn's explanation.

"There's so much that's going on, Tameka," Emma continues, "D'Shawn has to pick up more people who are essential to stopping this oppression. All he is asking is for you to remind Asir that his father…HIS father…will not abandon him."

Tameka crosses her arms and nods. Then she sheds a tear before wiping it off with her hand. D'Shawn looks at Emma and nods.

"Thanks, Emma, I won't be gone long." Tameka refuses to make eye contact as D'Shawn quietly leaves the home.

Afterwards, Tameka stands there while allowing her emotions to flow out. Emma, sensing how open she is, walks next to her, rubs her arms and comforts her. In a shocking displace of reciprocity, Tameka uses her other hand to touch Emma, as the two women bond together in this difficult time.

Chapter 22
The Shroud

A small sliver of light appears towards the east. The trees move with the breeze of the morning winds as the world begins to wake up for another day. As the sun begins to rise, Victor is staring at the window of his office. Awaiting the updates for the old Benson house purchase, Victor fixes his hair and walks towards the refrigerator.

He opens the refrigerator, takes out a bottle of cognac and sets it on his desk. Suddenly, a knock on the door interrupts his silence.

KNOCK KNOCK KNOCK.

"Mr. Goth, Mr. Goth?"

"Ugh," Goth groans as he reaches for a glass. Then he reluctantly responds to the knocking.

"Come in," he instructs.

Heather walks in to greet Goth. She is wearing a long-sleeved light brown sweater, a long, denim skirt that runs down to her shin, and a pair of brown, 3-inch boots. She is cautious and skiddish as she holds a stack of papers towards her chest. Goth shows some of his crooked teeth as he smiles at her.

"Ah, Heather. Good Morning, I take it you brought me some good news?"

Heather stutters, then, with prudence, shows Goth the stack of papers.

"Um…well," she continues, "there's been an issue…that requires your attention."

"Oh, I'm sure that anything you bring, regardless of how dire it is, will be graced by your presence," Goth says as he reaches for the stack of papers.

Goth takes a moment to look at the papers. Heather stands nervously by placing both of her hands behind her back. As Goth shifts through the papers, micro expressions in his face tense up as the blood vessels in his eyes get thicker. His face becomes red, so much so that he turns around to face the window. Despite the sun rising, there is a dark, cold entity in the air that clouds the mood of the room. Heather is shivering, awaiting Goth to respond.

After a few moments to recollect himself, Goth turns around, smiles and walks towards Heather. He places his cold, sweaty hands on Heather's right shoulder and addresses her.

"Thank you for what you do here. For this company and…for me," Goth says while rubbing her shoulders, " Now, can you be a sweetheart and grab my guards for me, please?"

"Um…sure, Mr. Goth. Right away, sir," Heather responds.

Goth smiles, then removes his hand. Heather turns around, but Goth lightly touches her on the small of her back.

"I really…REALLY…appreciate it, Heather," he says. Heather shrivels for a second, closes her eyes, then responds.

"Anything for you, Mr. Goth."

Then Heather makes her way out of the office.

Goth grabs his glass and walks toward his small ice compartment. He lifts the lid, uses the tongs to take out 4 ice cubes, and puts them in his glass. Afterwards, he pours his cognac into his glass, then smells the glass before taking a sip. Left alone while awaiting his subordinates, Goth begins to ponder the ramifications of the new while reevaluating his plans.

"*That son of a bitch Shadowmoor defeated Ayaka*," Goth reflects, "*and soon will make his way back to the states in his feeble attempt to redeem his doomed people*." Goth takes another sip of his glass while he chuckles to himself. "*Well, seems like we need to elevate our plans*."

A few minutes later, several men with black suits, white shirts, blue ties, and sunglasses enter Goth's office. Each of them stands with their hands crossed behind their backs, awaiting Goth's responds. None of the men shows any emotions or says a word. Goth turns around, places his drink on his desk, and then walks towards his guards.

"So, I just received news that our Tokyo building went into flames a few hours ago. Ayaka is dead, and now, one of our major chemical labs is utterly destroyed," Goth continues, "So…I come to you gentlemen, what should we do with this revelation?"

None of the men answered or showed any signs of participating. Goth becomes slightly annoyed by crossing his arms and pacing back and forth. A few seconds later, one of the guards clears his throat to get Goth's attention. Goth hears this, turns around and walks towards one of the guards.

"I didn't quite hear that," Goth says, "someone has something to say?"

The same guard who cleared his throat begins to speak with patience and with a level of respect.

"Sir, I think we should amplify the effects here."

"Really, and why do you think we should expend vast resources and put a target on us here to amplify the effects of the pandemic?"

The guard continues to speak while maintaining his composure and keeping his face forward.

"Sir, the other countries of the world don't have the sophisticated medical resources that we have here," he continues, "even though 2 of our out-of-country facilities have been compromise, enough of the pandemic has spread that the effects are nearly irreversible. Also, the majority of the opposition resides here in the States."

Goth rubs his chin and hums to himself. Then he continues to question the bold guard to test the limit of his resolve.

"So, what makes you think that this is the best option for us?" Goth asks sarcastically, "I mean, we already control the destiny of men. Why waste time on spilling acid on an ant hill?"

The guard once again clears his throat. Despite his reluctance to answer, the guard forges forward to answer Goth's probing questions.

"The enemy we face is also the face of resistance. If we concentrate our resources to completely eradicate the support system of Shadowmoor, then the rest of the world's melanated population will capitulate to the system or perish without a symbol of resistance…sir."

As Goth nods with this logic, he walks over to his desk and pushes a button on his intercom.

"Heather, can you bring me those glasses me please? It's a time for…a celebration."

"Right away…Mr. Goth."

"Thank you, Sweetheart."

Afterwards, Goth walks towards his guards. He smiles, then paces back and forth. Goth states his grievances while awaiting Heather to arrive.

"Gentlemen, we have a situation here that needs to be addressed, and indeed, it will be addressed, but in good time," Goth says, "But for now, we need to take time to…celebrate our success. I mean, what kind of boss would I be if I didn't take the time to thank those who helped me make it all possible?"

Again, none of the guards says or does anything. They continue to stand and face forward like obedient soldiers.

Heather arrives later with a tray of champagne glasses. Three of them have green handles, while the rest of them have red handles. Goth looks at Heather, then smiles again.

"Heather, can you be a doll and hand out the red handle glasses from that end to the men, please?"

"Sure, Mr. Goth. Seems a bit early in the day for champagne though."

"Oh, it's never too late to show appreciation to those who work hard for me." Goth answers. Heather then grabs two glasses at a time to give them to the men. Two by two, the men receive their glasses; all except the guard at the end, who spoke out.

"Oh dear, I don't have another red handle glass for you," Heather says.

"No worries, no worries," Goth states, "Just give him this one with the green handle."

Heather nervously nods, goes and grabs the green handle glass. She then walks towards the lone guard and gives him the glass. Once he receives the glass, Heather walks back toward Goth. Goth grabs a glass, then gives Heather a glass.

"Oh, Mr. Goth, I don't drink this early," Heather says.

"Nonsense," Goth exclaims, "You should be part of this as well. Please…I insist."

Goth smiles again as Heather reluctantly takes the glasses. She then rubs her arm holding the glass as Goth makes a toast.

"Gentlemen…and lady, let's celebrate where we were, where we are…AND to the future," he boasts, "Now, FOR RIGHT AND REASON…"

"We will achieve Elitetion," Heather and the guards respond.

With a nod, Goth prompts everyone to take a sip.

As each person sips, Goth looks at his glass and smiles.

"This is good, wouldn't you say?"

After a few seconds, some of the guards begin to cough and clear their throats. Soon their coughs get louder and louder. Then their coughs are followed by shattered glasses, as all but the lone guard, Heather and Goth remain standing. Goth continues to chuckle and sip his glass as the remaining guards begin to gargle spit and blood on the ground.

After the coughing ceases, so do their lives. Heather is completely frozen with fear while the lone guard starts to show some resemblance to concern and caution. Goth walks towards the guard, places his hand on his shoulder, and addresses him.

"You seem to be a great student of history, my friend," Goth says, "And as a student of history, you should know that history favors the brave and the bold. YOU SEE…your… so-called comrades were too soft, too subtle, too docile to make a declaration to what needed to be done. BUT NOT YOU…no no no. Despite whether or not you were right, you felt something within you to speak out and live with the consequences of your actions. I like that, I really do."

Goth then releases his arm then walks towards Heather as he finishes his light speech. She continues to shiver while the guard watches Goth. Goth continues to smile as he looks at the dead bodies on the floor.

"You see, nothing can defeat you faster than yourself, and those around you. People who are not as committed to winning as you are will effectively cause you to dwell in defeat. So in other words, those who are not committed to win are essentially dead weight," Goth concludes, then looks at Heather, "Heather baby, be a rose and send someone here to clean up this trash. And as for you (pointing at the lone guard), catch up with the others and meet me in the lab."

Both nod, place their glasses and walk out of the office.

Once again, Goth is alone. He drinks the last of his glass while looking down at the corpses. His face becomes red and sweaty. Then he shakes his head and converses with himself with devilish intent.

"He'll be back here soon. I need to make sure that his return is met…with several obstacles," Goth whispers to himself, "I'll need to get with my contacts in Atlanta and push our plans forward."

Afterwards, Goth places his glass on his table, takes one last look at his guards, and then walks out of the office.

Goth makes his way towards the bottom of the building. When he reaches the doorway, he is greeted with 2 more guards, wearing body armor, carrying .45 mm on their holsters, and wearing sunglasses. A hand recognition device is placed on the wall next to the door. Goth places his hand on it to allow it to scan. After the green light gives him access, the guard moves away from the door. Goth opens the door and walks in. The guards then close the door then resume their posts.

Goth looks around the vast laboratory and smiles. Several people with pure white lab coats move back and forth between working stations as Goth inspects the conditions. Some of the tables have test rats and syringes. Other stations have chemicals boiling with burners and heat lamps. Towards the back of the lab, has a golden sword attached to a machine, mounted next to a huge cylinder container 30 feet high. Goth smiles again as he walks towards it.

Goth is greeted by the lone guard, Heather, and Cecil, the head scientist of the lab. He is a short man with a bald spot, straight brown hair, buck teeth, glasses, and a slur. Despite his unattractive appearance, his intelligence and expertise make up for his physical deficiencies.

"Good Morning, Mr. Goth," Cecil says. "What do we have here?" Goth points. "This is a manifestation of the Pustula Flu. However, we bonded it with the Reintergon and added some strands associated with aggression."

Goth then walks towards the cylinder and places his hand on it. The mist within is a heavily congested mass of purplish, grey smoke. It swirls and swirls, while creating small sparks in it, mirroring that of a brewing storm. Goth is pleased with the development of this project as he re-engages with the conversation.

"Magnificent," Goth whispers, "So when will this be ready for spreading?"

"Actually, it's ready now, but we haven't developed a strong enough antidote yet to counteract the effects if we can't control it. Truly, the mysterious power emitted by the sword has…elevated the power far beyond our expectations."

"Such power is never meant to be controlled, Cecil," Goth explains, "We just need to make sure it's targeted to the right people. We have the resources and the blueprints to lessen the effects on us."

"Understood, Mr. Goth. When do you want to…"

"We'll know when the time is right," Goth interrupts, "In the meantime, use all of the resources at our disposal to make this compound as strong as possible. Spare no expense nor leave no stone unturned."

The lone guard, Heather, and Cecil once again leave to follow up on Goth's orders. Meanwhile, Goth looks at the mixture of his bioweapon brewing in the cylinder container. He smiles while he once again whispers to himself.

"The world will soon be shrouded in darkness, and no amount of light will dampen it," Goth vindictively gloats, "and the problem will be eradicated…and truly we will complete…ELITETION!"

Magnificent
So when will this
be ready for spreading?

www.ingramcontent.com/pod-product-compliance
Lightning Source LLC
Chambersburg PA
CBHW070821020826
48982CB00014B/143

* 9 7 9 8 9 8 5 8 7 5 4 3 0 *